Praise for

A Course in Freedom

"Everything man has ever built has just been un-built within these pages."
Kelso Coleman

"There are defining moments in life that call us to deeper levels of understanding and bring us into alignment with our very essence. Lawrence Lanoff's new work isn't a book, it is a defining moment; a journey home to our completeness."
John Alexandrov, CEO – Legacy Capitol Solutions, LLC

"Lawrence is red-hot, and so are his radical ideas. This book and his teachings have literally changed my life."
Kelly Russ – Massage Therapist, Yoga Instructor

"I read a few pages of Lawrence's book every night before I go to sleep. I pick at random and sometimes end up reading the same page over and over. Make this book your bible. It's all you need!! As the words sink in and resonate, you will be led to freedom. This is Lawrence at his best."
Marcia Slawson

"You know I am going to thank you like a thousand times and this is mmmm number three. Let me first say that your workshop was the most amazing five days of my life. Probably many lives! I've been playing with the energy of the world, and because I live in it, I figure I might as well put it to good use. I have been on such a power trip, it's great, taking energy here and there that people are throwing away and creating with it…creating and creating. *Thank you!* Love the book by the way. Peace, and keep doing whatever crazy thing you're doing. Cause it's working!"
Jeremy Long

"Working with Lawrence is like being led through the labyrinth of self-discovery. Along the way, I was kick started to release personal biases and points of view. Then I learned the art of deconstructing my own myths and stories. Now I travel the path of no path. *A Course in Freedom* is *priceless,* and an *unmatched* collection of tools to work with as I continue on my way to a life of love, joy, peace, and fun!! I have been privileged to learn from a true master energy healer, and I have no doubt that the best is yet to be."
Barbara Kerns

"Lawrence's workshops are amazing. He has a way of extending truth that is incredibly real and honest. And did I mention *fun?* I love it. Lawrence's support is heartfelt. His offerings have a way of shaking out the stories we've created that no longer serve us and helps us to remember the truth of who we are. *Yummy!* It is an honor to call Lawrence my teacher. I also call him a stir stick. Lawrence has supported me in living in a greater capacity of freedom within myself. It just feels so good. Thank you, thank you!"
Rita T. Henry, Inner Prosperity Inc

"It has been my honor to work with Lawrence Lanoff as a student, become good friends, and now partners in 'The CASH Flow Code.' I've told people for years that if Lawrence had a long beard and were from India, and he wanted it, he could have millions of followers. Lawrence is a master energy tracker. My favorite teaching of his is that fear, particularly fear of death and purgatory, is totally unnecessary. In fact, if you track that seemingly simple belief, it may be ruining your life! If a thought (any thought) doesn't serve you, if it hasn't given you anything of value, why believe in it? I know that Lawrence is working on his new book already and I am looking forward to his expansion and amplification on this particular subject."
Jim Lowitz, CEO – Permalean, Inc.

A COURSE IN FREEDOM

The Drunken Monkey Speaks

LAWRENCE LANOFF

IMPORTANT CAUTION

Although anyone may find the information in this book to be useful, it is written with the understanding that the author is not presenting specific spiritual, sexual, relational, financial, or psychological advice. The author is not responsible for and assumes no liability for any actions taken by any person utilizing this information, either expressed or implied. This material is intended for entertainment purposes only.

A COURSE IN FREEDOM

*** Please read this book at your own risk. ***

Copyright © 2007 by Lawrence Lanoff. All rights reserved. No part of this book may be reproduced or transmitted in any form or by any means, electronic or mechanical including photocopying, recording or by any information storage and retrieval system, without permission in writing from the author.

Published by Soullight Publishing, www.soullightpublishing.com. Illustration and cover design by Pamela Becker, www.pamelabeckercreations.com. Printed and bound by BRIOprint, www.brioprint.com.

Books are available at special discounts for bulk purchases in the United States by corporations, institutions, and other organizations. For more information, contact soullight@gmail.com.

ISBN-13: 978-0-9794051-0-5

First Printing, April 2007

Acknowledgments

When writing a book, there are so many things that go on behind the scenes to make the endeavor possible. I want to thank Marilyn DeMond for all of her brilliant contribution, diligence, and effort to the cause—from writing, revising, formatting, and editing—without her, you would not be reading the following chapters. I want to personally thank Marilyn for all that she has done, and continues to do in support of my wild, uncensored vision.

My deepest gratitude goes to my meditation partner, Dr. Jonathan Parker, www.quantumquests.com, who is an ardent supporter, co-worker, co-creator, mentor, and personal friend for over a quarter century. Thank you, my friend, for being a trusted soul.

Special thanks to David Chester, Attorney at Law, for pushing me to explore consciousness, and the universe, more deeply than I ever imagined possible, all the while asking bigger and bigger questions about the nature of reality. There is an ancient teaching that says, "When the teacher is ready, the student appears." David sought me out at Mount Shasta, appearing at my doorstep, and insisting that I work with him if for only five minutes, five hours, or five days. That is what finally dragged me out of the movie business and into teaching full time. Without David's love, sincerity, and generosity, this book would not be possible.

A shout out to my mom, Sherry Lane, www.caricaturesusa.com, who has always done her best to point me in the right direction spiritually. From est to Castaneda, from Seth materials to Semjase, to co-teaching our first workshop when I was 11, mom always pushed me to explore the universe open-mindedly. She is the one who handed me Dr. Jonathan Parker's brochure, Pathways to Mastership, so many years ago, and has been my confidant while developing the new materials that I am sharing with you now.

Thanks to Skip and Phyllis for their love and support.

A special thanks goes to Zeerak Khan, a.k.a. Vasumitra. Her fierceness taught me how to fight back for the first time in my life. She also helped me to integrate and unify sexuality and spirituality in my body, allowing me to finally shatter my freeze responses, pushing me to see through my limiting myths and stories around my body. Together, we laughed and cried our way through many life-altering experiences.

A sincere thank you to Joseph Campbell, whose body of life work helped me to see and break free of the prisons of my own myths.

I want to thank Sedona for opening her arms to me, and welcoming me into her inner world. She has given me a great, vast, and beautiful space in which to continue to expand and explore the unknown, infinity, and beyond.

In Infinite expansion,
Lawrence Lanoff
Sedona, Arizona
April 2007

Contents

	Foreword by Jonathan Parker	*xv*
	Introduction	*xvii*
1.	The Power of Myth: How you are Kept Prisoner by a Drunken Monkey with Sharp Teeth and a Big Bite	1
2.	Truth, Justice, and the Matrix	11
3.	Human Problem Underlying all Problems—It is All in Your Head!	15
4.	External World is a Projection of Your Inner Mind—That's Scary!	23
5.	What the Bleep Do You Want, Anyway?	26
6.	Mirror Brain Always Says, *Yes!* Except When It Doesn't	28
7.	Lies of the Self and the Field of Awareness	31
8.	Karma is a Gross Way to Work Out Anything—I Do Mean Gross!	34
9.	Life is Arbitrary—Get Over It!	37
10.	Space, Time, Speed, Radar Guns, and Planet Earth Day Planners	40
11.	Grasping Senses Make Us Human—They Give Us Headaches	44
12.	There Exists an Energetic Reality: Love It or Be Eaten by It	50
13.	Four Buckets of Mythology—Your Life Bucket has a Hole in It	53
14.	Major Functions of Religious, Systematic, Human Mythology	61
15.	Mythology and Society: Here Today, and Unfortunately, Here Tomorrow	76
16.	Collision of Past and Future Mythologies Means Dramatic Upheaval and Unrest, Otherwise Known as Change	79
17.	Masks of God are Actually Misunderstood Visions of the Ego	83
18.	God is a Reflection of the Disintegrated Ego—We are Really in Trouble!	87
19.	Life Myths are Your Prisons, Boxes, and Walls—Now Let's Eat Bread and Water	92

20.	Clear Insight: The Desire to See Your Life Clearly—Even if it is Foggy Inside	95
21.	Demons and Fears can be Your Guardians—Or Risk Ignoring Them	99
22.	There is No Inherent Right and Wrong on the Path—There Just *Is*	102
23.	Love and Be Loved—Infinity and Light are Everywhere—Including the Dark	104
24.	To Eat or Be Eaten—That is the Question	108
25.	Your Brain's Filters Interpret and Color Your Reality	110
26.	Field of Awareness in the Ground of the Infinite—The Answer to Manifestation of the Soul	112
27.	Life Simply Is—In Order to Receive, You Must First Perceive	114
28.	Personal Myths Define Your Reality—and, There is No Santa Claus	117
29.	Change the Timeline—Change Your Reality	121
30.	Question Your Myths—Wake Up from Your Deep Sleep	124
31.	There is No End to Anything—Except The End: Evolve, Integrate, Next Stage	126
32.	On the Quest for Spiritual Knowledge—There are No Rules	129
33.	Human Beings are Myth Generators—That is What We Do	132
34.	Your Story is Your Life—Your Life is Your Story—Make It *Fun!*	135
35.	Stop Taking Everything Personally—You are Not that Important—Really	137
36.	Baggage You Carry Around Weighs You Down—Drop Those Bags!	139
37.	Addicted to Pain—The Human Condition	142
38.	No One Controls Your Thoughts or Feelings—Even if You Think They Do	145
39.	We are the Center of the Universe—Not!	147
40.	You are Mostly Unconscious—So Pay Attention!	149
41.	The Primate Truth—On Bananas and Brains	152

42.	Your Brain is Paranoid: Look Out! Behind You! A Terrorist is Creeping into Your Bedroom Window	156
43.	Are You Talking to *Me?* Nobody Else is in Here, It Must be Me	159
44.	Know Thy Fear—Know Thyself—Know More Fear	162
45.	Life is a Perceptual Illusion	164
46.	Old Spirituality Versus Boundless Life and Sudden Death	166
47.	You are Not Your Myth and You Never Will Be	168
48.	Human Beings are Moralistic, Moralizing Machines	172
49.	You are a Symbol of God	174
50.	All Life is Symbolic Metaphor—Including You	176
51.	Symbols Evoke the Release of Energy in the Body	178
52.	Symbolism and the Brain	181
53.	History of the Ego/Mind	183
54.	Sacrifice—Your Main, Unconscious Operating System	186
55.	Religion, Spirituality, Enlightenment, and Slippery Slopes	191
56.	Enlightenment: What is It and Will It Kill Me?	193
57.	Say *Yes* to Life—Live in Your Freedom	197
58.	Illusion is a Trap—It Doesn't Exist	199
59.	You Exist Independent of Anything External—Maybe	201
60.	Core of Self—Living in Your Essence	204
61.	Inquire into Your Essence	206
62.	Loss of Your Essence	208
63.	Feeling Vulnerable and Helpless is Part of Being Human	210
64.	Drunken Monkey, You Shall Not Pass!	213
65.	The Brain, Like a Flower, Blooms when Nourished	215
66.	Shifting the Pain Paradigm—From Bananas and Peanut Butter to Star Fruit Jelly	219

67.	Love Is…	223
68.	Self-Love, Self-Deservement, Self-Creation	225
69.	Money and the Secret of the Sacred Wind Manifestation Tornado	227
70.	Money as Creation, Money as Love	229
71.	Cash Flow—The New Paradigm for Receiving Money in Your Life	232
72.	Our Experience of Money is Energetic Reality	236
73.	Energetic Reality and Manifestation	239
74.	How to Manifest—Create in an *Infinite* Field of Creation	242
75.	Given a Choice, Choose Conscious Manifestation	245
76.	Soul Manifestation and Creation Meditation	247
77.	The Human Need to be Right	250
78.	Humans are Addicted to Chaos	253
79.	Stop Beating Yourself Up	256
80.	Morality and Judgment—The Double Bind	259
81.	Sexual Essence	261
82.	Sexual Myths and the Unconscious Mind	264
83.	Relationship Mythology—An Endless Barrage of *True Love* Symbols	268
84.	Sex Drive: Source of Creation	273
85.	Articulating the Masculine Wound	276
86.	Desire: Secret Language of God	279
87.	Sexual Energy Creates and Destroys	281
88.	Relationships and the Pain Paradigm	284
89.	Pain and Suffering Do Not—and Will Not Ever—Lead to Bliss	286
90.	Seat of the Problem of Humanity—It is in Your Brain	288
91.	Be Conscious with any Discomfort—This is Stuck Energy	291
92.	Healing Sexual Abuse and Trauma	293

93.	Sexual Energy and Yoga	296
94.	Opening the Sacred Geometry of the Pleasure Centers	299
95.	Divine Feminine	301
96.	Defining the Feminine Wound	303
97.	Infinite Masculine	308
98.	Sex Drives Everything—Stop Trying to Control It	311
99.	Live the Fairy Tale—Drink the Energy	313
100.	Loving from the Inside Out	316
101.	Our Natural State is Buoyant, Abundant and Must Be Cultivated	318
102.	Awakening from the Dream—Some Reminders	321

Foreword by Jonathan Parker

Every once in awhile a book comes along that you don't want to put down because it challenges your thinking and opens your mind. The book you are holding in your hands is just such a rare book. *A Course in Freedom* breaks fresh ground to expand your life view. As you digest page-after-page, you will realize worlds of beliefs are being overturned by exposing and challenging the very mythologies everyone has unwittingly lived by.

Lawrence Lanoff makes no pretense to soften the challenges he presents in each chapter. Facing tough realities from an early age he unearthed solutions to break himself free (as well as those he counsels) from the conformity all cultures impose, and now he shares a lifetime of deep insights into the inner workings going on behind the curtain of our creations.

If you thought you would or could continue through life thinking as you always have, then don't read this book because it will confront you and change you. You may well find yourself pausing frequently and saying to yourself, "How did I miss that insight all these years?" In total, you will find yourself discovering dozens of new ways to think about all that you think.

Like me, you will probably find the content of the chapters that follow comprise more of an enlightenment handbook than most books addressing that subject. Chapter after chapter relentlessly reveals our hidden beliefs and secret questions and dismantles them one-by-one revealing the naked reality behind how we have all fabricated our lives from arbitrary choices and self-created illusions. Indeed, can anyone actually *be* enlightened when their lives are constructed of myriad unexamined assumptions and mythologies? No doubt, there have been few who have lived in those realms.

I have known Lawrence for nearly 30 years and have seen how tenaciously he has probed the inner workings of his life and the lives of the many he has worked with to unravel the causes for what works favorably and what doesn't. In reading this book, you will have a new outlook on your life and the lives of the rest of humanity all caught in the same warp of mythological thinking. This is a book about positive futures for this is a book that brings great hope for all that we can be, and while not only showing us the direction, it provides the ways and means that will take us there. So, prepare to be challenged. Prepare to shift your awareness. Prepare to awaken!

Jonathan Parker
November 2006

Introduction

Congratulations! The fact that you are reading this paragraph, right now, at this very moment in your life's evolution, is no coincidence. It suggests that you are on a path of freedom: A Path of Awakening. A life lived in freedom is a life lived consciously—outside of the norm. After pursuing truth for more than 30 years, I realize that no place exists outside of us to look for truth, wisdom, or knowledge. Everything that we need exists within.

I densely packed this book with spiritual and practical life advice and wisdom (that I intuited, meditated upon, and refined in workshops and individual sessions for the past 25 years) to help you navigate your own way, finding your own answers from the inside out. I call this path the path of no path—a life course in freedom—no place to get to, but rather continual evolution and expansion. Either you are consciously on your path of freedom, or you are not; and on that path, you are either awake, or you are asleep. You are either in clear light of your own truth, or the delusion of the illusion. Awake is awake. Asleep is asleep. Free is free. If you want to wake up and be free, then you are in the perfect place at the perfect time.

I invite you to awaken from your dreams. You have little to lose—except what you are not anyway. The dream is an illusory, perceptual experience about the way life appears to the parts of you that are experiencing this three-dimensional, holographic reality as if it is real.

The hologram idea suggests that we experience what we believe is real, not what is real. When you look at what is actually happening, it is mostly uneventful. Life simply is—we add meaning after the fact.

The physical universe does not care about you, one way or another. Pain or joy, fear or pleasure, despair or ecstasy, whatever you wish to experience, your brain will attempt to provide and validate because that is what you believe. You receive what you ask for. Your perception creates *yes*. The problem is that the brain often says, "Yes," to what is in the unconscious.

Life creates. Look around, and you see that life boundlessly creates in infinite directions and variations—infinitely. To be in accord with the infinitude of this natural expression, you must discover your unique, creative flow, and focus on what you want.

Through living your own life, you break yourself open to the mysteries of life. Step into your life and discover infinite talents. Come to know the mystery of life through your own experience.

Maturity consists of becoming one's own authority in one's

own life: the fulfillment of fully experiencing your unique life. Discover your own expression, throwing off the expectations of society, duty, obedience, obligation, and family.

The universe is neutral, random, if left alone. Act upon this neutral, random substance to create what you want and desire. Life is the structuring of random stuff.

Your brain is filtering, projecting, expecting, and structuring, and most of it is unconscious. Why not structure consciously more of what you desire? You are completely free to be exactly the way you wish, within the generally accepted rules and laws of your culture. Why not create what makes you joyous and happy? Why not tap into cash flow? Why not create freedom?

Webster's dictionary defines freedom as "the power to exercise choice and make decisions without constraint from within or without."

Freedom is your birthright and not dependent upon anything—not how much money you have or how moral you are. Freedom is independent of your life circumstances or constraints.

Life is typically lived from the *if only* perspective. "If only I had X (fill in the blank), then I could finally be happy." How many *if only* statements about sex, money, spirituality, religion, job, family, love, relationships, etc., impact your perception of wonder, happiness, freedom, and well being in this moment?

I invite you to take an inventory of your life. Pay attention to the places and spaces inside your body where you truly feel free, and where you feel constrained, blocked, or restricted.

The unconscious mind contains everything we can't accept in life. Any sensations that we feel are too overwhelming, for whatever reason, end up in the unconscious mind. Since the unconscious, autonomic mind makes up 90 percent of brain function, then we better pay attention to what it is saying and doing with respect to our sense of self, especially our spiritual, psychological, and financial freedom.

The conscious mind, on the other hand, contains everything we can accept. All sensations that we are willing to feel are contained in the conscious mind. The conscious mind represents what we allow ourselves to experience the sensations of—our comfort zone. Seeking the safety of our conscious mind, living within our comfort zone, dominates our whole life experience and perspective. Our life path then focuses on playing it safe.

Any path you follow will eventually become the constraint. You will find that your beliefs are the obstacles to freedom. Let freedom guide you on your path. Society will not agree with you on your path of freedom—avoid looking outside yourself for approval. Do what feels good and right, and leads you to expansion and freedom. Freedom happens when you discover your own path, your own joy, and destroy your old, outworn beliefs and mythologies that keep you imprisoned. When mythologies are destroyed, freedom reigns, and energy flows back to the powerful, creative self. Energy flows back to your center, and you can use that free flowing energy to create and structure what you want.

Human beings are completely dissociated from the modalities

of the past. New situations come up faster then we imagine. The world we live in changes rapidly. The models used 2,000 years ago no longer work—nor perhaps do the models used 20 minutes ago. We have to find our own way.

Ultimately, you decide what is right for you and what is not. <u>Take what you need and let the rest go.</u> Feel free to open this book randomly, playfully, and see how it answers your questions perfectly ... sometimes harshly, and sometimes gently, guiding you on your own path. You have to risk being alive to fully live your life.

Remember, if you are reading this book, then you are already on a path of freedom.

Infinite Love,
Lawrence Lanoff
Sedona, Arizona
April 2007
www.acourseinfreedom.com

The Power of Myth: How you are Kept Prisoner by a Drunken Monkey with Sharp Teeth and a Big Bite

The Drunken Monkey lives inside your head just beneath your conscious awareness whispering painful, paranoid, enraged, vengeful, confused, conflicted and often catastrophic guidance through an unconscious flow of myths, symbols, images, voices, feelings, and thoughts, flowing day and night through your body and mind—a suicidal back seat driver, clamoring for control of the steering wheel of your life. When the drunken monkey speaks, no matter how insane the thought, your *brain* has no choice but to listen. Up until now, you have been the drunken monkey's prisoner, and you are living on a planet of prisoners whose minds are plagued and paralyzed by the drunken monkey's distorted, terrorized thinking.

The operating system of the drunken monkey is based on myths. Myths structure the deep, unconscious brain, and thereby inadvertently structure the conscious, self-aware mind, and what we call our conscience. We are rendered helpless by these deep and powerful myths, the cute little fairy stories with teeth, that the drunken monkey seamlessly weaves into an unconscious nightmare of fear, anxiety, shame, blame, and guilt that makes life for billions of people nearly unbearable.

What we call the conscious mind, the new brain, is a relatively recent development in human evolution. As the prefrontal cortex and cortex evolved, they gave us the ability to build large social structures for mutual benefit, safety, and support. With our self-aware mind, we recognize and bond with people in our immediate group. We know when we hurt another's feelings or break moral codes—seeing the consequences of our actions through the eyes of others; we feel their emotional pain. We can also scan the world around us for potential threats to the group's well being. By having a self-aware mind and conscience, we can contemplate our own life, lessons, and destiny of death.

The new brain focuses on relationships, imagination, thinking, problem solving, possibility, potential, resource sharing, etc. The conscious mind interacts with stored memories and feelings, allowing us to learn, grow, adjust, adapt, and change our behaviors so that we fit in and thrive within our society. We have a biological drive to be part of a whole. However, an unintended consequence of the conscious mind is that it is weak when compared to the ancient brain. The old brain has highly developed neural pathways fighting for access to the parasympathetic and sympathetic nervous systems. The old brain dominates the new brain; the drunken monkey runs the show. The new brain is helpless to defend itself against the constant onslaught of the ancient symbolic language running rampant behind the scenes.

The language of the drunken monkey is myth and symbols, and our modern mind has been drugged, trapped, and programmed by myths and symbols thousands of years old that developed around the same time as the newer parts of the brain were firmly coming on-line. We have become slaves to our brains, and more accurately, the operating system developed by the drunken monkey to help us survive and not be annihilated by life.

Myths are the unconscious operating system. Myths are the shorthand symbols of fear, anxiety, and guilt that the ancient brain uses to control the body and mind. Myths are powerful, energy evoking symbols and stories about our ancestors' *severe misunderstandings and misperceptions* about life, told to other ancestors as if these stories were correct or worse yet, truth. Myths are a virus with no cure—unknowingly spreading lineage to lineage, family to family, city to city, state to state, country to country—continuously evolving over time to fit the language and imagery of the day. Myths keep people in an unhappy, ignorant, sleep state, thinking that they know the truth about this life. People fight, work, live and die for myths that they believe in—myths that they inherited and now take for granted as *truth.*

Myths swim just beneath the surface of conscious awareness and are nearly impossible to catch. Even when we do see our myths, it is only for fleeting moments. They seamlessly slip in and out of our inner minds, constantly influencing our moment-to-moment experience whether we are awake or asleep. We don't consciously perceive the myth's symbols working on our psyche; therefore, releasing ourselves from the myth's clutches is nearly impossible.

From the womb until our final gasp for breath, myths are cleverly implanted into the unconscious via cute little stories that mommy and daddy tell us about life. These stories comfort us, giving us the rules and laws that we need to survive and thrive in our culture. Myths compose the operating system of this human life and determine almost every decision that we make. We attribute the creation of this operating system, and the feelings within our conscience to God, but we have no idea that these feelings are actually composed of the energies from powerful myths, created by our ancestors, and passed down through the ages as absolute truth.

Let me give you an example. Suppose you know this *truth* about life: sex is dirty, bad, and shameful. Perhaps you feel guilty about self-pleasuring or engaging sexually with a partner. You've heard that it's immoral to orgasm—that God's purpose for sex is procreation only. Moreover, your own parents told you that God would punish you if you feel too good. You know this is the *truth* because any time you have sex or self-pleasure, you feel God judging you, or nonphysical beings such as angels or dead relatives watching you with displeasure. Therefore, you experience horrible feelings of guilt and shame flowing through your body anytime that you even think something sexual. From the drunken monkey's perspective, the feelings of guilt and shame prove to you that sex is bad, evil, and wrong.

The drunken monkey tells you that something external (God) is punishing you for having animal, lower chakra desires. You are taught that it's not good to feel good. After all, you *feel* God and your conscience pressuring your psyche about how evil your sexual impulses and behaviors are. The problem is that you don't know that your conscience is set by your *inherited and learned* core beliefs and mythologies about life. God does not set your conscience—*your ancestors do.*

You must remember to ask the simple question, "Is this myth, this cute little story that mommy and daddy told me about life, actually serving me? For that matter, is it even correct?" Mommy and daddy can't question because they have been commanded not to question by God's law.

Our religions, the spiritually oriented infrastructure of myths that we live by, appeared roughly 7,000 years ago. The key insight that priests propagated was a simple one: *as above, so below.* The science and mythology of that time taught that the Gods were in heaven, and that they moved the stars, sun, and moon in an orderly manner. The sun rose at a certain time and set at a certain time. The *heavens*, the ephemeral domain of angels and God, were predictable, orderly, and perfect, while the earthly plane was evil, irregular, and abhorrent. Earth had loss, famine, pain, suffering, sex, murder, death, war, and defeat.

The idea, the myth, the gross misunderstanding that followed was this: we should order earth to be like heaven—*as above, so below*. That is our job, and that is what God expects: *as above* (order, clarity, and predictability), *so below*. With this simple misperception, this simple misunderstanding of ancestral insight taken as truth, the entire modern world has been condemned to a psychological sentence of life in prison. The drunken monkey is running the show. From education to law, and everything in between, our modern society has been ordered around this gross misunderstanding, and the drunken monkey loves it.

Imagine using a 7,000 year-old road map to drive across the United States. The map would be mostly useless. Yet, we continue using maps of life and morality generated by our ancestors whose science and ideas are thousands of years old. How crazy is that?

Our entire modern world is structured around this ancient idea—*as above, so below*—which is incorrect. The *heavens* are not ordered by God, but rather by laws of gravity. Gravity is a physical force, not a spiritual one, and there is no *up there* anyway. Space is space. We live in an infinitely expanding universe that is expanding infinitely. Nothing is fixed in space, and there is no static point of heaven or anywhere else *up there* in the universe. There is emptiness and expansion. Our rules, laws, and morals are based on a misunderstanding of a spiritual story; yet the power of myth is that despite all human science and insight that have appeared in the last 7,000 years, the erroneous story persists, structuring and organizing our lives from the inside out. As a planet, we are lost in the delusion that there is truth *out there*, in the heavens above; lost in a vast illusion of the way we were taught to think about life.

The power of myth came to me through meditations, insights,

client sessions, and personal experiences. I asked myself the simple questions, "Why is it that some things change and other things don't? What within holds on tightly to certain beliefs? Who is really running the show in my life?"

Surprisingly, the answer I stumbled upon radically changed my life forever. I recognized it was not God running the show, but rather, my brain. God, it seemed, had little if any influence over the brain. I discovered that the deepest parts of my brain, brain stem, and limbic system were aware and communicative, but beyond my conscious perception. These parts of the brain behaved like a drunken monkey wrestling for control of my daily perception and experience, often winning out over my conscious thoughts, feelings, and behaviors. This is a huge insight because the ancient brain does not use verbal *language*, but rather uses symbols that are not recognized by conscious awareness.

There exists, in the brain, a language system of symbolic imagery that flows beneath the surface, communicating extensively and effectively, yet remaining unconscious and beyond detection by the new brain. The rudimentary symbols in the ancient brain cause the release of vast amounts of energy in the body in the form of stress, tension, shame, guilt, fear, anxiety, and worry.

For two weeks, I entered the world of this ancient, fear-ridden, and symbolic communication, and my life, as I knew it, fell apart. My awareness awakened: what appeared to be coming from *out there,* I discovered, was actually sorting, filtering, and assembling within my brain, but creating the impression that it was coming from outside of myself. Reality, I discovered, was not out there, but rather, being assembled by a drunken monkey inside my head.

I suddenly saw everything in life as a symbol of something else—a secret code of the ancient reptile brain. I began discerning and understanding this simplistic yet powerful language with my conscious new brain. I was shocked by the discovery that, though I thought I was in control of my life, there was an alternate life running a majority of my experience, and it didn't want to change. That part wanted chaos, pain, suffering, guilt, and shame. That's all it knew. After two weeks of communication with these parts of my brain, fear disappeared from my life, replaced by creativity, peace, joy, and ease.

For nearly two years, I was in free fall, unable to communicate to others the depths of what I was learning. I saw the symbolic nature of everything, and how people react to the drunken monkey symbols flowing unconsciously through the brain, communicating them with fervor to others in their daily lives. I no longer saw life as reality—I saw life as a collection of symbols, flimsily woven together inside of the brain, giving rise to the feeling of being conscious, and based in *reality*. (We know what we know because it feels real.) Furthermore, I noticed that other people were completely wrapped up in their inner unconscious symbols, seeing them as *truth!* I saw the way people's faces contorted when the drunken monkey ran the show. People argued and fought with dumbfounding rage, struggling with self-created symbols emerging from deep within consciousness—yet perceiving the symbols as truths emanating from the world outside.

The magnitude of influence that the drunken monkey has over our lives magnified and clarified for me while watching an image of the President on CNN. I watched the President's face contort as he unknowingly referenced the internal symbols being generated by the drunken monkey in his head, and vividly communicated those symbols to the American public. He awakened the drunken monkey anxieties and fears inside of his fellow Americans, and I knew then, nearly eight months before it happened, that we were going to war. The most powerful man in the world thought he was in charge; but in reality, the drunken monkey was running the show and controlling the steering wheel of an entire country. Even the most powerful, influential world leaders fail to recognize that they are reacting to symbolic communications emanating from deep inside their own brains, and being projected and perceived as coming from outside of themselves. When the drunken monkey speaks, everybody listens.

In the following chapters, I attempt to help you become aware of the power of your own myths, to see, hear, and feel the drunken monkey in your head—giving you the chance to let it go for a minute, for a day, for a year, or for a lifetime. My basic guideline is this: people need their myths. So, use the myth if it serves you. When the myth traps you in a prison, limits your freedom, your finances, your ability to love, or your experience of pleasure and joy, when the myth affects your health, then drop the myth. Choose new myths that serve you. You can learn to wrestle back control of your life's steering wheel from the desperate, chaotic grasping of the drunken monkey in your head.

All myths are stories, and all stories are incorrect—all of them. Myths, stories are guesses about the way things are from a very limited perspective of inherited or perceived truth. Expand your vision to encompass the possibility that you don't have a clue, and neither does anybody else—especially the drunken monkey in your head.

Truth, Justice, and the Matrix

At a recent workshop, a student asked the innocent, provocative question, "What is truth?" This question cuts to the heart of the human experience. What *is* truth? Truth is the belief within self that you have things figured out. Possibly, you believe that we are all one, or that love is the highest path, or that you are not the body, or that the ego is bad, or that vegetarianism is the right way, or that there is a gigantic conspiracy of some kind intended to control you. Everybody thinks that they figured out the truth and emphatically insist that you believe their truth. This gives you a hint that the question of truth is a question of mythology.

Truth is a story, or a bunch of stories about reality, a myth. The problem is that if you were taught myths of truth as a child, if you were raised with *the truth* in your household, then *your* truth is *the truth*. The stories that you learned at an early age from school, society, culture, family, and religion become cemented in your consciousness as inherited truths. These truths set the boundaries of your moral, ethical codes of conduct—your conscience. The stories appear real and concrete in your inner psyche—but the stories are not real. The stories and truth exist in *energetic reality*. Therefore, your truth can be changed.

The problem is that the brain interprets the truth, in energetic reality, as unchangeable physical reality. The brain confuses energetic reality with physical reality because when you are young and listen to stories, you create vivid images about the stories in your head and perceive them as if they *actually happened*. The stories didn't actually happen in three-dimensional reality; you just see the images vividly happen, in energetic reality, in your mind's eye. This is especially true when you hear these stories as a child. You grossly misunderstand the images inside your head to be truth—a documentary of the story that you are hearing as if it actually occurred—but the truth is inside your head.

We can summarize truth in this way: truth is whatever you believe it is because it *feels real* to you. You were there. You saw the story *happen in your head*, so it must be true. You concretize your stories and turn them into external events—news stories and facts. You know the stories are truth because that is what you were told by mommy and daddy, what you saw in your head with your inner eyes, and what feels real to you in your body—and you expect the rest of the world to agree with your truth. If other people agree with you, then you think that confirms the three-dimensional, newsworthy reality of your truth; but this is nothing more than a shared hallucination about reality. You see what your brain is

Truth, Justice, and the Matrix

structured to see.

Let's say that you have the insight that reality is an energy matrix—we are all one with life, and that real life is actually the matrix—the web of oneness. The matrix is *the truth*, and because you saw that idea in a movie, and other people agree, then it must be true. Also if you take any kind of hallucinogenic drugs, then you personally have seen through this life, and you have seen the matrix with your own eyes. The drug experience confirms the *truth*. Now, it becomes truth with a capital T. However, the harsh reality is that your truth is just another story about the way life is; that is, in this example, facilitated by drugs.

We live on a planet of competing truths—each person believing their story about reality is *the right one*. Truth is a story about a gross misunderstanding about life and the universe. It is scary trying to get a handle on the fact that there may be no truth out there. People want to feel safe and secure in this universe, and want to believe that they, or someone else, have it all figured out.

People are trying to engage you in their hallucination. They want agreement in their gross misunderstanding of reality, concretized by other delusional people. As more people agree with a reality, you see a cult or a religion develop.

Basically, truth is a mythology. A mythology is a story about a gross misunderstanding about life. The problem with truth is that you think your truth is the right way when it isn't. You live in an infinitely expanding universe, expanding infinitely. Whatever is truth today will not be truth tomorrow. A few years ago, some people thought that the Internet was the work of the devil. The people who believed that truth left themselves far behind technologically, and are now forced to catch up. The Internet is an integral part of everyday life. Everything that we do is Internet based. Therefore, the myth had to change. Now it is okay to use the Internet. What changed? Not reality. The Internet didn't change; just the story, the myth, that the Internet is evil changed.

Truth is relative, based in the moment, and comes and goes. What has the desire to know truth given you up to this point? What has pushing your truth on others given you? Desiring an answer will take you nowhere. The so-called truth never took you anywhere, and never gave you anything except a muddled mess. The irony is that as you realize that there is no truth, you can find your freedom in the unknown and rest in awareness. As you bring in that awareness, you are free. Beyond truth, there is a space of peace, freedom, and the feeling of relaxation that allows the mind to be still. There is nothing to search for. What you are looking for is already where you are—the freefall of the unknown.

Truth is nothing more than a story, a mythology, about the way life is. You think that you have things figured out, but you don't. Moreover, whatever you think that you have figured out will change soon enough. Truth is just a gross misunderstanding about life. Nobody really knows much of anything, including you.

Human Problem Underlying all Problems— It is All in Your Head!

On the journey of freedom, the most important truth of all is that human beings, and human brains specifically, have an amazing inability to distinguish what is real from what is not real. This problem arises from the very act of thinking—the active process of generating and storing symbolic mental imagery. Thinking is not reality, but rather the generation of symbols woven together by various parts of the brain, in an attempt to approximate three-dimensional reality.

This idea came to me while meditating in Sedona, Arizona. I asked myself the simple question, "How do I *know* anything?" It occurred to me that life is a commingling of experiences and sensory inputs, perceived as reality, but stored in the form of symbols. Each part of the brain has its own symbolic system, and some of those symbols override other symbols. In general, the older, more ancient symbols in your brain take over. For example, you are walking alone on a dark city street late at night. The brain stem and the reptilian parts of the brain awaken and offer their symbols to help you sense, perceive, and most importantly, survive any potential threat. If your experiences of dark city streets are mostly good, then the symbols that show up while you walk are mostly good. However, if your experiences of being alone on a dark city street are mostly scary, then the brain stem will offer images that are frightening and adrenaline provoking; overriding your prefrontal cortex, your thinking mind, and putting you in a state of high alert. Simply reading these words about a dark city street has an affect upon you. If the thought scares you, the fear symbols will overwhelm your rational mind. In general, ancient symbols win out over recently formed symbols and experiences stored in the brain. Everything is symbolic of something else—a reference to a feeling, a past experience, an emotion, or a thought. From a neurological perspective, in a stressful situation, the more ancient parts of the brain will take over.

Open in your life to the idea that all life is metaphorical, symbolic. Nothing is what it appears to be, ever. Life is symbolic, connotative. The literal interpretation, the denotation that we inflect on life through cultural stories, personal myths, religious beliefs, etc., is simply a misunderstanding of the way life is. The moment that you think you have it all worked out, you are lost in the desert without water.

Denotation pertains to the literal meaning of things, something heard or read and taken as *reality*—the absolute truth, the final word (including news, entertainment, books, fairy tales, dreams, religious teachings, family knowledge, learned wisdom, psychic readings, etc.).

Human beings share their inner symbolic insights, spiritual truths, and wisdoms in stories, songs, writings, and symbols. Most human beings misinterpret these teachings as reality—*truth* with a capital T—especially if they adopted them as their own truths, if they are living their lives based on these truths, and not seeing them for the cute little stories that they actually are.

Connotation has to do with the inflection of the story, the symbolic meaning behind the story, the inner wisdom of the story—the original insight that gave birth to the story. Spiritual insights, wisdoms, and guidelines told in symbolic, story form reflect the inner psyche of the person writing them. All things written are projections from deep within the ancient, symbolic brain. In understanding life in a symbolic way, nothing is taken as real—all is understood as poetry, metaphor, and symbolism. The stories represent expressions and reflections of the inner energies and potentialities within each of us, driven by our deepest longings, desires, needs, and drives. Whether it is the drive of the pleasure seeking organ, or the drive for community and love in the heart, or the desire to connect with God, each organ is often in conflict with the needs and drives of the other organs. Each organ struggles to assert control. The entire organization of the brain/mind/body/central nervous system reflects this struggle for control. Different parts of the brain struggle for control over other parts of the brain, competing for neurological and chemical resources. The body is composed of competing systems, each in its own way struggling for power, control, and dominance—each trying to assert its own *truth*.

For everything revealed in a story or religious truth, something deeper is hidden, concealed, and covered up. From morality to hidden agendas, your organs, chakras, and desires have ulterior motives to everything that they do. Always ask yourself, "Why am I doing what I'm doing? What God will I follow? Which organ is trying to assert itself, and lead the charge right now, and why?" The answers to these simple questions determine your experience of freedom and happiness in your life.

Most individuals involved with world religions are tangled in this problem of connotation versus denotation. The elders and books teach us that what we read in *Holy Scripture* is *literal*—the final word of God—factual, actual, a documentation of events. We are riveted when told these old stories are real, historical events, similar to a movie beginning with the words, *based on actual events*. We love this type of teaching, but it reduces the potential spiritual insights to news reports about events from long ago—as finding an old newspaper from the 1800's is interesting, but not at all relevant to our life now.

All stories are metaphors, even if we believe them to be fact and reality. For example, we hear an engaging premise to a story—the end of the world is coming in 2012. Focusing on the denotation of the story is simple misreading of symbolism, interpreting a mythical image—the end of the world—and taking the story as reality, a fact. We, as humans, are part of the dramatic through line—will the human race survive or not? Who will be the *chosen people*? These are very compelling story lines, but have nothing to do with reality.

I promise you, the world will not end in 2012. How can I say such a thing with unwavering fortitude? First, I have spent years training myself to clearly detect the metaphor, to recognize the symbols passed down through the ages emerging from the deep inner brain; however, the second and most obvious reason is the earth doesn't keep a day planner—but more on that in a later chapter.

Armageddon stories and the end of the world mythologies have been told since the beginning of humankind. Perhaps you remember the millennium individuals who believed the end of the world was coming in 2000. (That's what Prince's song, *1999*, was about.) They predicted this for over 20 years. Then there are the technologists who believed the end of the world would come through the collapse of the modern technology infrastructure because of Y2K, the two-digit date that didn't include a new millennium. We all remember the San Diego cult that believed spaceships were behind Haley's comet, and killed themselves so that they could join the hidden mother ship; or those who believed Nostradamus's prediction that Los Angeles would sink into the water in 1973, 1979, 1981, 1986, 1987, 1996, and of course 1999. I was living in Los Angeles during the 1987 prediction—and it nearly cleared out Los Angeles that weekend. In my lifetime alone, the end of the world, as *predicted* by the Mayan calendar, has happened seven times.

I have seen and heard at least 45 different versions of these deep brain stem symbols that deal with the end of times. Individuals believe that their interpretation of the myth is the *real one*, the right one, and that this time is different from all the others because of the confluence of events, planets, astrological signs, and X (fill in the blank). In the 1970's, my best friend's mother left New York City because the Bible predicted that God would make *satanic* New York City fall into the water. Each generation, since the beginning of Christianity, believes that the second coming of Christ will occur in their lifetime.

All great religions of the world share the same elemental myths and stories as their moral building blocks, but fight one another because the same biblical, *rules and law* based God, has different names. We kill each other in the name of our God, because we take the symbolic references within the storybooks as absolute truth.

We are conflicted when science proves repeatedly that these stories did not, or even worse, could not have happened. External reality says definitively *no*; internal beliefs and symbols say unequivocally *yes*. We may be disappointed, confused, uncertain, or more often in denial when time shows us that what we expected to happen didn't. Typically, our inner realities and beliefs win out. We deny three-dimensional reality—what actually happened—and go with our internal gut feelings and hallucinations.

We do this because the brain experiences *reality* in two directions—externally and internally. Images inside our brain are perceived as real, and images outside our brain are perceived as real; however, the brain perceives all information as externally produced, whether it comes from the inside or outside. The nature of the brain's function is that whether the image is internally manufactured or externally experienced, it is all perceived as if it is externally experienced. The result is that we interpret stories, internal images, and symbols in our heads as external, historical, natural, actual events—and this is where things get really messy.

Our brains project upon and add to external reality—it is the only way we can make sense of the data entering the senses. We *must* categorize, interpret, shape, add to, cross reference, associate, deny, process, filter, anticipate, judge, contrast, compare, expect, structure, and seamlessly experience reality as coming from outside of ourselves—*out there*—as if coming through the five senses. This is how the brain operates. It is not bad or wrong—it is simply the mechanics of the brain.

Those who came before us expressed their internal insights and understandings about the world that they were living in as if they were real, external, and historical facts—because that is how they experienced them. Our spiritual leaders of the past thought their internal insights, the images in their heads, were actual reality.

Mythology is the symbolic language of spiritual insight, communicating about the internal dynamics and spiritual forces that shape us. All myths and religious metaphors are true in the sense that they speak of internal transformation and possibility—the death and rebirth of consciousness—not about external reality.

In order to make sense of our lives, we must learn to read the imagery and tales as symbolic of spiritual powers and potentialities within us. We have to teach our conscious brain to read all external situations symbolically, because much of what we experience is actually projection from internal depths of the symbolic fear based brain that we perceive as coming from outside of ourselves, including what we think of God. This creates denotation confusion. We think everything is completely external and real. We live in a very loosely cobbled together, arbitrary reality that we think is *fact*—it is not.

Thinking is simply the process of accessing and combining internal and external symbols to give you a perception of external reality. Think poetically, artistically, and metaphorically—act responsibly. Nothing is what it appears to be, ever. Nothing.

External World is a Projection of Your Inner Mind—That's Scary!

A cold, unloving, dangerous world is simply a projection of your inner mind. Your sense of self, your identity, is a projection. Your life is a projection. Allow for the awareness that you are the cause of your own life, and your own experience. Where are you focusing your attention? Who is focusing?

If we attempt to receive nourishment from an externalized projection, that is to say from the world outside, we will always remain hungry. We are like a child, lost in an adult world, trying to figure out a way to survive. We can never thrive as a child, because we always project our needs outside of ourselves in an effort to change and heal our past experiences, which is hopeless, and not helpful. We want somebody or something outside of ourselves to save us—as mommy and daddy used to. We are still looking for the milk to suckle from the breast.

I first discovered this learned helplessness while working with a client who I saw symbolically as a body with no legs or arms. This was a very disturbing symbol. To the person experiencing it, it felt real. I quickly recognized it as a symbol of the limbic system—a symbol of helplessness and fear. From the limbic system's perspective, being trapped without arms and legs is a feeling that it knows all too well. For eons, our ancestors dealt with limited mobility, always on the verge of extinction and annihilation.

We are born helpless, and this orients us to the idea that the power in life is somehow out there—for someone or something else to give to us. Mommy is our savior, our rescuer, and our life. Mommy comes to assist us when we are helpless, and this creates the feeling in the brain/mind/body/central nervous system that the answer, the savior is out there. This is a misunderstanding about the way life is.

Consider that you may be mistaken in your approach to life, with the focus on looking outside of yourself. Why do you do it then? Why do you do the very thing that you don't want to do? You go to the movie theater marked pain and suffering, and that is the movie that you watch. If you want to change your experience, you must do something different that is outside of your zone of comfort. Fear of sensation is the fear of life. What you are afraid of happening externally is actually happening internally, and being perceived as if it is happening externally. The projector inside you must change the movie. Changing the way that you interact changes your reality. Insanity is doing the same thing, over and over again, and expecting a different result.

An infinite number of possibilities exist about how the

projector will work, or not work, but you must recognize them. The world is infinite, filled with endless possibilities. You are creating your world exactly the way you have been structured by the drunken monkey.

The world we live in is the world that we deserve. If we live in a world void of love, then that is the world that we are creating and the world that we are structuring. If we think that we deserve a better world, then we must do what is needed to create that world. If we change the world that is structured inside our heads, then external experiences will shift to reflect the new structure.

If you want a juicy world, filled with freedom, then you must create that. Change the movie. What are you afraid to experience, feel, or say right now? You can have anything that you want, anything at all—yet you do not. Why?

What the Bleep Do You Want, Anyway?

What do you want? This may be a difficult question to answer—especially, if you are immersed in a spiritual mythology (e.g., personality dissolves upon enlightenment, focusing on money is not spiritual, sexual desires are to be denied and suppressed, etc.).

As you clear your mythologies, abundant energy becomes available for you to use—to focus on what you want. Your sense of power comes from creating what you want. Your potential to create comes from your ability to focus your energies on receiving and creating; but to do that, the energy must be available. Energy is power. Power is creation. Creation is getting what you want.

As you de-mythologize your life, energy flows back to the center of your being. You use the flow of energy to create your life. The more energy in your center, the more energy you have to create and receive what you want.

Another way to discover what you want is to ask yourself, "What am I passionate about?" I asked a client this question, and he responded that he was passionate about acting and Latin dancing, but not writing. For 15 years, he tried to write a book, and he expressed passionate anger about not being able to write. He created a lot of *not writing* in his life. Are you more passionate about what you want than what you don't want?

What do you want, right now? In your freedom, allow yourself to ask this question. Your birthright is to know what you want, and to pursue that. You create in your life all the time, so defining what you want is extremely important. What you want directs your life. Every decision you make determines what you receive. Either you are working your life, or your life is working you. When energy flows towards what you want, you feel peace, power, pleasure, and joy, in your inner being. You are working your life. When you block the energy flow, you tend to feel angry, depressed, unfulfilled, and compressed in your inner being. Life is working you.

Again, I ask the question, "What do you want?" Internally and externally focus on what you want, and you will create that.

When energy flows towards what you want, you feel peace, power, joy, and pleasure in your inner being. Passion is a creative force. Be passionate about what you are against, and receive more of that—or be passionate about what you want, and create that. From the brain's perspective, it is all the same.

Mirror Brain Always Says, Yes! Except When It Doesn't

Your brain is a mirror reflecting back exactly what you give it. I discovered this while in deep meditation. I noticed an echo. No matter what I threw out or thought about, it was echoed back to me. As I pulled my awareness further and further back in an attempt to understand this echo effect, I saw in an instant that the brain is a mirror. Like the distant sound of my voice echoing back to me in a red rock canyon, I realized that whatever I asked for, the brain very lovingly sent back to me with a *yes*. I would say I want love, and within seconds, massive amounts of love flowed back to me. If I saw hate, hate came flowing back.

The problem is that our mythologies, beliefs, and unconscious send impulses to our brain, too! The brain bounces these feelings directly back to us, exactly as we sent them out. Whatever we experience is something that we created, and the brain is simply mirroring back to us. In a way, what we call God is simply a mirror that says, *"Yes."*

We structure mythologies, stories, beliefs, and feelings inside of us, and then turn around and perceive them as coming from outside of us—as facts—caused by the outside world. When the myths are perceived outside of us, they are perceived as real objects. We create a monster with horrifying detail exactly the way it scares us the most, and when complete, we turn away from it, count to three, and then turn back. We now see an external, horrible monster that is the worst thing that there is in the world—our monster—and it scares us deeply and intimately. We conjure the worst of the worst, and then forget that we conjured it. We are terrified when we see the monster, having forgotten that we created it in the first place.

The brain structures, conjures, and creates reality, then perceives this conjured reality as *absolute, unchanging external reality.* The nature of the ego is that it is a field of changing stress. That stress, bouncing off the mirror universe, is reflected back directly to you.

The natural human state is pain, suffering, addiction, stress, and retraction—feeling out of control, helpless, and fearful of the external and internal worlds. It is not about the actual world itself, but how you feel about the world that you are seeing. That is what clues you in on your perceptual window. If you feel judged, it is safe to say that at the deepest levels of self, you are judging yourself, and so on.

The external world is a reflection of your inner consciousness—wounded parts within you desperately trying to heal by constantly re-creating hurtful circumstances, hoping to change the outcome. Your conscious mind says one thing and your unconscious, feeling world, says something quite different. Stop looking outside and blaming outside; instead, look at what is being reflected from inside.

A mirror doesn't care what you think about it, what you wear, what you do. It simply reflects back exactly what is in front of it. In a mirror universe, the answer is always *yes*.

The brain is an associative organ. No matter what you focus on, the brain reflects it back instantly. Over time, your external reality will change as you live in silence, in awareness. As inner quiet is mirrored back to you, you have more of that in your life, and therefore, more energy to create what you want.

Lies of the Self and the Field of Awareness

The shift into the field of awareness is crucial. Awareness encompasses the brain/mind/body/central nervous system. All of those exist within awareness. Awareness itself is similar to the page on which you are reading these words. The page itself is unchanged, but what is projected, seen, or read changes your experience. If I say, "I love you," that will be experienced one way. If I say, "Your feet smell," that will be experienced another way. The page hasn't changed, only your experience of what is on the page has changed.

As we come to know ourselves as the field behind the projections, then what appears on the screen becomes less important or volatile, because there is always the screen. This is awareness.

Take a moment to feel into the field upon which everything is being projected. Your senses are projecting. Your emotions are projecting. Your brain is projecting. Feel into the field that the projections are occurring upon. Be aware of being aware. Feel the screen that your brain is using to perceive. In truth, there is no way to perceive anything directly. Sit with what you are actually experiencing right now. Who perceives? Are you the perception, the content of what you perceive; or the awareness, the field upon which the projection occurs?

Life is basically an assemblage of data/input from the physical senses, filtered through our worst, most painful, empty, lonely, and impoverished life experiences that are then again interpreted by the brain/mind/body/central nervous system in a kind of semi-closed loop. We are in trouble if we don't find a more conscious path, because the brain/mind/body/central nervous system is basically a storage device for pain and fear, which from its perspective ensures our survival.

Life on earth developed with the idea that pain is the way. Survival depends on avoiding pain, suffering, and death. Religion grew out of this need in humans to control the pain/death continuum; however, this place isn't real. If you are a soul, then you are already whole and complete. You can't be a more complete soul. How can a human illusion, resting in God awareness, create a sin? How can a human illusion create karma? You are not real in an ultimate sense. If you were, then there would be no death. The physical existence that you are living is impermanent. If physical existence is impermanent, then it can't be *real* with a capital R. The form that you are living in, the container that moves through physical life, will cease to exist.

What you are seeking is much closer than you think. You already are that which you are looking for. What you are looking for is a perception, a feeling, or a knowing, which is completely arbitrary. This life is a lie, a complete fabrication. Karma, or the game of life, is probably incorrect.

Karma is a Gross Way to Work Out Anything—I Do Mean Gross!

Karma is a waste of time, one illusion supposedly hurting another illusion—then creating more karma for whatever else it does while paying off an earlier debt. Karma is a double bind. The nature of all life is that it creates pain and suffering for someone or something. Life feeds on life, so by definition karma is created constantly.

I discovered this while working on a friend. He was recovering from a bad divorce. I looked at how much he had lost and suffered. He felt it happened because of *bad karma*. When I looked at his *karmic* body, and what had actually been *paid* against this supposed debt, I was shocked to see that this entire life of pain and suffering barely made a dent in the karmic pool. This one life had already made more karma than it had burned. "Karma is wrong," I said. "If we use karma as the path to salvation, we will remain on this planet forever, trapped in a downward spiral to a life of hell."

Our understanding of karma must be incorrect. If you follow the law out, you see that there is nothing that you can do that creates no harm. Just existing creates some harm to someone or something, even if it is to yourself or your body. Harm is done always, and energetically the pain outweighs the payment. You are always accumulating debt, but burning up very little.

Karma only works because you are asleep. You live in a state of continuous illusion, thinking it is real, and judging yourself by this sense of reality—what you should have done versus what you actually did. Basically, you are screwed if you believe that this is your real life. You, in this illusion, could suffer a lifetime to pay the debt that you owe from a previous lifetime, and not even scratch the surface of diminishing the debt that you collected in this lifetime. Karma is not pound for pound. Karma is a strange system, because the life that you think you are living doesn't even exist. No one here is real. How could you possibly collect karma for a life that isn't real? You don't collect karma on a movie; you are just acting—pretending that it is real, and so it is with life. There is no inherent reality; this life is an illusion.

Furthermore, why would God need these illusions to suffer? We are not real. Everything that we know about ourselves are stored symbols—memories that when accessed cause a release of energy, feelings in the body. We are trapped in the gravitational field of beliefs and emotions, based on the human created morality stories of God, fear, pain, and suffering—as if suffering will magically change karma. We are here because we are here. If we are deluded into thinking that our being here makes a modicum of difference in the universe, then that is our illusion. If we are already whole and complete, then why the pain and suffering: to have a good life, another time, someday in heaven?

The idea of heaven is a mythological image—not a reality. Heaven relates to the idea mentioned earlier: *as above, so below.* Heaven refers to a mythological, misunderstood image, not to an external place where we can find peace. Heaven refers to a state of consciousness: here and now—a state where you experience peace *now*, in this life, in this moment. Heaven is a psychological state of awareness, not physical reality.

Our life, everything that we know about who and what we are, is a lie, a consideration, and part of the illusion, a complete fabrication. Life is arbitrary. This life and our culture could easily have grown out of love, peace, joy, orgasms, ecstasy, fun, play, Samadhi, etc. Why not?

Forget Karma. There is nobody here to collect Karma. Life is no more than a story about the way that it is. Your stories are your prisons. Release the story, and release yourself from prison. Release yourself from prison, and gain life force energy to create what it is that you want. What the bleep do you want, anyway? For that matter, what the bleep do you know?

Life is Arbitrary—Get Over It!

Life, and whatever spiritual path you choose to believe in, is an arbitrary construction, a myth. A myth is a spiritual insight—*a misunderstanding about the way life is*—expressed in story form that people (including the author of the story) believe is real, right, and true. All content that you tell yourself about this life is a myth. The universe is infinite possibility. The key life questions are, "What am I creating in this arbitrary place? How am I choosing to live?"

Early on my path, I often related to and valued my painful past as a teaching tool. I believed that the more I suffered, the more I would grow spiritually. This mythology came from Christianity and Buddhism. Then I had the breakthrough understanding of symbols and realized that the only ties to my past are the symbols that I have stored in my brain. If I change the pain-charged symbols of my past into positive, life affirming symbols, then the experience of my past, my present, and my future change, too. You have to learn to rewrite what you call the past—which is really a collection of long-term stored symbols in the brain that you interpret as reality. (When the brain experiences a debilitating disease such as Alzheimer's, the sense of reality changes, too.) The brain fabricates your past history to the best of its ability based on the stored symbols. You can take your consciousness, your awareness, and bring it to bear on your past, changing that which doesn't work for you. Go back to the future, and forward to the past to create the life that you want *now*.

Choosing your life is giving structure, or more accurately, extracting structure out of the random stuff that life and the universe are made of—extracting structure from infinite possibility. You are extracting your structure out of nothingness. Choose wisely. The physical universe doesn't care, so have it work for you in a juicy, fun, and joyous direction.

If you could do anything, what would you do?

If you could be anything, what would you be?

If you could create anything, what would you create?

What is it that you want, right now?

What are your deepest desires?

What if you realized that your desires are expressions of energies wanting to move through your body and be experienced? What if you gave yourself permission to experience what you want right now—energetically—in thought?

Life is arbitrary—space/time is arbitrary. Recognizing this offers you the opportunity to create what you want at any given moment. The purpose of life is to create. Creativity is rewarded on this planet. What do you want to create, right now?

Space, Time, Speed, Radar Guns, and Planet Earth Day Planners

As I said before, the earth does not carry a day planner. The starting point of a calendar is a completely arbitrary human creation based on observable, seemingly unchanging patterns, such as phases of the moon, cycles of the sun, temperature changes, seasons, crop harvest patterns, etc.

No *real* calendar exists in the universe. That is why every culture has a different religious New Year, based on the point in time when that culture began paying attention to the cycles of nature and writing them down in symbolic form.

Space/time is an arbitrary distinction that gives us a model for negotiating our way through three-dimensional life—gross physical reality—but is nothing more than an overlay, a vivid hallucination. The paradox is that space/time exist, but they aren't *real*—even though they feel that way.

Simply put, the human perception of time, as a sequence of consecutive moments, is an artifact of a still developing brain.

Space, Time, and Speed

Space/time is an outgrowth of the natural tendency of the brain to *chunk down* reality into manageable parts, symbols that are key to the perception of our reality. The concept of space/time is inherently flawed because it is a concept—an overlay appearing real.

In one of my shifts of consciousness, I began to perceive time as an expansion, a wave that ripples through the universe. Time is not linear, but rather something that fluctuates with our experience, expanding and contracting, depending on what we are doing or where our awareness is focused. Time is relative. To me, time is experienced as simultaneous waves. I see the whole of my life, from womb to death; yet experience the focus of the moment. On one hand, I am already dead, and these words are those of a dead man speaking. On the other hand though I am technically alive, I am in a process of dying, and I will cease to exist in this form eventually. The part of me writing no longer exists—in a way is dead, and the only evidence of its existence are the words written on the page, which will also at some point cease to exist.

Getting back to the earth, it hurtles through space in multiple directions simultaneously, at unfathomable, mind-bending speeds. To think there is a fixed point in space/time is ludicrous. We live in an infinitely expanding universe; however, the only way that we can know and understand the speeds at which we are moving through space is to measure them in reference to other objects that are also hurtling through space—one of Einstein's realizations.

If you somehow fixed yourself in the universe for a moment, the earth would hurtle by you at over 70,000 miles per hour. The entire planet would blur past you in less than a blink of an eye, and that is just one of the movements affecting the earth at this very moment.

Space/time/speed are human creations and have nothing to do with anything—except functioning comfortably while here on the planet. In consciousness, in meditative spaces, there often is no sense of time, an altered sense of space, and a sense of boundaries changing. Perception itself is what creates sensation. If you don't know it, or don't perceive it, then essentially it has no impact.

To expand your own consciousness, you must consider things beyond those perceived by the five senses. To understand why the world will not be destroyed in your lifetime is to understand that all perception is relative, and has little to do with what is actually happening in the physical world. In order to make a date with destiny—that is, the destruction of the world (a misunderstood metaphorical image)—the universe would have to fix itself in space/time, and it would have to agree on an exact time and location to destroy the earth so that you could be there to see it.

Imagine that you have a date with friends. They don't know where they are in space/time, and they don't know where they will be. You don't know where you are in space/time, and you don't know where you will be. Furthermore, you don't know where they are, they don't know where you are, you don't know where they will be in space/time, and they don't know where you will be in space/time. Neither of you know date, space/time, nor location. What kind of date do you think that will be? Welcome to life in an infinitely expanding universe. The earth will in fact end someday, but that has nothing to do with you.

You think something is real because it appears real to your senses. However, senses can be erroneous—often, and so can you. In fact, if you pay close attention, you will see that you are mistaken most times about everything ... so relax. Pretty much, you are incorrect about the whole thing. So stop worrying about it, and stop fighting about it—from some perspective or point of view, your beliefs and ideas are just plain old.

Grasping Senses Make Us Human—
They Give Us Headaches

Our essential being is one with nature. We are more impulse systems of nature than we are the *developed, enlightened humans* that we imagine ourselves to be.

The modern ego/mind, the sense of self-awareness, is a relatively new development on the human timeline. When we consider the total history of life on earth, from the development of the first single-celled organisms, which current fossil records suggest began roughly three billion years ago, to the beginnings of the modern human, which began some two million years ago, to the modern homo-sapiens, which began roughly 300,000 years ago, to the current human form, which may have begun as recently as 37,000 years ago, it is clear that we spent most of our genetic time simply being and then not being, coming in and out of existence. Putting it another way, there was no self-awareness for a majority of the last three billion years. As the need developed for more complex systems and societies to work harmoniously together, we began developing the modern ego/mind/brain, with the pre-frontal cortex and cortex being the most recent additions to the brain—a majority of which came on-line in the last 7,000 years.

From this vast time perspective of three billion years, we can see that the modern ego/mind/brain is still evolving. We are a work in progress. Scientists recently discovered a brain evolution gene that may be responsible for helping the brain evolve 70 times faster than the rest of our genetic code—we are *still evolving*.

Nature, that is not self-aware, is simply being. If we look at a dog, a cat, a monkey, or a bird, they are just there. They are in this natural state of being. A tree is also just being, as are rocks and mountains. Quite frankly, what our spiritual leaders call enlightenment is nothing more than reconnecting to the state that our ancestors experienced for three billion years. This natural being state is where we come from. Our nature is of this, so we really don't have to work all that hard to get back to it. It is more who we are than the modern ego/mind is.

When you come from the perspective that you are your body or mind, then this prison of the ego limits you. However, the instant you know yourself as consciousness, the instant you know yourself as being, as alertness, as composed of the particles of the universe, you are outside the prison. The prison then exists inside of you— not you existing within the prison.

I worked with a student on a regular basis who often suffered from depression, anxiety, and the mind taking control. I explained to the student how chemicals flowing through the body create feelings of anxiety and depression. After several sessions, the student told me that when driving to work the mind started to take control and the chemicals began to flow. The student said, "I finally understood. I got it. The chemicals flowing through my body are not who I am. It's happening, but it's not me. The chemicals flowing through my body make the anxiety feel real, but it's not real." The student no longer existed within the prison. Each time after that when the symptoms recurred, the student let go of the story faster and faster.

Let go of the story that you are somebody. Whoever you think you are is composed of energetic thought reality anyway. Whoever you think you are is constantly changing, updating, and evolving. So, who are you right now? Moreover, where are you right now? It is the grasping parts that inform you of this question.

The five senses are always grasping. That is their job. The eyes grasp, the mouth grasps, the hands grasp, the skin grasps, the ears grasp, always trying to get information about something. The ego living in the body is the ultimate vehicle of neediness.

Take a moment to feel the tension of the grasping. Feel the parts of you that are trying, struggling, and wanting to figure it all out. Your prison is composed of all of that: your neediness, your fear, your grasping. "If only I could get one more X (e.g., dollar, understanding, friend, relationship, etc.)." That is the realm of the senses, because the senses come to life through grasping. Feel into the field of tension that is the grasping of the senses. Feel the senses grasp for air, food, money, shelter, pleasure, pain, etc.

Grasping is what makes senses, senses. No morality is attached to the grasping. The problem for us is when we concretize the grasping of the senses and try to make the external world responsible for our happiness. This is another description of learned helplessness—wanting and waiting for something in the external world to save us.

The field of tension created by the grasping of the senses is what we typically find ourselves living in. We live in the realm of not human beings, but human doings. Call all of the components of this grasping, addictive quality that is the modern ego/mind, into the present time, and give it permission to let go.

You are not this grasping—no matter what. No matter how much you infinitely grasp, you will never grasp enough. The ego/mind is an endless pit that can never be filled, no matter how much you need or try to fill it. The ego/mind lives in energetic reality. Moreover, physical reality will never fill energetic reality.

Ask the simple question, "Who am I beyond this grasping?" What is the field of consciousness that the grasping exists within? Become aware of the part of you that is aware of the grasping. Notice that the grasping lives within your awareness.

Feel into the grasping, but let the grasping float away as a ship on the horizon. Let the part of you that grasps be set adrift in the field of consciousness. Feel into who you are who is beyond the form. When you are no longer compelled by fear, desire, or obligation, when you release the need to believe that you are the mind or the body, things begin to open up.

If you find any part of you trying, notice that. All the effort in the world will not take you over the threshold. Shift your focus to the space in which that grasping exists. It is similar to straining to see the path in front of you by flashlight, searching for every rock or potential threat. That is what the ego/mind experiences, but when you turn the flashlight off, and begin to direct your attention up from the constricted path, you look into the vastness in which that path lives—the vastness of the universe, of which you are a part and only for a short moment that we call life. By making that simple adjustment, the body begins to vibrate in the hum of the universe. You can't be anything other than what you are, and that is a child of the infinite, expanding, and creative universe.

The cells, atoms, and molecules that vibrate in you, are the same ones vibrating in the infinitude of space. Expand your field of view to the magnitude of the infiniteness. Your life exists within the field of vastness. The body lives in consciousness, in awareness, in the vastness of the nothingness. As nothingness approaches, you may feel some resistance, unconsciousness, fear, or grasping. Let that come and let it go.

Recognize the vastness of the universe that you are a part of. The dust that is in you is the dust that is in the infinitude of the universe. Let the dream of the body go. Let the dream of the mind go. Let the dream of your identity go. Feel into the vibration that is emerging in your body as you connect to your being nature. Let that vibration begin to vibrate you. Surrender more deeply into that vibration, and spill into the hum of the universe.

This is a death of the ego having control—bless the ego, release it, send it love and compassion, but let it drift away, like an iceberg on a distant horizon slowly disappearing, melting into the sun. Feel deeply into that vibration. Keep surrendering into the quietness. Surrender into the silence. Recognize the silence and welcome it as your being. Feel the depth of nothing.

Happiness exists in the realm of energetic reality, and therefore must be met energetically. Give yourself what you want and need energetically, and paradoxically, you will give yourself freedom and happiness now.

There Exists an Energetic Reality: Love It or Be Eaten by It

The energetic reality of life is the most influential and powerful reality within you. Energetic reality is experienced as flow throughout your body. Energetic reality is similar to an alternate life that is being lived right now through the physical experience. As you think about these words, there is an energetic reality that is in effect, teaching you as you read.

You may think that you are experiencing *reality*, the words flowing in front of you, but this is only a part of the story. This paragraph and my words have an energetic reality behind them, and the energies are awakening and stirring things within you. Some of you may actually tap into my consciousness. Reading this sentence, if you are quiet, you will notice a flow, a tingle, as the energetic reality teaches you. As you comprehend the truth of energetic reality, you see why it is important for you to cultivate your ability to discern, understand, and track the language of energy.

There Exists an Energetic Reality

You interact with energetic reality everyday. Everyone you meet and speak with, everything that you think is affected by energetic reality. Energetic reality changes with everyone that you interact with. Individuals carry around an energetic *flavor*. Notice how you feel when thinking of a family member or a best friend, someone that you are attracted to, or the person standing next to you. Every person has their own energetic reality, a flavor that they carry with them, and it is as unique as their fingerprints.

At the level of this reality, we are all one. We are all God. Energetic reality is what connects us to everyone and everything in the universe. Learning to understand this energetic reality opens us to tremendous spiritual freedom, because it allows us to participate in the life behind life, the energetic reality of the infinite, to interact with others in total freedom.

In this respect, humans are similar to the Internet. We are each interconnected through our energetic relationship to source, which is where we exist, a network within a network. We are nodes, Internet connections within the context of source. We exist within infinite creation, everything and nothing. As a result, we are plugged into energetic reality, and can instantaneously travel the universe—visiting everyone in it who has ever been, or ever will be. We exist within (and because of) the vast network of source.

Learn to follow this energy, and all things will come to you. Everything that you need appears in the moment that you need it. All information is yours. Infinitely.

Closely track energetic reality—you feel peace in your body when living in your freedom or tightness/constriction when concretizing a mythology—one of your misunderstood stories.

Four Buckets of Mythology—
Your Life Bucket has a Hole in It

Mythologies (misunderstood stories thought of as real) can be assigned to four major categories. These four categories/buckets will assist you in easily recognizing mythological symbols and images, the metaphors that repeatedly appear in society and religion.

Mythological bucket one says that the world—in all its horror and beauty—is perfect the way it is. Many of the early tribal cultures looked at the world in this way—finding mystery and God in all things, including the horror. They recognized that life feeds on life, and therefore, all life needs to be honored and respected. Early ritual came out of this understanding about life: life feeds on life, and all things return to the earth. This way of looking at life affirms life, and everything in it. According to this misunderstanding, life, family, and tribe are dependent upon the animals and elements, subject to the whims of God and nature, and all things must be seen as sacred. Everything is to be respected, and the Gods are swift in their punishment for not following the rules and laws. So mythological bucket one can be captured in the idea that all life, with its beauty and horror, is sacred.

Mythological bucket two is the kicker. The idea of this bucket is that there is a struggle for good over evil in the universe, and good must overcome evil. This idea comes from thousands of years ago: *as above, so below*. Above includes goodness, Godliness, order, angels, cleanliness, and heaven. Below is earth with its horror, temptation, sex, money, evil, death, and destruction. According to this misunderstanding about life, humans are animals until they overcome their earthly desires, which they must do for their reward someday in heaven—or else suffer the consequences of eternal damnation in hell. Unfortunately for us, this is the nature of the major world religions that we inherited. Everything is seen from the viewpoint of the fight of good over evil. This idea spills into all areas of the human psyche, and most current mythologies. This myth literally structures our modern society, from law to justice.

This myth reappears in various forms throughout the planet. The names and characters change—file off the serial numbers a bit, and you can re-use the same tired old story of the struggle for good over evil, and nobody will be the wiser. It shows up in the form of belligerent alien beings from other planets, crop circles, and conspiracy theories: as above, aliens, so below, humans; and as above, God, so below, humans. All kinds of mythological images come from above, such as chariots in the sky and killer meteors. The symbols change but the story remains the same. You can see it in the bad energy that so many new agers are afraid of. The lower consciousness of people versus the higher consciousness of the enlightened ones—it's a struggle for supremacy. Each system believes that it is the way, the true way, the only way, to conquer evil and restore the balance of goodness to the earth.

The basis of bucket two is the story that the world was once in a state of Eden, perfection, and the snake and woman messed it up for the rest of us; and because of this ridiculous, misunderstood mythological image, women all over the world are still paying the price, stuffed into bags that hide their dangerous forms so they don't call any attention to their bodies, and therefore their evil nature. In this way, we can overcome the evil oriented physical plane, and rise up to the spiritual, heavenly, correct existence that awaits us—without any further temptation. If you think this isn't true, I will share a couple of examples with you.

Let us begin with the bag. In Islam, the bag is called a burka; in Catholicism, it's called a habit; in Buddhism, it's called a robe. In Buddhism, women don't necessarily cover their heads, but instead shave them to make themselves as asexual as possible. Whatever name you give the bag, it is intended to hide sensory, sexual, and shape cues about the person underneath it. The idea is to not tempt anybody into lower, animalistic thinking.

Recently, a senior Muslim cleric compared women who go outside without a headscarf to uncovered meat. The statement, needless to say, outraged people. The implicit idea here is that women are to blame for sexual attention and rape. Essentially, from a spiritual perspective, having a body with curves is bad, and must be overcome. The joke of this is that the very purpose of curves, shapes, and hair on the head is symbolic—a symbol that is intended to create a release of energy in the body that ultimately results in a fertilized egg and the continuation of life.

From this misunderstanding of bucket two, woman, who gives life, is inherently bad and evil, especially if she enjoys any kind of sexual pleasure. In addition, there are all kinds of words to describe this kind of woman. The bottom line is that this is the bucket of shame, guilt, blame, fear, punishment, and retaliation—and fundamentally is the refusal of life. Any human impulse is to be overcome for the higher planes. Of course, this myth doesn't work very well for the life that we are living, which may account for the fact that the population has doubled on the planet within the last 50 years. Apparently, neither the bags, nor the shame are keeping people from having sex. In 2006, the population in America crossed over the 300 million mark. Since it is likely that these new Americans weren't born from Immaculate Conception, it's safe to say that people are having sex, and apparently lots of it. This is a perfect case of the myth not relating to life. All this myth does is make people ashamed of their bodies, unconsciously spreading disease, confusion, and conflict through denial of their sexual impulses. Sex is not the problem. The problem is we are not talking, because shame structures our sexual mythologies, keeping us bound, gagged, and in the dark, helpless to experience conscious pleasure.

Summarizing bucket two—if it has anything to do with life on planet earth, it must be overcome. The religious mythologies tell you that life is to be resisted so that you can have your rewards in heaven. If the myth you are following has any kind of power struggle within its stories, then it goes into this bucket. If there is something that must be overcome so that you can have a reward later, then it goes into this bucket. If there are levels that must be risen to, then the myth goes into bucket two. You should pay close attention to this bucket, because it appears pretty much everywhere in modern culture. The stories change, the characters change, the name of God changes, but the underlying idea is exactly the same.

Mythological bucket three is another common mythological view. Simply stated, bucket three says that we can affirm the earth, but only if people do it our way. If you don't agree to our way, then we will kill you. This is the basis of most of the 40 some odd wars currently being waged around the planet. Mythology makes us think that we have come a long way since our hunting and gathering ancestry. In reality, of course, we haven't. We continue waging endless tribal wars and border skirmishes that have to do with mythological bucket three: do the world our way, see the world our way—or else die. Even the world religions that preach love and peace fall into this category. If we don't believe in their God, then he will kill us when judgment day (a mythological image) arrives. We have to ask ourselves, what kind of God needs us to believe in it anyway?

The more awake and aware I become in my life, the more I

want to share the awareness with people, and the more compassion and understanding I have for those folks who aren't yet awake. It's my intention to make the awakening process as simple and easy as humanly possible. I know that if people are freed from the prisons of their cultural mythologies, they will be truly free. I want to do whatever I can to help—including writing this book. I certainly don't need people to believe in me. I'll put the information out there, and if they are interested, they will find me, or I will find them. I don't feel compelled to test them, nor have them do stupid things to prove their love and faith. So why does a God need to do such things? We misunderstood the underlying meaning and purpose of the myth to begin with.

Bucket three includes activist groups, vegetarians, religions, cults, and systems of thought such as communism, capitalism, socialism, Marxism, Buddhism, etc. Each is the only way, the right way, and the world would be a better place if everybody did life the right way. People who are living their lives from mythological bucket three often walk around with an air of spiritual superiority, and pity for the rest of humanity. You can always tell people who are in this mythological bucket because they often have a spiritual arrogance about them. They think that they have it all worked out.

Summarizing bucket three—do it my way, or else suffer the consequences of doing life the wrong way. Oh, and by the way, X (fill in the blank) is, of course, the only right way to do life.

Mythological bucket four is science. Scientists suffer from the same mythological delusions that the rest of us do; however, they don't think that they do. There is the belief in science that science has already figured everything out, or will figure everything out, and maybe it will. However, there are endless scientific theories parading around as truth that have nothing to do with reality at all.

Science has some very interesting stories and ideas about the way life is that are all potentially wrong—including quantum theory. Yet entire philosophies and self help books and cults have already arisen out of this notion that the universe is a quantum field, a potentiality that doesn't solidify until it's perceived. If you walk around seeing this life as a quantum field, you are fundamentally wrong in your story about the way life is.

The only good thing about science is that, in general, even though scientists are often wrong, their wrongness refines with new information, revised theories, and new data. For example, though there are people who still believe the world is flat, current science sees the world as round, which is also not exactly true. However, the speed and ease of modern aviation and the Internet are possible because the earth is round. We can literally be anywhere on the planet within 24 hours, and via the Internet, we can contact any place on the planet at the speed of light.

If you are human, you are biased in some way, and that bias prevents you from seeing clearly. Keep these four buckets in mind as you read the next chapter. You will begin to recognize a pattern.

Not all incorrect mythologies are equally incorrect. Some are substantially more wrong than others. Just because two incorrect groups are equally passionate in communicating their mythologies, it doesn't mean that the truth lies somewhere in between them. One of the points of view could simply be wrong. If you are living from bucket two or three, you can be fairly sure that you are incorrect about life, and if you think your mythology is the way that it really is, you are probably more than wrong, which is really quite wrong.

Major Functions of Religious, Systematic, Human Mythology

Humans need stories. As long as there have been modern humans, there have been myths. In fact, it appears that natural selection has allowed for those with a proclivity for believing in, and making up stories, to survive. My guess is that the belief in stories enables us to help one another, and therefore ensure our ability to survive as a species. Stories help us get through this strange and crazy life. Stories help us make sense of our surroundings, who we are, and why we are here. To understand mythology, we have to understand that a mythology is a spiritual insight, an observation or *ah hah*, that a person had then shared in story form, a misperception about the way life is. Mythologies are stories, and all stories are incorrect.

Another way to look at mythology and see it clearly is by looking at another person or culture's religion. For some reason, it's easy to look at another's religion and see how strange their beliefs can be. A concise definition of all religion, *including the one you believe in,* can be said to be a misunderstood, concretized mythology—a series of misunderstood stories that you *believe* to be the truth.

Putting it another way, people tell stories so they feel safe in a crazy, often hostile world. Human beings are born too early. They do nearly a quarter century of their development outside of the protection of a mother's womb. Spiritual mythology, or what we call religion, serves the function of an external placenta, a safe zone, filled with rules and laws—guidelines for a safe and righteous life, in alignment with cultural and religious moralities.

Mythology gives an emerging consciousness more time to develop safely outside of the mother's womb. A well-rendered mythology guides you through all stages of life, from birth to puberty, marriage, adulthood, death, and then plagues you into the afterlife. It tells you what to do every moment of every day to ensure your entry into heaven.

The problem is that the mythologies we currently use are outdated and useless to a consciousness interested in expansion and freedom. There is a continual internal struggle to make sense of this life—a collision within concerning what is actually happening in the face of completely outmoded rules and laws. Most of the mythologies that people are attempting to run their lives with were created for a different people, living in a different time, with a different set of concerns. Let's take a look at the major functions of mythology in the life of a human.

One, mythology orients the new, incoming soul—telling the

Major Functions of Mythology

new being about the universe, offering an understanding of the location in space and time that the soul finds itself in. Consider that the first purpose of mythology is to create a great story as to why we are here. For example, we are spiritual beings having a physical experience in an effort to get back to God.

Two, mythology orients the new soul in its surroundings, the physical universe. Mythology explains why things are the way they are in external, physical reality. It tells of the unchanging physical laws of the universe that must be accepted. For example, the sun rises in the east and sets in the west, supposedly as ordered by God, who created the physical universe.

Three, mythology orients us in the rules and laws of the culture. In a well-structured mythology, ideally, the cultural rules and laws reflect the rules and laws of the physical universe as explained by the religious mythology. This is captured in the ancient idea: *as above, so below*. The rules and laws as handed down by God cannot be questioned any more than one would question the rising of the sun, the phases of the moon, or the movement of the tides. These are laws from God, whose word structured the universe, and that's that. Of course, in reality, the rules and laws were created by people and the ego, and attributed to God, but that's another story. The Ten Commandments, for example, are rules and laws for structuring society, laid out by a pretty smart man. If you said the rules and laws came from some smart guy, we'd say, "Who cares?" However, if you said they came directly from God, and we'll go to hell if we don't obey them, well, now you have our attention.

Four, mythology guides us through the various stages of life, from infancy to old age, and urges us forward into the great mystery of death. This idea is reflected in stories of our loved ones waiting for us on the other side, beckoning us forward. "Don't be afraid to walk through death's door," the stories go. "Mommy and daddy will be waiting for you there." "Go into the light." It's a cute story, encouraging us to please keep moving towards the exit.

Five, mythology helps us make peace with our inadequacies. Mythology assists us in covering up or suppressing our darkness. For example, we can say Hail Mary's to atone for our sins. Even if we just beat the kids before we left home to go to church—all can be forgiven.

Six, mythology helps us tell stories about our lives and past to keep us from fully experiencing the trauma of early childhood. We can look at our past through rose-colored mythology glasses, and tell ourselves cute little stories about *why* things did or didn't happen to us. We say things about our parents such as, "They did the best that they could," or "I have to forgive them, for they know not what they have done." These are great little stories to help us let go of the past. Of course, they don't really work that well, but that doesn't stop us from using them.

Seven, mythology structures the human central nervous system and brain to reflect the moral conditions of the society and system that we live in. We are *taught to see* life the way we are *told* that life is, and from the perspective of our inherited society, everything *appears* to be the way we are told that it is. The brain sees what it is structured to see. Through mythology, we see things the way that we expect them to be, which has nothing to do with the way that they are. For example, the Bible teaches that the world was created in six days and is only 6,000 years old. With a kind of spiritual arrogance, our myths teach us to see the world through this perspective and that's that. Of course, it has nothing to do with physical reality, but who cares? The story is cute and many people believe it—so it must be true. This is a classic case of more than wrong. Yes, people are very vocal about their ideas, but they are still mistaken. Our brain structures what scientists call an unconscious confirmation bias. We see what we expect to see. When we thought the earth was flat, even though all of our senses and myths confirmed the truth of a flat earth, we were, in fact, incorrect.

Eight, mythology serves the function of hiding what society and the system can't explain or doesn't want around. Society does this by calling anything within its own system good or God like, and anything outside of its system bad or evil. Mythology allows for suppression of scientific ideas, technological advances, and individual freedoms. Basically, a good mythology marginalizes whatever it doesn't want around. In some religious circles, the computer and the Internet are considered instruments of the devil (a mythological symbol) and therefore subject to punishment by God if used. This is a perfect mythology for keeping followers uneducated, and therefore docile and obedient. The general rule of thumb in mass religion is to shut up, do as told, read the holy book, don't ask too many questions, and donate a good portion of money. If we ask too many questions, then we are being influenced by the devil. Basically, when a mythological system doesn't agree with something, it is called the work of the devil.

Nine, mythology imbues us with an internal moral compass, what we call a conscience. We constantly worry about what other people will think of us. Morality is enforced by guilt, shame, and blame from our elders, our surroundings, and our inner feelings. When a friend of mine began asking too many questions in her inherited religion, her grandmother grabbed her by the ear and dragged her out of the room in front of everybody. She was made an example of what happens when a child asks too many questions. If grandmother had not taken action, she would have been ostracized, judged for the behaviors of the little girl. After all, children are to be seen and not heard. The conscience is actually a human creation, one that reflects the system of the mythology that we are raised within. The use of unquestionable mythological stories and images to embed the moral code and conscience deeply within our psyche creates a seamless, natural, and incontrovertible illusion that our feelings are coming from a God who knows our every thought.

Ten, mythology gives us a system of self-inquiry, a scale of truth, thereby allowing us to make sense of our lives, and know exactly where we are on our spiritual path. We are told that we can know who we truly are through the mythological symbols and images that seem to point to the bigger reality. We know who we truly are from the stories and mythologies of the system. We can know where we are, within our system, by seeing where we are on the scale of the mythology. The bottom line is, we understand ourselves, and where we are on our spiritual path, through our inherited stories and myths. For example, if I use muscle testing as the system, I can come to know myself as a specific number on the path to 1,000 on the spiritual evolutionary scale. The system gives us a sense of where we are on the path. Once you abandon the system, of course, you are no longer bound by the system. When I was muscle tested using the scale of 1 to 1,000, I stopped at 27,000—and was still running strong. All scales are arbitrary. The brain structures your experience and once you break free of your inherited structures, you are free.

Eleven, mythology hides our morphology. Mythology covers up where we actually came from with stories. Mythology covers up the science that we evolved from a common ancestor. For example, the mythologies of Adam and Eve are an attempt to hide the dirty secret of sex in our evolutionary past. We don't want to have evolved from filthy animals, which are of nature, and therefore evil. If we admitted that evolution was correct, then we would have to admit that the Bible is not, so mythologies tell us sweet creation stories. God placed us here in bliss, in a heavenly state—and we messed it up for ourselves. Actually, the poor little snake messed it up for all of us. We ate from the tree of knowledge against God's command so we must pay the price for our sins. A cute story (with the talking snake and all) but incorrect, as are all stories.

Twelve, mythology hides our inner impulses. Mythology keeps us from deeply listening to what is actually going on inside of our being. We are conflicted and often don't follow the inner impulse, overriding it with a thought such as, "What would love do now?"

Thirteen, mythology hides human nature. Many mythologies pit humans directly against nature. Many world mythologies have nature as being evil and bad, and something that needs to be corrected. Our nature is suppressed through mythology—whether that is the need to raise the energy out of the lower chakras, or to focus on love and the heart—either way, we are directed to rise above our human nature based on the incorrect idea: *as above, so below*.

Fourteen, mythology hides the differences between men and women. Mythology keeps us from clearly seeing what is actually happening with the different needs of differing sexes through stories about Prince Charming, finding a soul mate, the princess waiting to be rescued, or how men and women should behave according to local morals. What is actually happening is quite different from what we are told by the mythologies, and what is happening has more to do with biology and genetics then the stories lead us to believe.

Fifteen, mythology hides what is actually happening in physical reality by telling us that what we perceive is wrong. That yellow wall is not yellow, but blue. Moreover, if we are not seeing it as blue, then there is something wrong with us—we are under the influence of evil. When I was nine, I went to Egypt and saw death and poverty beyond my wildest imagination. I saw children my age, running wild—living and dying in the dirt streets of Cairo. When I asked *spiritual* people about why this was, the answers they gave me were unacceptable—they didn't make sense. When I said so, they tried telling me that it wasn't the way it appeared. Uh huh. So, I didn't see children dying in the streets? Not.

Sixteen, mythology hides the fossil record of the planet. Religious mythologies obscure the truth by telling us that science is wrong, that the world is only 6,000 years old, and that the fossil record is simply misunderstood. Religious mythologies pit us directly against the fossil record of our geological history.

Seventeen, mythology teaches us to project our rage and hatred outwardly—outside of our community, culture, religion, or social structure. The bad people, bad energies, bad religions, bad beliefs, bad countries, bad leaders, and bad systems are *out there*. We ultimately must get them to see things our way (bucket three), or God will take care of them, with a little help from us. In addition, we can, through our mythologies, justify attacking those bad people in the name of God, and killing them if need be. Whether it's suicide bombers, or stealth bombers, the stories that motivate us come from the same tired old place.

Eighteen, mythology keeps us acting psychologically as a child. A good mythology keeps us in a state of ignorance and innocence—as if that were somehow a good thing. When did we last allow a five year old to drive a car, much less guide our life actions?

Nineteen, mythology gives us reasons to live and die—from

gangs and turf wars, to religious struggles—it is stories that call us to action in our lives. Mythologies make us think that we have *evolved*, but we are a tribal culture that continues to fight tribal, belief wars.

Twenty, mythology attempts to control us, for our entire lives into eternity. Mythology wants to tell us how to behave forever and ever.

Twenty-one, mythology allows us to stay in pretend mode for our whole lives. We can pretend to be whatever we want, and forget that we are pretending, and everyone else will forget that we are pretending, and agree or disagree with what we are pretending. The entire planet is playing a game of pretend—pretending that the emperor is wearing clothes so that nobody notices that not only the emperor is not wearing any clothes, but we are also not wearing any clothes. I once saw my cousin standing on the lawn. He said, "Don't walk there." I immediately stopped in my tracks. "Why not?" I asked. "Because I'm a tree, and you'll walk on my roots, and it will hurt me," he replied. Not wanting to break him out of his innocent delusion, and not knowing how far he was willing to go in his make believe game, I immediately turned and walked in another direction. I often think of that particular event when I look at a religious person dressed in full garb. I wonder what they are pretending to be, and how far they are willing to take it. Most people take their pretend story to the grave.

Twenty-two, mythology hides the fact that nobody really knows anything. People just think that they do, and are very happy to emphatically tell us what they think they know, even going so far as to start religions around what they think that they know—enough said.

Twenty-three, mythology abolishes our guilt for doing what we *must do* in the name of God, country, or survival.

Twenty-four, mythology hides the fact that as a global culture, we suffer from paranoid schizophrenia. Due to our current state of brain evolution, humans are delusional. We can't see that things happening inside our heads are just that—interior experiences.

Twenty-five, mythology hides the truth about our society—that life feeds on life, and that if we are to live, something else must die. We tell ourselves cute little stories about humane killing, raw foods, or vegetarianism. We tell cute little stories about how our system of mythology is better than another system. This falls under the *do it my way and then the world will be the way it should be—the way I want it to be.* We can't eat rocks and get any nourishment. We can't eat concrete. We have to eat something that was or is alive. Welcome to life, and welcome to the various ways in which mythology rinses away our guilt about what we are doing to survive or thrive.

Twenty-six, mythology ensures our survival by helping the group bond, and therefore, survive. Typically, the people with the better mythologies created stronger bonds, which allowed more people who thought similarly to thrive. Mythology is a bi-product of survival. The strongest mythologies rose to the top. The ones that weren't so good didn't make it. As a result, mythology is implanted in our DNA. There is even new evidence that suggests that one of the reasons the Neanderthal line didn't survive was because they were too individually focused, and didn't know how to work together in larger groups. They were bigger, stronger, had larger brains, and yet they didn't survive because they were too selfish. Perhaps they hadn't developed a mythological oriented brain.

Twenty-seven, mythology provides us with simple little rules and laws that keep us psychologically intact. Human beings are very fragile, and what we call human consciousness is tenuously held together. Mythology provides us with a safety net—an external womb. No matter what happens, we can rely on this womb space, these simple, childlike rules. For example, suffering is good and what God wants. Sex is evil and to be sublimated—not for pleasure. The ego is bad. No matter how insane the rules sound, if we don't examine them too closely—as long as we don't ask too many questions, as long as we don't think about them—we will be fine. We will never have to see life the way that it is, because we have our little, sweet rules that we can rely on to explain why things happen in life. We call this faith, trust. It's very sweet, but has nothing to do with anything. These cute little rules keep us psychologically intact.

Twenty-eight, mythology controls the religious experience. Our experiences are structured by what we are told the religious experience should be. We are held in place on our path by the boundaries of what we are taught. What we are told influences our experience, which influences our life possibilities. Religion is a protection against an individual having his own experience. If, for example, you are told that the earth is flat, then you will act as if the earth is flat, even though what you were told is erroneous. It will determine the way in which you approach your community, your decisions, and your horizon. Your world, if you are afraid of falling off the edge, will only be as wide as your limited, flat earth belief allows. You are basing your world, your decisions, and your perceptions on an idea that is incorrect, yet it totally controls your life experience. For example, if you believe that spiritual people shouldn't get angry, you will be contained by that experience, perhaps beating yourself up, and harshly judging your experience whenever you feel the natural, human emotion of anger. The fact is that you are human, and therefore, human emotion is a natural consequence of being human. So what. Spiritual or not spiritual is just a story. Human emotion simply is.

Twenty-nine, mythology promotes monogamous relationships through ritual ceremony, commonly called marriage, that tells us we are obligated to care for our partners until death due us part. The ceremony of marriage is also about ensuring paternity and protection, plus sharing status, wealth, land, and resources. Religious mythology will guilt and shame us into staying together, even when the marriage isn't working out or feeling good. Additionally, it exerts control over the natural sexual impulses that drive us to create and pro-create, change partners, and have other experiences. Fundamentally, religious mythology attempts to control the marriage experience from ceremony to grave.

Thirty, if we think that there is no way to explain things other than our mythology, our religious orientation, our group, or our system, then we are trapped in the prison of our mythological viewpoint of the world.

Perhaps you are beginning to understand the importance of mythology in daily life. Mythology is the life blood of how to live within *The System*—whatever system you are born into, be it Islam, Judaism, Christianity, Buddhism, Hinduism, socialism, racism, prison, drugs, Communism, capitalism, etc. Being human, you are bound by a system of order. Even if you are an outcast, you are bound by that system of rules and laws. The system structures your brain that structures your experience.

As spiritual adults, we can practice the realization that everything we know is a mythology, a human created structure of rules and laws. We must choose our myths wisely, because the myths and systems that we live by are either our keys to freedom, or our prisons. Our myths and stories keep us from experiencing life directly, on its own terms.

Remember, mythology structures your central nervous system and brain, and ultimately the society that you live in. Your own mythology seems like *reality and truth*. You have inherited your mythology, so it is likely that you don't even see it. Mythology is similar to your car windows—you only notice them if they are dirty. If you don't see your own myths as myths, or think that your religious myth is *the real truth*, or your people are the chosen people, then you are still living in mommy's belly, wrapped in a placenta of other people's stories.

In learning to detect, listen to, and understand our own mythological stories, we can heal ourselves and connect to others in an empathetic way. To be human is to tell myths and stories about our lives to others, and more importantly, to ourselves.

Mythology and Society: Here Today, and Unfortunately, Here Tomorrow

One of the major roles of mythology is to create the rules and laws of society. We use mythology to rigidify, fix, validate, and maintain social order.

Complex societies are built by using strong mythological symbols. The symbols evoke powerful emotions and reactions. These are the rules and laws that supposedly come from God. The rules and laws are unquestionable, as the rising and setting of the sun.

Mythology functions as a strong and thorough system designed to answer interpersonal and societal challenges faced during the course of a lifetime. Mythology is similar to a protective coating that surrounds the psyche and helps to organize our lives around the system of laws given by God.

The religious myths that we are using today are thousands of years old, and are not necessarily capable of escorting us through the culture that we currently find ourselves living in. The world is ever changing, infinitely. The myths that define our lives are failing against the pace of constant, rapid change. The crisis of religion is that it hasn't adjusted to the world that we are actually living in now. Frankly, it can't. *No system can contain boundless life.*

At the current pace of change, every two years we find ourselves in a completely different technological generation. To understand the implication of this, it is helpful to know Moore's Law. Moore's Law is the prediction that the size of each transistor on an integrated circuit chip will be reduced by 50 percent every 24 months. This can be taken as far back as the invention of the abacus. The result is the exponentially growing power of integrated circuit-based computation over time. Moore's Law doubles the number of components on a chip as well as the speed of each component. These aspects double the power of computing, effectively *quadrupling* the power of computation every 24 months.

The relentless advances in technology affect every area of life. No religious mythology can keep up with the rapid change. Issues of sexuality, safety, security, relationship, marriage, consciousness, spirituality, meditation, nanotechnology, cloning, neurogenesis, stem cell research, genetics, border wars, technology, television, entertainment, capitalism, computers, communism, space travel, weaponry, warfare, separation, tribalism, terrorism, war, on-line trading, the Internet, music, creation, recreation, on-line gambling, the human genome, same sex marriage, Aids, fear, workaholism, reaction, pornography, neuroscience, symbolism, life, and death are coming into question on a daily basis.

The world is changing so rapidly that our mythologies, our

Gods, and our consciousness can't keep pace. Our mythologies can't keep up with the boundless, ever expanding life that we are faced with, so we tend to revert to the basic childhood mythologies as a catchall. Anything that we like or agree with is good, and everything that we don't like, or don't know, or don't understand is potentially evil.

The advance of technology will eventually kill our Gods. Inevitably, as technology advances, more and more of the magical thinking that we live our lives by will be reduced to rubble, held helpless by the rapid pace of change. Begin to embrace change now. Change is the only thing that will never change, until it doesn't.

Collision of Past and Future Mythologies Means Dramatic Upheaval and Unrest, Otherwise Known as Change

Most of our societal and personal problems are emerging from the energy of the collision of outmoded mythologies, religions, and familial beliefs thrown into conflict with our radically changing external reality. Mythologies align us with the group, or an idea that is against someone or something evil. Mythologies put the bad stuff *out there*. The religious *right* is the tradition of health, wealth, and war. We have inherited a system of aggression. We believe our system is right, and we will impose *God's* will upon the other—the devil worshippers, the bad people. In our current world mythologies, we must always fight and defend against something or someone. We must overcome, exert our will over, and ultimately defeat what our mythologies consider evil.

Each mythology and belief that we have makes us defend the opposite of that belief or mythology. If there is good, there must be evil. Where there is dark, we must fight for light. From a mythological perspective, it is the battle for good over evil (bucket two). We must stand against all that isn't spiritual, isn't familial, isn't religious, isn't morally *right* from our perspective.

Within and without, we remain conflicted. We must protect our health, wealth, and progeny—we must protect our own. We must protect this life. We must also impose our will upon our natural internal impulses. So not only are there wars in the outside world owing to the collision of mythologies, but there are constant internal wars among the principalities of our various needs, wants, and desires.

In one of my workshops, a student struggled with letting go of the religion she was taught as a child. She asked me, "What if I'm wrong in choosing not to believe in the Rapture? My family is concerned that when they are snatched up by God and taken to heaven, I'll be left on earth alone. I don't want to be left here alone." Courageously she persevered in examining how inherited beliefs had shaped her life, her emotions, and her unconscious, child mind. After sitting with the feelings, emotions, and sensations for a while, she was able to see the possibility that the Rapture, the end of the world, was a misinterpreted mythological image that was mistakenly taken as reality—another example of the idea: *as above, so below*. When she gave herself permission to acknowledge the Rapture as a myth, she experienced an enormous release of pent up energy that had been holding her trapped in the belief that she would be left behind. That energy, once released, was available to her to create things that she wanted in her life.

This system of inheritance does not reflect the world that we are currently living in. The main idea of this planet is that there is one *true* God who is a historical fact. That historical fact named God created the world, and sent energies into the world. Those energies must defend against evil. Our duty is to overcome the world and all its temptations and evils.

When a religion transforms a metaphor into a fact, the world is in trouble. We kill one another in the name of our God. The problem is that to create the world the way we want and need it to be, we must convert, overpower, or kill everybody who doesn't think as we think.

We have lost touch with the fact that we are not the metaphors that we believe we are. No one myth exists that is *the way* for everybody. Life is boundless and infinitely creative, in a state of constant change. It can't be controlled by any single story, religion, or mythology.

If you are unable to see that your inherited religion is no more than a collection of stories and myths of dead people, then you are still suffering under the power your myths have over your life. You are trapped in the prison of your mind until you can see that whatever you believe is just another myth about the way things are—stories. Moreover, all stories about life are no more than misunderstandings about the way things really are.

When a mask of God says, "I am the way," and you take that literally, you are lost. No one system of belief, religion, or thought can possibly encompass boundless life—so take back your power from all of your searching. You must always come back to your true self that is transparent to the transcendent—beyond the image and the symbol.

Masks of God are Actually Misunderstood Visions of the Ego

A mask of God is a constraint applied by the human ego/mind, upon the infinite unbound life source, in an attempt to give that formless, timeless source a shape that the human mind can accept, comprehend, and relate to. Humans need a human-like God.

As the body is a mask that our formless soul wears to experience earth, so are the many faces of God costumed and masked to contain the infinite, allowing us the chance to step down its boundless energy into a form that we can understand. In this sense, God is a condescendence of the infinite into a form that the human mind can relate to.

The human mind is unable to comprehend infinity. We, therefore, inflect the infinite, unbound with a mask, and that mask is cross culturally named God. The most basic, elemental form that man uses to contain the infinite universe is named God.

The masks of God are many. The religions that worship the masks of God are many. Humans worship masks of God that are mostly composed of pain, suffering, and retribution. Cross culturally, each mask that God wears is a mask that creates and fosters separation, fear, duality, and repercussion. God is seen as punitive, judgmental, and unforgiving. (If you had a friend who behaved like God, you wouldn't remain friends for long.) The way God is worshipped around the world is a brutal reflection of the worst parts of our inner selves, mistakenly perceived and concretized as existing outside of ourselves. Our own internal symbols and inflections upon the infinite within us are projected outside us as a vicious God. The darkest and worst within us is projected out upon God—a mean and vicious God that drives us to be *good*.

I was in a profound session with a client when I came upon the truth that God, in all its forms cross culturally, is an awful God. As we looked at the attributes of God, we began to wonder where God began and the devil ended. God is always asking us to sacrifice, to have blind faith and trust—and if we succumb to our human fear in any way, we are severely punished. There is no compassion. God is always watching us, waiting for us to screw up in some way so he can banish us to hell. Moreover, the devil is always looking to catch us screwing up so he can take us to hell. Basically, different names mirroring the same attributes. One is testing and expecting obedience, while the other is testing and expecting failure. God and the devil are humanized projections of conflicted energies within the body. They are two sides of the same coin. When we consider the world's religions, we see a pattern of people worshipping a vengeful, moral, wrathful, angry, easily pissed off,

Masks of God

willing to kill, inflict suffering and punishment God. We are told to be faithful—or be wiped out.

What is it within people that causes them to worship such a cruel being, begging for its mercy, praying that God will be merciful and not smite them? What is the need in humans to see the world in this way? What is the need to suffer internally?

The most elemental need of humans is to inflect the unknown in a way that it appears as a God. Humans have a biological need to worship a creator. The ability to communally worship a creator creates strong bonds between people. The problem is with the ways in which we worship this God. We see this creator as a being of extensive rules and laws that must be followed, in trust and faith, or risk unending hellfire. The faces change, the masks might not be human; however, God is always moralistic in his rules and laws.

We clearly see that rules and laws were created by man, and ascribed to the unknown in the form of God. God becomes the holder and enforcer of rules and laws of man, now forgotten, and projected outside. We are taught that faith is the reason that God behaves in the way he does. We are told to have faith in these unseen forces, and they will guide us into the after life—but only if we are good, according to the system or society that we are part of.

When we look at what God really is, we are left with a version of the ego/mind: judgmental, fearful, vengeful, angry, etc. This is how we know that God is a mask of man, a symbol imposed upon the infinite. The mask is composed of the worst traits of man reflected by and in God.

Why would an enlightened being such as God have so many rules and laws in so many different forms, many in conflict with one another? Rules and laws don't make sense to an all powerful, all seeing, all knowing being who *is* infinite truth. That's because these are rules and laws of humans trying to protect whatever it is that they are afraid of experiencing.

God is a mask. The rules and laws that you believe and follow were created by humans and the vivid human psyche, and ascribed to a form, a mask, that is given the name God. Do not be so attached to the mask of God that you can't see beyond and through the mask. The mask is an illusion.

Only four real Gods exist in this earth life: sex, death, cash, and the unknown. The problem is we don't understand any of them, but think that we do.

God is a Reflection of the Disintegrated Ego—We are Really in Trouble!

Here's the big question: what are the differences between God and the ego/mind? Here is a list of properties that individuals have ascribed to God over the years:

Judgmental
Unforgiving
Angry
Vengeful
Conditionally loving
Abandoning
Willing to kill to prove a point
Holding a grudge
Spiteful
Tribal
Separate
Dualistic

Afraid of others not like itself
Dependent upon ignorance
Don't ask questions
Endless rules and laws
Demanding
Believes in the reality/truth of external circumstances
Believes in causation of events
Cares about what you do in your private life
Never satisfied
Never happy
Demands suffering
Demands pain
Doesn't want you to have pleasure
Fun is bad
Any type of personality is bad
Money is bad
Ego is bad
Selfishness is bad
Be afraid
Out to get you
Ready to throw you to the devil at a moment's notice
Rage filled
Constraining
Compressing
Hates anyone that doesn't agree with its viewpoint
Believes in absolute truths

God is a Reflection of the Ego

Believes in sin

Punishes for sin

Punishes for eternity

Willing to crush you at the smallest infraction of a rule or law

Willing to kill your family

Willing to destroy nonbelievers

Makes you carry your cross

Isn't at all compassionate

Doesn't understand the human condition

Believes its way is the only way

Believes its own myths

Reads minds and punishes accordingly

Willing to kill masses of people to reach its end game

Will destroy the world and anybody who isn't a true believer

Will damn non-believers to eternal hell

Demands sacrifice

Hates sexuality

Hates nature

Abhors nature

Constantly pits groups, places, and things against one another in the name of faith

The world is to be overcome

Nature is to be overcome

Lets the devil try to catch you and mess you up

God will not be satisfied until you are destroyed

If we examine the above properties of God closely, we will detect the properties of the ego at work. God is the byproduct of the ego projected on the infinite.

God did not create the ego—the ego created God. All of the above properties are really properties of the ego. The ego projects on the screen of nothingness and creates on that screen an image of a being that is the worst of the worst.

We have no way to distinguish what is real from what is imagined. We have no way to distinguish connotation from denotation. When we project the darkest aspects of our inner mind upon the field of the infinite, we see whatever we think we see. God is a projection of the deepest, darkest, and most awful parts of the ego. God is a fabrication of the ego, by the ego, for the ego.

We have a biological need to believe, because believing allows societies to form, create, share, and bond. Humans who believe in God have a higher likelihood of survival and success. They even live longer. The need for God really fulfills the need for the organism to thrive and survive.

Our God is not outside. Our God is inside, and it is created by the ego. The ego projects and creates God in the *outside* world—not being satisfied until we are beaten, humiliated, and destroyed, because by being destroyed somehow we will be saved by God. This is why many spiritual paths emphasize suffering now and paying the price, so that we can have an eternal reward at a later time—after we're dead. The ego is about concretizing the symbol,

God. Meanwhile, the brain is unable to distinguish between what is internally or externally projected upon the screen.

When watching an explosion on a movie screen, the screen doesn't explode, but it looks as if it does. The screen we are watching in our heads also experiences the images as real; however, the images are not real. Human beings created the symbols and images of God. The screens of the olden days were tablets and scrolls. The inner projections of God were written on scrolls, projected on the screen, and taken as fact by those who looked at the screen of the scrolls.

Humans have created it all, and all of it is a projection of the worst, most suppressed parts of the ego. God is a projection, by the ego, upon the neutral infinite universe. When we look at the attributes of God, we are looking at ourselves.

The universe is a mirror. We project whatever we want upon the mirror. None of it is real, but all of it seems real because we are stuck in our inability to recognize the difference between what is real and what is imagined. Mythologies, composed by the ego, define our comfort zone and inhibit our freedom. If we want to break out of our comfort zone, then we have to challenge our deepest beliefs.

Life Myths are Your Prisons, Boxes, and Walls—Now Let's Eat Bread and Water

Our myths are dense, conscious and non-conscious stories that we see, feel, act upon, and believe are real; but are not real at all. We perceive them as literal, factual truths; however, myths are the compositions of the ego. Myths are the non-conscious collections of elemental symbols, woven together as stories that guide our lives as if they are facts. Myths compose a majority of our unconscious mind and guide most of our human decisions and experiences.

To live in your freedom, you may want to move towards living outside of your life box, outside of your comfort zone, outside of the denotation. To live in your freedom is to uncover and unwind your myths about who and what you are, uncovering the various identities that you perceive as you.

For example, how do you know who to spend time with? What foods to eat? Who to marry? Where to shop, what to buy, how to shop? Would you go to a biker bar to meet friends? Why or why not?

The answers to these simple questions have to do with your personal comfort zones and your personal myths about the moralistic symbolic images and identities that occupy your life.

Your personal stories about the way life is, guide you in your moment-to-moment daily life. Your sense of self, how rich or poor you are, how loved you feel, are all determined by your myths and stories about who and what you are.

Myths give our lives meaning. Myths structure our brain's storage centers. Symbols and images are highly compact, efficient brain storage methods—that allow us to pack as much data as possible inside a three pound gelatinous mass called the brain.

Myths bring order to our central nervous system. Myths structure and defend our sense of self, well-being, God, and life. Our myths determine the quality of our lives.

Additionally, myths are our internal prisons projected outwardly. We project our inner myths upon the external world, seeing our inner myths as facts—constantly blaming things outside of ourselves for our actual life conditions and our experiences.

I listened as a student in a workshop talked about an unfaithful spouse. I asked the student for specific examples. The student could not give one concrete example. The student was imagining behaviors in the mind, unconsciously projecting them onto the spouse, and then blaming the spouse. The student believed the spouse held the same mythologies and stories. I asked those in the workshop to do a simple exercise—describe the word dog. Each person described a dog that they knew, their reality of dog. The student then understood that just as everyone has his or her own description of dog, everyone has his or her own relationship reality. The student finally saw the closely held beliefs defining the relationship, and the morality being projected. The student then understood the spouse did not hold the same mythologies and stories.

We see our myths rear their heads whenever they are challenged, either by another person's myths, another culture's myths, or another's religious myths. When myths collide, we wage war—internally and externally. Again, we have confused connotation and denotation. We take symbols as reality and consequently are forced to live that conflicted life.

A myth is a story about life. Your brain mistakenly interprets these stories as real. Your life is a myth. Everything that you think that you know about anything is a myth: a misunderstood story about spiritual, emotional, and psychological insights that are mistakenly perceived as real by the brain. They are not real. They are representations and symbols of how you are told it is. Stop listening to mommy and daddy, and find out what this life is about for you. See clearly.

Clear Insight: The Desire to See Your Life Clearly—Even if it is Foggy Inside

Clear insight is a key piece of the equation. You must be willing and able to see your moralities, myths, symbols, life, and consciousness clearly. The truth, seen clearly, sets you free. Seeing yourself clearly is no easy task, yet is one of paramount importance. Seeing clearly is the difference between living a life of freedom, and living a life of imprisonment. When you are blinded by pain, desire, ignorance, fear, guilt, sacrifice, shame, doubt, and blame, you are not at all free. You are trapped by inner demons that hold the chains of happiness in their hands.

The inner demons appear as friends, but in reality they are internal enemies, masquerading as friends—and, once seen clearly, they truly are friends again. These dark scary parts of yourself only have power over you if you give them that power through your fear. Fear is contagious. Once you start down the path of fear, the ancient parts of the brain take over. Recently at a party, several children were hunting ghosts. They took me deeply inside a cavernous haunted house. I watched as terror flowed through their bodies—unabated. A wave of chill ran through the kids, and when the chill of fear hit me, the hair on the back of my neck stood up. From the reptilian brain perspective, fear is as real as whatever you imagine. The brain can't tell the difference between reality and imagination. However, once you know the truth about anything, it is no longer scary—that's the beauty—the dark is only scary when there is no light. Turn the light on, and the dark is instantly gone! See the wave of fear consciously, and take control of it with your conscious awareness. Fear is just the release of energy in the body caused by a symbol either outside or inside the head.

Clear insight is a principle, and clearly stated it is this, "No matter what is going on in my life, inside or out, I am willing to shine the clear light of truth upon it at all times. If anything scares me, I will shine the light of clarity upon it—no matter what." If you shine the light upon the darkness, then you will be in charge of the fight. Shine the light, and keep the enemy off guard. Be willing at all times to shine the light of clarity upon whatever is happening in your life. Face what feels un-faceable. Turn and face your darkest, deepest fears. You live as if your deepest fears are truth, reality. They are not.

I recently woke up one morning and for some reason was afraid of losing a finger. I resisted the feeling until I recognized that the cutting off of fingers was a symbol. The reptile brain was feeling disempowered, so it kept flashing the danger of losing my fingers in my head. If I had taken the symbol literally, I would have been worried about some kind of accident; however, I recognized the image as a symbolic communication. In energetic reality, I gave permission for all of my fingers to be cut off, until the energy and fear of the symbol discharged, which took all of five minutes.

Symbols in your head are energy, and can be worked with. Yes, they feel real because, as any good symbol should do, there is a release of energy in the body when the symbol is recognized, either consciously or unconsciously.

Everyone hides secret pains. Things that you feel if others knew about you, they would disown you. Laughter, or a good mask may cover it, but everyone has hidden pain. Be willing to shine the light of awareness upon your hidden pain, and set yourself free from that pain. Awareness integrates back into the whole, back into being. Awareness is all that there is, so you must discover the light of awareness in even the seemingly darkest places. Light is the underlying reality of all things.

On the path of freedom, as spiritual adults, we must learn to find the light, where it at first appears not to exist. The light is there, in all things, and our job is to reveal that light. We live in fear when we look inside and see frightening, scary, and seemingly insurmountable symbols of darkness. We come to know ourselves intimately, completely, and fully through exploring our deepest fears with awareness. We become free of our demons when we finally learn to turn the light switch on—no small feat. Surrender to the symbol until the energy that it evokes has lost its power.

Light is a state of awareness—a metaphor for seeing clearly. Each time that we are willing to look into the dark and face our fears, with clarity, we become more and more integrated as a whole person, and can walk clearly on the path of freedom.

Demons and Fears can be Your Guardians— Or Risk Ignoring Them

Your perceived demons, deep limbic brain symbols, are asking you to live a larger dimension of your life. In recognizing that your demons are actually your guardians, your cheerleaders, you will conquer much of your fear of your own shadow selves, the parts of you that you deny and hide from yourself, others, and the light.

When you recognize your demons, your deepest fears about your power and desires, and see them directly lighting your path for you, you give them a way to express their hidden energy into your life to support you, and send energy to your inner space. You do this by making peace with your fear of your own power and desires.

We are human, and we all have dreams, fears, passions, wants, and desires. We have been taught that these energies are evil and bad; but, of course, this is just a misunderstanding about how life really is. Our dreams, obsessions, passions, drives, impulses, and desires have the potential to light our path.

Your demon becomes a monster if it is repressed and not dealt with. If the demon remains hidden, it helps fashion your creative hell. You must grab hold of the demonic form, facing it fully, frontally, and directly. When you face your demons, your demons lose their negative, repressive powers over you. The repressive forces only work when you are afraid of them—which are what your inherited myths tell you to be. Fear of your impulses keeps you in prison; see the impulse, give it room to breathe. Explore it energetically, in consciousness, where you can safely explore anything.

You can't let your impulse system control your life, for disintegrated monsters are the forms that eat you up. I worked with a student who was suppressing sexual impulses, desires, and thoughts. The student initially could not see the correlation between the suppression and the physical symptoms manifesting. When the student began experiencing panic attacks, I assisted the student in releasing the stuck energy. We then started to explore the student's sexual mythologies. When the student learned to release the energy that was so long suppressed and allow impulses to express, the energy started to flow and all the physical symptoms disappeared. The student experienced a surge in creative energy. When you understand, breathe in, make room for, and recognize your demons, you can actually make your demons your source of energy.

As you integrate your demons and worst fears about yourself, you come to know what gifts are hidden for you within the energies that you have been forcing yourself to hold back. Recognizing demons is part of integrating the powers within you that they point to. Your demons hide your own personal buried creativity and treasures.

Once you integrate your demons and deepest fears, the energy contained behind the demon and behind the fear becomes your energy to use, however you desire. Often, as you step out of your demons, you step out of society and find yourself beyond good and evil. If you follow the adventure of the impulse system of your life, you live on the path of freedom.

By living your life fully and completely, with demons integrated, you give the world your true self, innovating the self in a beautiful, unique way, bringing something to the world that it didn't know it was missing: your unique self, forged beyond expectation, society, and culture.

On your path to freedom, there are no constraints other than the ones that you take on as your own. When you define anything as good or bad (right or wrong), you set the boundaries of your personal prison. Inner demons contain massive amounts of potential energy for internal change, transformation, and freedom.

There is No Inherent Right and Wrong on the Path—There Just *Is*

The most basic elements of myth are our stories of what is right and what is wrong; this is good and that is bad. Bucket two.

A fundamental need in the human mind is to separate experiences into light and dark, good and evil, right and wrong, God and the devil—every moment of every day. Myths are the stories that we tell each other, and ourselves, to help us sort through our raw, sensory input experiences.

Your myths make up your comfort zone. Your comfort zone is holding you in place. Myths are your sense of safety in the harsh, uncaring physical world. Your myth is who and what you know yourself to be. Your myths determine your daily actions and daily behaviors, thereby influencing your overall experience of reality. Myths tell you when you should wake up. For example, there is the myth: early to bed and early to rise, makes a man healthy, wealthy, and wise. This is a simple, interesting myth about the way life is, that works for some of the people some of the time—but it doesn't make this story true with a capital T.

No right and wrong exists, per se. There just *is*—what is right and just for one is an act of treason or sin for another. Every human action is bad for someone or something.

For the infinite, all is good and just—all is birthed out of the infinite creative flow. For humans, however, we must operate within the constraints of our society. Some things are just and right actions, and others are not. This takes incredible discernment on the path of freedom.

When you know who you are, you are free. When you are free in life, then you learn to see what is. To see what is, is to look directly into the vastness of the infinite unknown.

Love and Be Loved—
Infinity and Light are Everywhere—
Including the Dark

Another problem that individuals have on their path to awakening and freedom is the following: owing to the confusion of connotation and denotation, individuals believe that there is inherent darkness and evil in the universe, absolute right and wrong.

For most individuals, simply reading the word evil feels scary and threatening, but consider this: infinite consciousness is everywhere. Infinite consciousness creates all things, including darkness and evil. Everything exists within the infinite, so you never need to be afraid. God consciousness, awareness is in everything, even within the darkest spaces and places of the universe—the darkest places within you.

Do you think that all things are contained and created by God, but there's somehow a box outside of God consciousness where evil lives? It is simply not possible.

When I first understood this, it was life changing. I was working with a student who was having difficulty understanding

Love and Be Loved

this concept and integrating it. In meditation, I led her to the darkest place I could find—a demonic, hell-like environment, where there was no light at all. It was dark and scary—her skin and my own crawled like furry spider flesh. The room became cold. We were in the darkest and scariest demonic realm I had ever visited.

Then I asked her, "Where is God consciousness here?"

She stumbled for a moment, having great difficulty answering the question. Fear had overcome her. She was convinced that she would die in this place.

Again, I asked, "Where is God consciousness here, now?"

"It isn't here," she replied.

"Well, how is that possible?" I asked. "Does this evil, demonic, hell-like space somehow live outside of God? Are you saying that God contains all life, except for the demonic realms, that somehow they are extra real, that they managed to carve a little zip code for themselves outside of infinite God consciousness?"

She thought for a moment.

"Can you see," I began, "that God consciousness is everywhere, including here, in the darkest darks? Infinite God consciousness is here. Know this and find it."

She looked in the darkness, and suddenly saw a pinpoint of light. I told her to expand that pinpoint, to focus on the light until she saw through the veil of the demonic darkness. The energy in the room began to shift. Soon she was feeling peace. After about an hour, the deepest, darkest, coldest, and hellish space transformed back into the underlying truth—infinite God consciousness.

The infinite is infinite because it is everywhere, in everything—from the lightest lights to the darkest darks. Your job is to integrate this realization, and take it into life. Everything is of infinite God consciousness, including all of you. Your lightest lights and darkest darks exist in infinite consciousness.

You are. You exist within all that there is, as everything else does, light and dark.

We all want to experience the ecstasy of love, even the darkest creatures. Love is a beautiful experience to integrate into the body.

Love is. Our deepest drive is to know love—to love and be loved—to feel the depth of who and what we are. Love has no opposite. Move the love energy through the body, towards the deepest, darkest parts of self, that are hiding in fear of being seen for who and what they truly are.

You are, and you will always be. Bring love and be loved to every aspect of your internal reality. Love it all, including the parts of you that you hate, that are darkest, or that you are afraid of. These are the parts of you that you believe unlovable, unacceptable, especially if seen by others.

We tend to concretize within ourselves the thing that we have decided about ourselves. We concretize our internal myths about ourselves and make them real.

Exercise: list ten beliefs you have about yourself, that if someone knew about you, they would absolutely not accept you, much less love you.

Love and be loved in the being that you are. Unfold in this love, and fear will wash away from you. Compassion is not towards another, but towards self. The body is merely a vehicle of consciousness. Know yourself as that, and you will know yourself as compassion.

To Eat or Be Eaten—
That is the Question

Your body is nothing without your soul that lives within it and through it. Part of the freedom to play comes from the realization that you are not this body of flesh and bones. Your body is simply a temporary vehicle through which you experience this virtual reality called life, and it will eventually decay. Therefore, the body, in that respect, can't be who you truly are.

I helped a group of students understand this by taking them on a field trip to the Body Worlds exhibit. Body Worlds is Gunther von Hagens' anatomical exhibition of real human bodies. We had the opportunity to see the human body displayed in ways that helped us understand what an amazing machine it is. The bodies were dissected and placed in various everyday poses: chess player, skateboarder, cowboy on a horse, basketball player, etc. We saw our mortality reflected back to us, and it was difficult for some of the students to acknowledge that one day the body would die. The exhibits helped us understand that the body is a temporary vehicle, which should be well cared for to enhance our life experience. This is why exercise and eating healthy is important. We take care of the body so we'll live longer and have time to explore consciousness.

Your body is an energy processor—a filter that either processes energy currents moment-to-moment, or is being processed by life. That is to say, either you are eating the energy of this moment, or the energy of this moment is eating you. You'll know if you are being eaten, by how your head feels and the amount of tension and stress that you hold in your body, which is a storehouse for suppressed and unlived feelings, thoughts, and emotions.

The body also houses all of your beliefs and filters. Seldom, if ever, do you actually encounter *reality*. Too many filters prevent you from completely experiencing the fullness of the moment—the reality of your true being-ness.

Who you think you are, is different from who you really are. Almost everything you know about yourself is unclear at best; an amalgam of thoughts, beliefs, emotions, desires, stories, and myths that you have been holding onto and defending. Moreover, that may be all that you are.

The body is intended to carry the light of your divine, infinite soul, to experience joy, pleasure, love, ecstasy, freedom, bliss, and sing the joys of creation. Pleasure is a birthright.

Your Brain's Filters Interpret and Color Your Reality

A complete description and understanding of mood and emotions is still far out of the reaches of science; however, there are principles emerging that we do know. For one, there is no unfiltered here and now. Science tells us that external information, from the eyes and other senses, is highly processed before the identity becomes aware of it.

Saying it another way, past, present, future, unconscious, conscious, fear, pain, body sensation, feelings, hunger, desire, emptiness, etc., are flowing and mixing back and forth within the deepest structures of the brain. This rough fabric is hewn into something called the experience of this moment, the remembered experience of the past, and the imagined experience of the future.

Although we assume that we perceive the world directly, information from the senses goes through a myriad of systems, manipulations, and computations in the brain before reaching the conscious mind.

Become aware that if it is processed through your senses, you are hallucinating your experience—it is *not reality* with a capital R, but rather a shady approximation of what is actually going on.

You are awareness, your true self. Within your awareness appear your body, your mind, your ego, your brain, and your identities, both conscious and unconscious. When you first wake up in the morning, before there is body, identity, movement, yoga, or a story, there is awareness. Awareness is the background of who you truly are. Awareness is the only thing that is real.

Your awareness, however, is covered up by the dream, the illusion. This is Maya. This is life. Your identity, the filter through which you perceive and live your life, is an accumulation of past experiences, your belief in karma, future expectations, roles, goals, beliefs, fears, worries, job responsibilities, power or lack of power, sexuality, relationships, problems, money, exercise, etc. You are what you do, who knows you, and the amount of money in your bank account today; however, this identity isn't a fixed reality at all. Who and what you think that you are, is in a constant state of filtered self-interpretation, readjustment, and flux, that seamlessly overlays itself on top of your truth in your awareness.

Know that all exists in your awareness. Experience this for yourself, and you will see beyond the form.

Field of Awareness in the Ground of the Infinite— The Answer to Manifestation of the Soul

Everything, ultimately, comes back to the being that we are—to the realization that there is only one thing that does not change, and that is the field of awareness that we live in. That is the only thing that doesn't change: the background that our brain/mind/body/central nervous system lives within. The only thing that doesn't change is the truth of who and what we are. Everything else changes. Constantly. Continuously. The more we clamp down, the tighter we contract, the further we move away from the truth of what we are.

You are a field of consciousness that exists as God. That is the truth of who and what you are. However, that field is simply a field.

The soul is, in its simplest form, a potentiality, a field of possibility. It doesn't thrive until we allow it to thrive through perception. Prior to that, the soul seems trapped in a field of possibility that is concretized, until it is experienced and perceived, and therefore, free to flow. The soul must be experienced and allowed. When the soul is perceived, in a deep and profound way, there is created a sense of the sacred. The soul is a powerful transformer of consciousness once it is perceived, but seemingly not very effective until then.

The power of your soul emerges from your ability to perceive it and receive that perception. Perceive it and you will see it. Allow yourself to be touched by your soul.

Life Simply Is—
In Order to Receive,
You Must First Perceive

Here is the question. If there is nobody to perceive the physical universe, does it, in fact, exist? Without perception, without somebody to recognize its existence, there is nothing. Physical matter needs perception, as does energetic matter. In other words, your soul is called into existence because you are there to receive it and perceive it, as are all mythologies. What happens if there is no perception? Without perception, is there anything?

To call our soul into existence, we must both open our receptivity to the soul and perceive it; that is, call it into existence. The energetic field of perception doesn't have to do with the conscious mind. We perceive and receive subtle realms of consciousness through the field of awareness. We must develop the subtle energies of perception and receptivity that call the highest aspects of exalted states of consciousness into being. That is to say, without us, the perceiver, there may not be a universe that exists at all.

Our perceptions not only influence our experience of ourselves, but they influence our experience of others. To perceive, even the act of perceiving, influences outcome. To perceive is to influence. To know something is to create its existence.

Our myths, stories, moralities, rules, laws, beliefs, knowledge, and understanding influence our experience of life. Our experience of life influences the outcome of the perception. Essentially, our perception creates our reality. To perceive is to create causation. Perception causes existence. Causation is the act of creation.

How this applies to daily life is that the act of perceiving influences our experiences of the external world, which influences our inner experience, which affects creation in the external world. We know ourselves through these windows of perception. The perception itself influences our decisions. Our decisions and perceptions call into creation manifestation. What this means is that reality is a possibility, not an actuality. Our experience of reality is determined by our perception of reality. To perceive is to create, at least at the level of experience.

Imagine that you are walking down a city street. The buildings are unchanging. Myriads of individuals pass you by. The only thing that determines what happens to you is your perception. If you are in a place of fear, then individuals will look menacing. If you are in a happy space, then individuals will appear open to you. If you are angry, you will see angry individuals. The act of perceiving influences what you perceive.

Everything external simply is. The brain projects history upon that external reality in an effort to make sense of what we are perceiving, all the while not understanding that the act of perceiving is influencing what we perceive and therefore, what we experience.

Meaning is something that we add to life, depending on our mythologies, our past, what we believe, what we perceive, and how we feel in the moment. There is always a lot of background noise in the psyche.

Personal Myths Define Your Reality— and, There is No Santa Claus

Your brain frames and stores your past experiences in story form. Myth is impersonal and tries to speak to society as a whole, but our dreams and personal stories are the dynamics of mythological, symbolic themes operating in our own consciousness.

What you think that you know about yourself is a collection of stories and myths that you, your ancestors, your body, and your brain have told you about yourself. The modern ego/mind is an accumulation of experiences, reactions, fears, pains, grief, shames, doubts, worries, traumas, and drama passed down through the ages. In fact, current brain research shows that the child brain is extremely unstructured at birth, acting more as a field of unlimited potential, with infinite ways of being wired by experience.

Adult life is a remembered collection of mythological, symbolic stories and images. Your entire life is a myth that your brain/mind/body/central nervous system created, recorded and stored. None of it is real—it is an after the fact creation, recollection of reality as *denotative*, absolute truth.

With a limited number of image symbols within your brain, perhaps as few as a thousand, you come to know everything about your inner and outer worlds. Mythic image symbols are efficient ways of referencing and storing vast amounts of data. When it comes to efficient storage, a picture is worth a thousand words. The brain has a small, contained space in which it must learn to compute, store, and access memories and teachings for a lifetime.

Prior to now, you have been unable to determine that your myths aren't real. Your brain has been stuck in the denotation—the reality of what is perceived.

The human brain is still evolving, and someday the human race will naturally and clearly be able to differentiate between myth and reality, connotation and denotation; however, this is not yet the case. It takes a tremendous amount of conscious effort, attention, and energy to recognize this hidden, symbolic language of your brain; however, it is well worth the effort.

Nothing that has happened to you in the past is happening now. The past is symbolic, connotative, and referential. Your memories refer to images, symbols that evoke sensations, and cause the release of energy in your body, and vice versa. They are not facts. They are ever changing, ever evolving symbols. They refer to your past, but are not actually happening now; however, from the brain's perspective, when you review a memory you perceive it as real. Your body re-experiences the trauma, wound, or pleasure as if it were happening right now. In this way, it is happening right now, only inside of you, symbolically.

I was teaching a small intensive group when I asked one of my students to remember a traumatic event. By simply remembering the event, he was immediately thrown into the trauma of the event. He relived it completely in a matter of seconds. Suddenly, he was light headed with racing pulse and sweaty palms. Pain contorted his face as he relived the trauma rapidly, four or five times in about a minute.

The brain is unable to distinguish reality from memory. The brain sees the memory as fact, denotation of what is happening right now. Of course, the traumatic event wasn't happening right now, but the memory triggered sensations and stored symbolic images in the brain that in turn created an internal experience in the moment. In truth, the actual event passed by, in a matter of seconds, decades earlier.

You are living your life by referencing symbolic images that your brain is interpreting as real. Nothing you believe is inherently real—it is all a symbol. A symbol is composed of energy, thought patterns. Energy is perceived, and therefore can be changed and transformed.

Another name for symbols is stories. Stories are how we remember. We tell vivid stories in our imagination and these become our reference points for our lives. The more vivid the story, the more emotion and sensation flow through our body. Stories are how we evoke our past, understand our present, and prepare for our future.

Through our stories, we connect to our humanness. Our stories pack the emotional punch in our lives. Life has meaning through our stories. Stories create our experience.

Pay attention to the stories creating your reality. See your life as symbolic connotation referring to internal experiences, not external reality. Internal experiences are energetic reality and can be changed and altered.

If it exists in energetic reality, then it can be changed. Change energetic reality, and you will change your experience. Change the symbol, change the myth, and change the reality. The only thing that is real is what is unchanging—and that's change.

Change the Timeline—
Change Your Reality

All time exists in the here and now. When we make a change in the present, it affects our past and our future, which in turn influences our experience of the present. The illusion here is that the past has been written. On one hand, this is true: the actual act/event has come and gone. It cannot be changed. However, how we experience that event, how we feel about that past, what symbol flashes in our mind as a reminder, is in a constant state of flux.

Everything that you think you are, everything that you know about yourself, is in a continuous state of flux, constantly changing, but giving you the impression that it never changes. If you are on a path to freedom, then you are changing your present experience by changing the symbols flashing from your past. (If you want feedback on how quickly you change, it's helpful to work with people on a regular basis who know you well and can reflect back to you how you change. For example, they can share with you when they notice a change in your body posture or voice, facial softening, or feel an increase in your receptivity and connectedness.) If you feel that your life experience is focused on pain and unchanging, question why you believe that.

The limbic brain is the holder of these looped thoughts, images, and beliefs that you feel can never change. The brain does this so that you *never forget* the trauma and pain of the past, as if that will somehow prevent you from experiencing that trauma or pain again in the future. The limbic brain is making you re-experience the pain and trauma—moment-to-moment, day after day—beneath the surface of your awareness by constantly producing a flow of unconscious nerve impulses and images that seamlessly flow, mix, and blend with actual, external sensory nerve impulses, keeping you in a continual state of hyper-alert terror, well below the surface of your conscious awareness.

The limbic brain feels that if it keeps you steeped in continual pain and suffering of high terror alert by endlessly reliving horrible events that happened in your life, somehow you will not have to experience some imagined potential future pain. Forget that you are constantly in pain now, trying to avoid future imagined, possible pain—somehow the limbic brain doesn't have that understanding ... so you continually suffer, day-in and day-out.

When you change your reality/perception/experience in the here and now, you can take that change into your life stream, thereby changing your past reality based on your new current realization of energy, which then changes your future reality, which in turn further changes your current reality and experience, which influences your experience of the past.

Who you are now is completely different from who you were yesterday. You exist in this moment with what you bring with you, consciously and unconsciously. Change the present and you will change your past and your future. Life is constant change.

Question Your Myths—
Wake Up from Your Deep Sleep

Life is ephemeral. Life comes and goes. Experiences are temporary, everything in life changes. What is the lesson here? The soul is infinite, complete already. Your soul is already in a state of infinite, integrated bliss. Therefore, there is no place to get to. In your truth, you are already *there*.

Everything here is an illusion. It all comes and goes—like cardboard cutouts. Everything on planet earth has value only because we say it does. The universe is infinite. Expanding in all directions—infinitely. The infinite, expansive universe is beyond our capacity to even imagine.

There is no inherent value to anything. Value is an arbitrary distinction, a myth or story that you give to things such as money, homes, property, etc., to give structure to your life. The entire life you are living is a creation. What is it that drives this creation? What forces are moving you to create the life that you are living?

Why exactly are you here on this planet, having this

experience? This is the question. Yet, if you meditate on this question, you begin to understand why all life must crumble in the face of pursuit of the spiritual path. Your myths must be shattered in order for you to move in any direction. Sticking a flag in the ground and saying any myth is truth is not helpful. For example, one of my students held the mythology of angels and masters, which caused the student to look externally for assistance and answers. When the myth was shattered, the student realized that everything is an internal experience. Instead of calling out to angels and masters, the student calls to that energy which is within consciousness. This was a major shift for the student in taking back suppressed, compressed energy.

Your pursuit of freedom is a way of knowing about the natural world and your place in it. Base your freedom on what can be tested and experienced. Keep open to the possibility that your spirituality and myths are erroneous. Be willing to release spiritual patterns and beliefs when they no longer serve you. They no longer serve you when they cause you pain and suffering. Pain and suffering are arbitrary. Base your path to freedom on observations and experiences.

Nothing is sacred, especially the sacred.

There is No End to Anything—Except The End: Evolve, Integrate, Next Stage

If you are ready for a revolution, you are in the right place—face your life directly, as a scientist, and listen to yourself dispassionately and accurately. You know nothing about your life. Who you think you are will change many, many times over the course of your life—especially the closer you come to understanding your inevitable death. It may even change by the time you finish reading this chapter.

You are not a fixed point in space and time. No fixed point in space or time exists. The universe is expanding infinitely in all directions with no fixed points anywhere, just infinite movement and change.

You never again have to worry about the end of the world coming in your lifetime. You simply aren't that important. The end of the world will come whenever it comes. The world is not looking at some arbitrarily created human calendar (which all calendars are), checking its date, "Oh, I'm the world, and I have to end on December 12, 2012." This is misunderstanding of the myth, looking at the denotation of mythological stories, instead of the connotation.

The end of the world that humans have been predicting in their lifetime since the beginning of time has to do with internal change and transformation—it is not about external change and never has been. The brain's inability to determine this is the problem for civilization right now. Human beings are still unable to determine what is real from what is imagined—what is reality from what is symbolic, mythological reference. We, as a race, still perceive symbols, myths, and references as reality. As long as we do, we will be lost in the dream.

Every realized human being continues to work on inner development, which is unending—the development of essence, being-ness, is-ness, and presence. The development proceeds by exposing more and more subtle aspects of remaining personality to the truth of who and what you are as consciousness. After the basic personality is broken down, the process of dropping increasingly subtle aspects becomes easier. It results in greater and greater expansions. The more personality is exposed and its boundaries dissolved, the more essence develops. The fulfillment is boundless, infinite, and expansive. Evolve, integrate, next stage.

Orient your work on your spiritual path towards freedom, self-compassion, and self-deservement—approach yourself with gentleness and respect. Avoid pushing, struggling, straining, or suffering, which takes you nowhere. Struggling and suffering are old school.

Let them go. Suffering is mythological reference for a different people, in a different time, with different needs. Suffering is arbitrary. Feel free to choose and create something else.

You can do this by working from your heart center. From your heart, meet yourself exactly where you are. Have no effort or desire to change. Simply observe where you are right now; because the place where you really are right now is exactly where you should be, simply because it is where you are. Meet yourself here: in your body—in your heart.

You are not your expectations of where you think that you are or where you should be. You are exactly where you are, perfectly for this moment. If you don't work honestly and directly, meeting yourself exactly where you are, then you will always be trapped by the bondage of your mind and the tyranny of your conflicted mythologies and illusions—never questioning the rules that you live your life by.

If you are here on planet earth, you have more work to do. So, relax. Do the work. Keep it simple.

On the Quest for Spiritual Knowledge—
There are No Rules

Okay, I have good news, and I have bad news.

Are you ready?

There are no rules!

Rules are myths and symbols created by the brain/mind/body/central nervous system. If there are rules, those rules came from myths compiled by the ego/mind to brace against the fear of sensation—overwhelming feelings and impulses—our fear of fear. Any time there is containment, such as this type of person versus that type of person, it comes from fear-based myths. Boundaries, categories, and distinctions are examples of containment. Containments are created by our myths. Likewise, myths create our containments. Containments are the boundaries of our comfort zone.

As stated previously, myths tell you that this action, belief, or thought is acceptable and that action, belief, or thought will send you straight to hell. This is good. That is bad. Bucket two.

I have done a lot of yoga in my life. In class, you are often shown how to do an exact yoga posture in a certain way, and then pushed towards the advanced posture. I counter this way of thinking by asking the teacher, "If the advanced version of yoga is the key to enlightenment, then why aren't all the people from Cirque du Soleil enlightened? They can do all the advanced postures better than anyone I have ever seen. Why isn't the US gymnastics team enlightened? Does this mean that a paraplegic person can never awaken?"

To put it simply: it is not about the act or the action or the posture—it is about the field of consciousness in which they take place.

Our mythologies inform us, as beliefs, to do things in certain and specific ways so we are good, right, and just. Yet there are hundreds of thousands, if not millions of individuals, doing it a different way, experiencing no ill consequences. Most individuals live in a numbed out trance state, seldom questioning the rules, feeling safe in their comfort zone of what is acceptable and not acceptable—because that is what mommy and daddy told them. Marriages have broken up over silly things that are taken as truths—such as which direction to face the toilet paper on the roll. One woman I know neared divorce over this issue. She saved her marriage by putting the toilet paper on a floor stand. Therefore, nobody was right or wrong. Similar things happen every day. We take our mythologies as absolute facts. Unchanging truths.

Here's the deal. There are no rules, including that there are no rules. I know ... it is a paradox. Perceive your rules as symbols and myths, so that you can break free of them. Which direction does your toilet paper roll face?

Human Beings are Myth Generators—
That is What We Do

Human beings are myth creators. Myth is the energetic structure that holds our psychological life together. The mythic structure exists behind all human life and helps us to determine, sort through, and categorize our life experiences. Myths inform us as to what is good, and what is bad in our personal, business, financial, and spiritual affairs. Myths tell us whom we are, whom we should love, when to go to sleep, when to wake up, who to spend time with, and who not to spend time with. Myths underlie all thought and action.

Mythic structure is your prison. Mythic structure is your freedom. This is the power of your myth. Your entire life is composed of a continuing, ever changing, ever evolving myth. The more persistent the myth, the more that you think your myth is who and what you truly are.

The key to freedom is unlocking your mythical structure, and separating that from your true identity. You are not your myths.

Human Beings are Myth Generators

You never were, and you never will be. When your body dies, so will most of your myths. Who are you beyond the myths?

We understand ourselves through our stories and myths. We compress years of experiences, thoughts, emotions, and histories into a few compact narratives that we tell others and ourselves. In learning to detect, listen to, and understand our own stories, we gain understanding about how to heal ourselves and how to connect to others in an empathetic way. To be human is to tell myths and stories about our lives.

If you had to tell your story simply and fast, what would you say? Write a poem about your life story—50 words only. Poetry is beautiful, because it forces us to see behind our narrative, behind the story of our life.

Take a few minutes to craft your life poem. Here is an example.

A life Lived

A world,
Rough, untamed
Tough streets and life

Mean cars, small body
Time alone, in my head
Split from pain

Walking to kindergarten,

Finding Egypt,
Pyramids and rebirth

New York at night
Transvestites, dance,
Dogs into men

Wild west sexuality
Spiritual wisdom
Integrates within

A new way…
I am still uncovering.

Your Story is Your Life—
Your Life is Your Story—
Make It *Fun!*

We each have a story that we are both blind to, and completely committed to. That story determines the outcome and the outflowing of our lives. The uniqueness of each story separates us from others. We feel as if everyone is similar to us. When we tell our story, we feel that others understand us, and what we are talking about—but they do not.

In one of my workshops, we did a seemingly simple exercise, where we listed ten common words such as love, peace, friendship, money, sex, etc., and asked each person to give ten words that defined each of those easy words. I offered 100 dollars for each of the descriptive words that all six persons matched up on. Simple.

Take a guess—how much money do you think I gave to the group? Out of ten simple words, each with 10 one-word descriptions, how many words did all six persons share?

None of the six persons had the same definition for any of the supposedly simple words. I didn't have to pay out one dollar.

Language reveals as much as it conceals. We think we know what somebody means when they say, "I love you." When, in reality, the story that makes up their definition of love is completely different from our own. We make complex decisions about our lives based on our stories every day.

Erasing your story is the idea of understanding the story of your life that you have been manifesting from, that you have been creating from, and grappling with that story to eventually change it into something more consistent to what your true life desires are.

Take a moment to reflect on the stories that are defining the flow and course of your life. When you tell your story completely, in total abandon and surrender, you begin to see life patterns that have been running the show of your life. Go into your pain stories, your hurt stories, your blame stories, and your shame stories in all areas of your life: physically, sexually, emotionally, mentally and spiritually. Reflect on the areas in which you blame God, your relationships, your job, your spouse, your parents, your teachers, etc., for the circumstances of your life. The areas with the most energy and charge will inform you of the story that is running your life. However, do remember, it is a story—perhaps a convincing one, but a story nonetheless.

Everything that you define yourself as is a construction. Your life is a fabrication, cobbled together by your brain, mind, body, fears, memories, emotions, etc. It is not reality. Since it is a fabrication anyway, perhaps it is time to stop taking things personally.

Stop Taking Everything Personally— You are Not that Important—Really

Perhaps the biggest flaw in the human condition is that we take anything and everything personally—as if someone is out to punish us, specifically. We act as if all that happens to us makes sense, that God or the devil is out to catch us, and that nothing is random. We behave as if others do things to hurt us—our childish parts are the parts that believe this.

Nothing is personal—it just is. You make it personal. Your friend or spouse says something, and you take it personally. Why? Even if somebody does or says something stupid to you, is it really personal? Do you think they would say such things if they knew you, the plight of your life, and walked a mile in your shoes? Others say and do things all the time that have nothing to do with anything. The car breaks down or has a flat tire. Someone bumps into you. Someone looks at you, cuts you off, goes slowly, or stops fast. *None* of it is personal. Taking things personally makes things personal. If your spouse complains about something concerning you and you take it personally—I have news for you—you just made it personal. What's going on has little or nothing to do with you.

Stop placating mommy. Stop being a good person so daddy will love you. Unconditional love means that it is there no matter what you do. You are an adult now. Love yourself unconditionally, no matter what you do. Mommy and daddy aren't watching you. They are leading their own lives. You are an adult now—behave as one by realizing this simple truth: nothing is personal. Nobody cares. They are living their lives, and you are living yours. That's it.

Occasionally, our paths cross for one reason or another. Even if our paths cross, it doesn't mean that I know you, or that you should take something that I say personally. I still don't know you. Whatever my projected reactions are, they can't be about you. I don't know you. They can only be about me, and what I'm feeling.

Exercise: for one hour, live as if you take *nothing* personally. Live for an hour as if nothing is about you. If an hour is too long, then try ten minutes. For ten minutes, act as if you are impervious to everything. No matter what happens, who says what, what you do, in the next ten minutes act as if it is not personal.

Nothing is personal. Nobody cares. Taking something personally only creates problems for yourself—problems that emotionally weigh you down.

Baggage You Carry Around Weighs You Down—Drop Those Bags!

What are you walking around with that is calling itself you? What are the stories, the frustrations, the pains, the sexual issues, the lack of joys, the ugliness, the self-loathing, the fear, the doubting, the emptiness, and the problems that you are taking personally?

We are continually cloaked with problems. Layers and layers surround us and tear us up from the outside in. We are filled with a pressure or fear that keeps us in a small place in our lives, in a small life box. We are shocked when we realize how much the baggage of past problems and future worries weigh us down.

In a session, I listened as a student talked about her children, listing the problems each child had unconsciously inherited from her. The student was still working on some of the issues and it tore her up to see her children suffering from the same problems. She expressed more passion about wanting her children to live in their freedom than she did about living in her own freedom. The children were young adults and it was time for the student to release the guilt and shame she felt about their problems. In letting go of the pattern, she let go of the obligation and mythology she was defining her life by as *mother*. She experienced a release of energy and an expansion in her freedom that enabled her to be with her children in a different way, that opened them to their freedom because they were not obligated by the myth of *child*.

Notice that we focus on what we don't have or don't want. We live in a continual state of having and becoming, needing and wanting; which is why Buddha said, "All life is suffering." Not because of what we have, but because of our problems—what we don't have. We suffer for the goals we impose on ourselves. We suffer for all the time spent wasting time.

Imagine a girl on the beach holding a bottle. The bottle represents the mind. The beach represents the subconscious and the ocean represents the universe. As we try harder to do things and accomplish more, we identify ourselves with the bottle. We become the mind and the mental aspects of ourselves. We find ourselves inside the bottle, trying desperately to reach the ocean. However, it is impossible. It simply cannot be. The finite, the bottle, can never know the infinite, the ocean.

We long for the ocean, but we live in the bottle. And every time we escape the bottle during the course of meditation, or some other way that makes us feel alive, the bottle calls us back, like a pusher, pushing the security of all that can never really be had.

The mind lives to satiate. The mind lives to be right. The mind lives to survive. That's its purpose. The mind is born of the flesh. It exists because of having a physical body. Unless we learn to let the mind do what it does, without reacting, or struggling, or trying, we are doomed to live in the bottle.

What does the mind do? The mind creates fear, judges, self-talks, self-hates, fixates, retaliates, and lives in a constant state of war and agitation. So what! You are not your mind. You never will be. Stop fighting it. Let the mind be and do exactly what it wants. Who cares? The mind is not who you are. You are not the drunken monkey inside your head. Stop paying attention to it. Let it do its thing in the corner. Let the drunken monkey sit and play with crayons in the corner, while you, the conscious, spiritual adult moves ahead, free of all noise. If you stop feeding the mind with further war, the mind will stop growing in its influence and power. Let the drunken monkey be a drunken monkey, and stop feeding it. Forget about it. Move on. There are much more important things to focus on—like what do you really want?

Consider for a moment how your life would be if you dropped all your baggage, right in this instant. Just for five minutes. Who are you? What are you without baggage, without the drunken monkey? Where does the addictive part of your personality want to run? Why does addiction feel like the focus of your life?

Addicted to Pain—
The Human Condition

Out of the infinite possibilities that we have for this life, why is this the life we are living? Why do we keep choosing the same things with similar individuals over and over again? What emotions are we addicted to? Anger? Fear? Sex? What is it that keeps us going at it over and over again?

If you are stuck in your mythologies, you are addicted to pain. You are addicted to suffering. You recreate that pain and suffering over and over again in relationships and in life, an endless cycle that you are unlikely to give up. This is what our inherited life on earth is all about—pain.

The part of you who lives in fear and suffering is communicating with the rest of the individuals in your life, also living and experiencing the universe of pain. The part of you in pain is calling out to the external world to bring you the energy that you don't really want. The part of you in pain is fed by the energy of pain and suffering—it is the way energy works. The pain and suffering wants more pain and suffering. Energy attracts like energy. Life is a mirror. You are inadvertently attracting the thing that you don't want as long as you are living in the universe of pain.

Your body suffers the brunt of this universe of pain by holding tension and stress due to avoidance and denial. The addiction, the story of pain, runs your life. As a result, you spend your life running from the sensations, wanting to not feel the magnitude of the pain.

One of my clients unconsciously and consistently acted out to create situations that were deeply painful. The client did this to shift the focus from the deep internal pain to a superficial external pain. The client was addicted to the experience of pain. In a session, the client came to understand the addiction to pain. The client created painful external situations as a way to feel alive and fill the emptiness inside. The pain felt familiar and safe. The client perceived the insanity driving the addition to pain.

Inside, you are completely flipped out. Ask yourself, "What is driving my fear and addiction?" Feel into the pain and agony of your life. Feel into your secret pain.

Look for the space, a tiny gap between what you truly are, and the mind's universe of pain. Begin to ground yourself in the field of your true nature, your infinite awareness, your field of being, living from the being that you truly are.

You are either in your infinite self, or in the finite darkness of the mind. As you begin living grounded in the being that you truly are, a whole new group of individuals will appear around you, supporting you in the reality of who you are becoming now. When integrated, embraced, and healed by the soul, the energy that you invested in the universe of pain (by feeding the addiction) will come back into your life as an energy that supports and uplifts you. The energy reinvests in your life as possibility, potential, and resource.

If you are living in the finite darkness of the mind, addicted to pain, then your brain is controlling you—you had better learn how to run it.

No One Controls Your Thoughts or Feelings—Even if You Think They Do

Nobody controls your thoughts or feelings—nobody. You think and behave as if someone outside of you controls your thoughts, feelings, and behaviors, but in reality, nobody *out there* does. Nobody controls your brain. You do. Unless you don't; then, the brain is controlling you. You let the drunken monkey run the show. You live your life accepting whatever the brain offers up as *reality*, the way it is—a reaction caused by circumstances outside of your control.

Nothing is outside of you—it is all just perception in your brain, and your reactions to that perception. The only way this makes sense is to realize that there is nothing that you perceive directly. Everything is filtered through the brain/mind/body/central nervous system, aura, and energy field. Every brain is different, as a finger print, because each brain is composed of different life experiences, expectations, histories, family origins, survival skills, abuse patterns, neglect patterns, religious patterns, location patterns, country patterns, state patterns, school patterns, friendships, training, military, chemical exposures, environmental issues, health issues, lineage issues, womb experiences, genetic predispositions, etc.

Human beings call this life. We accept anything that the drunken monkey randomly offers up as reality—reality that we are helpless to change—as if this reality is from God, a guardian angel, the devil, or something outside of us.

All fear flowing through your body is your unconscious, nonconscious, autonomic nervous system's creation. How do I know this? Just look around you—nothing is happening. You are reading a book. Big deal. What you are feeling *must* be internal.

Please contemplate and digest this: whatever you are feeling right now is your own personal experience caused by nobody and nothing; just as others' emotions are their own creations. Nobody has control over you unless you give it to him or her. Most of the time, you don't even control you—the drunken monkey is at the steering wheel. Yet, you believe that you are in control and everything revolves around you. It doesn't, and you aren't—unless you are.

We are the Center of the Universe—Not!

Humans believe that they are the most important things in the universe. How many times have we heard stories of aliens abducting humans? Many believe that aliens are trying to figure out how human emotions work. I am amazed that an advanced alien race, that conquered the speed of light, and regularly makes transdimensional shifts, would abduct us, and anal probe us, to figure out our emotions. I guess, according to this information, the seat of the soul is not in the head at all. We've been looking in the wrong place. If we follow the cue of the aliens, the seat of the soul is in the seat. Now I understand.... For a moment, think back to the buckets. This has to do with bucket two; something comes from above to either save or destroy humanity. Yes, the characters change (aliens, God, Jesus, etc.), but the essential story is the same.

Humans think that they are the center of the universe and that everything revolves around them. Hence alien stories and end of the world stories abound. We think that we are so important that all major earth and universe changes will happen in our lifetime. Yet, in geological time, all human history is only a blink of an eye.

Thinking that we are important is both a good thing, and a super blind spot. The idea of God works because we are filled with the sense that we are the most important point in the universe. We are so important that God cares about every thought and feeling, every hair on our heads. To be human is to feel that we are the center of the universe.

In summary, your ego thinks that you (your brain/mind/body/central nervous system) are the most important thing in the universe, and as a result, everything else in the world cares about you. The terrorists care about you. The IRS cares about you. The government cares about you. The earth will end in your lifetime—that's how important you are—the whole planet will crumble before your eyes. This type of thinking and believing makes your brain extremely paranoid and insane.

Look up at the stars in a night sky. Take in the fact that there are an infinite number of universes being created infinitely, and expanding infinitely. That's how significant we are.

Uncontrolled, and un-awakened, your brain is paranoid and insane. You are not the center of the universe. You're not that important. You simply are.

You are Mostly Unconscious—
So Pay Attention!

One of the reasons you fail to awaken from the dream state is because of your brain. The brain is an incredible machine made up of the ego, by the ego, for the ego—a mechanism designed to function perfectly in the physical dimension. The brain's existence is based on retaining and circulating the historical knowledge of all human pain and suffering, fear and shame, guilt and blame throughout the multi-body system (conscious and unconscious) in an attempt to keep those things from happening to you ever again. The joke is that as a result of its nature, the thing that the brain doesn't want to experience, it damns itself to experience over and over, in endless loops that are desperately trying to heal—and there are thousands of lifetimes of these loops. Re-read this paragraph. Your own brain is in a constant state of PTSD—Post Traumatic Stress Disorder. The problem is that you don't know it.

Your brain is speaking in multiple languages that do not inter-communicate, similar to attending a meeting in the United Nations without translators—no one leader will understand what the other leader is saying. You can imagine the mess it creates. What does this mean to you? It means that your brain is having the same problem. It doesn't understand the language of the other parts of your brain. Each part of the brain developed out of needs at different stages of human evolution. Ontogeny recapitulates phylogeny. Your development from egg to person exactly and sequentially repeats the entire human evolution. This is true with your brain as well. Your brain is a three-dimensional incarnation of all human history.

You have heard the modern saying that you only use 10 percent of your brain—this is not accurate. You use 100 percent of your brain, but you are only conscious of 2 to 10 percent of what is happening. That tiny percentage is called the conscious mind. Everything else is functioning at a level that is other than conscious. Your brain is actually functioning quite well—that is the modern human's problem. What is being communicated unconsciously, in a language that you don't consciously understand, is devastating to your conscious, emotional life.

The most reptilian, fear based, unconscious parts of your brain are running your life, creating a nightmare. Every day your brain is deeply triggered by external images that also affect that trigger and stimulate the darkest recesses of your own brain. You are in a mass delusion, a mass sleep, and a nightmare of sorts, from which you cannot wake.

Your life is being lived by your other than conscious minds. I say minds, because similar to the United Nations, they are different territories, areas of the brain that speak their own languages and do not know how to intercommunicate. Please understand this. Digest it. Meditate on it. Read it again, aloud. Become conscious that you are mostly unconscious.

The darkest recesses of the brain, when un-awakened, know only fear and terror. Your daily life reflects the mostly unconscious parts of yourself.

The Primate Truth—
On Bananas and Brains

At the core of the mind is absolute, cold terror. That's where the drunken monkey lives. I call this *primate terror* because the mind is always focused on fear, especially fear of death. I was in a phone session exploring core issues with a client, when I felt compelled to shift my attention to the center of his mind. When I tuned in energetically to the center of his mind, I perceived a stem-like object vibrating in fear. I energetically removed the vibrating stem of fear, and behind that, I discovered this primate terror—symbolized as an endless stream of drunken, screaming chimps rioting in the center of his head.

The chimp fear is an extreme fear that creates terror inside of our psyches. It makes mountains out of molehills, creating huge, wild, fear storms that terrorize us. The terror is beyond language, beyond conscious thought, beyond reason—pure primate fear knows only total terror, constantly on hyper-alert, freaking out over the smallest things. For example, let's say that there is a rumor at your work about job positions being eliminated. The drunken monkey mind immediately takes this information as fact and you feel a flash flood of terror that you are the one who will be losing your job. Of course if that happens—the drunken monkey terror story continues—you will not be able to find another job, you will never work again, you will lose your home, you will have to live on the streets, and you (and your family) will die from lack of food and shelter, but not before suffering for protracted periods of time in horrific pain.

If the primate terror of the mind is not healed, we are triggered by the smallest infractions that catapult the body into terror sensations that feel as if the stakes are life and death. The mind lives in complete darkness most of the time—no light, no consciousness, just endless fear, and fear of fear. The brain is filled with background noise, neuro-static, that is often interpreted as primal terror. We are afraid of the very thing that we think is real, but it only exists as fleeting symbolic images in our mind.

Deep brain symbols are powerful because they emerge from the unconscious darkness of the mind. To give you an example, I recently had a dream where I saw a little girl walking on the side of the road. I could tell that the little girl was a ghost, and as I was driving past her on the road, her face swelled into a ball, her eyes became glassy, dead, and weird. When she turned her swollen blue face to me, her popping red eyes made my skin crawl, and my hair stand on end. She frightened the limbic brain. Even though my conscious mind, which was still aware during the dream, saw the little girl as a symbol, my unconscious mind, my drunken monkey brain was still terrified by her face—and took over my sympathetic nervous system, increasing my pulse rate, and raising the hair on my skin. There was something about the way she looked at me in the dark, about her blue skin and red eyes that made the drunken monkey begin to question everything about life. I took care of this by comforting the monkey, and telling it to relax, that it wasn't in control of this situation. As soon as I took conscious control back, my pulse went down, and the monkey relaxed.

Symbols are the language of the limbic brain, and they are only meaningful to the limbic brain. My own inner brain created the little girl, but the limbic brain thought it was seeing something that truly existed outside of itself. The brain was terrified because it couldn't tell the difference between what's inside, and what's outside. If that little red-eyed, blue faced, eye-popping girl were real, then there would have been something to be scared of. This language of symbols bypasses the conscious mind, and even though I fully understand the meaning of symbols, I am still limited by the conscious mind's inability to interpret and take control of the symbols of the limbic brain while in a sleep state.

The limbic brain is completely at the effect of its own manufactured symbols. We must train ourselves to take back control of these symbols as soon as our conscious mind comes back on-line. We have to go back into the dream, and create things exactly the way we want them to be, and continue to do this until it becomes second nature.

Be aware as the drunken monkey's primate fear expresses itself in strange and paranoid ways in your life—especially in the dream state.

Your Brain is Paranoid: Look Out! Behind You! A Terrorist is Creeping into Your Bedroom Window

The brain seamlessly moves your awareness from the highest highs, to the lowest lows many times throughout the day. The drunken monkey brain believes, "I am the center of the universe. The world revolves around me." Your drunken monkey is completely paranoid. Right now, there are images that are subconsciously flickering across the screen of your inner mind, ready to take you over, and take you down. You are making decisions in your life based on images in your mind, and putting your joy, ecstasy, and peace on hold for some imagined future time, with different physical conditions other than the ones you have now.

Understand this: your drunken monkey brain is narcissistic and lives in continual fear. To retaliate against this terror, your mind often becomes mean and vicious. The drunken monkey mind lives in continual fear of annihilation, and copes with aggression and attack thoughts projected on the outside world. The drunken monkey believes that everyone and everything has the potential to kill you. The terrorist, with a bomb strapped to his waist, is on *your flight,* or attacking your town, or stalking you. The terrorist is coming in your bedroom window.

Subconscious images faintly flickering in your inner vision right now are affecting how you feel. Realize that your brain is naturally geared to attack, protect, defend, judge, shame, blame, and guilt you and others into submission. Just know that this is a fact—it is not personal—just the way it is. The drunken monkey speaks, and your brain has been helplessly listening. Your awareness of this fact will help you change your relationship to the brain and your mind's natural tendency towards paranoia.

You can make a game of it—practice and have fun taking control of the symbol being vomited out by the deep unconscious brain. You know it's a symbolic image because it causes tension to build in the body. The inner image puts the drunken monkey on high alert, and that causes a release of icky feelings in your body. When this happens, take your new mind, your conscious brain, and put it to the fun job of wrestling back control of the steering wheel. You have full dominion over energetic reality. You have full dominion of the symbols that create fear, stress, anxiety, and worry in your inner space. You have to have fun taking back control. Play with the inner symbol. Tweak it. Turn the symbol into a furry bunny rabbit with purple ears and a clown nose. Then kick it in the butt and tell it to play in the fields. You are free, and always have been. Symbols have been controlling your life, and with practice that will change forever.

The brain is unable to recognize the difference between internal and external images projected on its screen. The internal screen of images triggers emotional responses within the body. Emotional responses directly affect how you feel, moment-to-moment. Feeling is not reality; it just feels that way. Feeling is another component of this skin suit that we wear that makes the inner myths and symbols seem real.

Are You Talking to Me? Nobody Else is in Here, It Must be Me

Another challenge is that the body is affected by the internal images projected on the inner screen of the brain. As we said previously, the brain can't recognize the difference between what's going on inside itself, and what's going on outside in actual, tangible, three-dimensional reality. The problem is with what we see inside the brain. The inner images create all kinds of sensations in the body that make us believe that the inner images are real. The internal symbols cause a release of energy in the body, in the form of feelings and sensations that make us believe that these inner horror images are reality.

Body sensations are what make this inner brain illusion so profound and the sensations from inside the skin suit feel so real. To the drunken monkey inside, everything looks real, and worse yet, feels real. What the drunken monkey sees in our heads is the worst of the worst, because the monster is being created from deep inside the ancient brain that imagines, creates, and stores our darkest fears, symbols, stories, experiences, and horror loops that continuously run on the vision screen within, beneath conscious awareness—but mistakenly appear to come from the external three-dimensional world outside our skin. These are the worst kinds of monsters—the ones that have free reign inside our heads, but that are projected upon the outside world. Don't think that this only happens to others, but not you. It happens every day and is happening to you right now.

You can see it in yourself, and in another, when these monsters take over. They terrorize us with their images of fear, pain, trauma, danger, suffering, and death. I see this all the time in the sessions that I do. When clients are close to releasing a myth that they were taught as children to be truth, the clients experience an upsurge of fear that feels debilitating. Their faces often contort in terror, as the image in the head exerts its power over the sympathetic nervous system. This is caused by the flow of chemicals through the brain and body.

The sensation of fear in the body is another hook. The body shakes from the flow of adrenalin. The drunken monkey is in full control. I see how hard it is for clients to believe that a myth, a symbol inside their head, can be so engaging. Clients often hear voices inside their heads saying, "No, this isn't a myth. This is truth." These voices become very loud and convincing. Clients feel as if they are going to die. They ask me repeatedly out of their fear, "Are you sure X (fill in the blank) isn't real, that it is a myth?" They intuitively know that it is a myth and are ready to let it go, but releasing childhood conditioning is tough because as children they knew the myth as truth with a capital T.

I believe that someday the brain will adapt, and the images that are inside our heads torturing us will clearly be identified as internal noise, brain static, and not something to take seriously.

Training yourself to see and recognize your own internal noise and brain static is difficult, because the sensation of pain is intense in the body. When you feel intense sensation, the body interprets that as real. If the body's experience is taken as real, then you become lost in those unhealthy, unproductive feelings.

We call these fears. Psychology calls it neurotic fear; that is, fear that you can do nothing about changing. However, we can change anything and everything—especially if it is brain static. Brain static is just energy, and the realms of energy can be changed, manipulated, transformed, and re-interpreted. You just have to know that you can change energy.

Your deepest fears are your doorway to freedom.

Know Thy Fear—
Know Thyself—
Know More Fear

The more you run from fear, the more you have to fear, and fear becomes your way of life. If you are attached to money or sex, then fear is the glue of that attachment.

When we speak of attachment to things, we find ourselves in the realm of duality; I am attached or non-attached. Individuals in the new age movement are fond of saying that we should not be attached. Nevertheless, attached or non-attached, we are in a bipolar realm, a realm of resistance.

To understand attachment, you must understand that there is an underlying need in attachment. That need is the addiction for more money, sex, love, food, pain, etc. The attachment point, the ligature to all attachment, is fear. When you understand that fear is the underlying focus, the underlying connective tissue, then you begin to understand the strength of attachment. To say this in another way, all attachment is connected by fear. The attachment leads you into the underlying consciousness that is fear.

Know Thy Fear

Deep unconscious fear is the connective tissue behind all attachment. Look at what you have a strong reaction to, and you will find yourself in the realm of deep unconscious fear. Track the reaction to the fear point. Look at what it is that bonds you to money, sex, eating, needs, desires, relationships, situations, and things. If you were to sincerely look at the attachment point, you will see your deepest unconscious fears. Attachment is a doorway to our unconscious fears.

Follow your attachment until it leads you to your deep unconscious fear. Track your reactions to their fear point. Understand that the fear projected in your mind is incorrect 100 percent of the time. To see this, it is helpful to keep a journal of the horrors and fantasies expressing in your mind. Be specific and reconcile the internal fears with what actually happens in external reality.

Hold all fear in love and bring your conscious mind to that fear. All fear is sensation. Sensation is just energy. Energy can change. All fear can change. The deepest fears are your doorway to freedom. Give yourself the freedom to live a juicy life.

If you are not feeling juicy and orgiastic, or at least at peace in this instant, then track the attachment to the underlying fear of poverty, loneliness, or suffering.

Life is a Perceptual Illusion

Why suffer? Suffering is arbitrary, and its value is limited. The world doesn't really exist. Who you were ten minutes ago doesn't exist in this instant, unless you are carrying it with you. If you are in the infinite flow of now, where is your suffering now? Jacqueline Bisset, when asked if she would have done anything different in her life, said, "I wish I had been naughtier."

Life is a perceptual illusion. Everything that is messing you up is in your head, because frankly, what's going on right now? Nothing. You are reading a paragraph. If you are not feeling downright orgiastic, or at least at peace, then you are stuck somewhere in your brain/mind/body/central nervous system's processing loops, which are based on fear, loneliness, poverty, pain, and suffering. However, you are none of that. You are the screen, an infinite field of potentiality that the brain/mind/body/central nervous system decodes through its *life experience.*

Take control of the vomit of the brain/mind/body/central

nervous system, because it is not real, just a collection of stored energy patterns. Change it, until you feel juicy. Stay with the simplicity of what is happening right now, which is not much.

You are infinite awareness. The finite, the mind, is trying to understand the infinite, the truth of who and what you truly are, which is simply impossible. Everything else is an ego creation, including all spirituality and religion—trying to justify or explain the unexplainable.

Old spirituality, based on ancient religious mythologies, is unhelpful in modern mythology, where we want to explore our complex totality.

Old Spirituality Versus Boundless Life and Sudden Death

Today is the perfect day to die. In the past, this fact would have been depressing. However, in modern mythology, this is a fact that must be integrated into your conscious awareness. In order to live fully, you must fully die.

The old spirituality includes confusion, duality, pain, suffering, fear, manipulation, retribution, and will power. God is all knowing, but only helps certain individuals some of the time. Miraculous healings are easily explained by simple statistics. Old spirituality is fear based and clouded with dogma. Old spirituality is filled with empty ritual. Old spirituality says donate cash to save your soul.

The new path says take care of business. Take care of your physical reality so that you have time to take care of your spirit. The new paradigm looks at all aspects of self. No part is disowned.

Life itself is your mystery school. The days of cave dwelling teachings and cloistered monasteries are history. The new spirituality asks, "If I sit in meditation, in a monastery, how do I know that I have really healed an issue in my life?" This is key. I remember being startled by an image of monks fighting one another in the street. When I saw that, I realized they had learned peace by sitting in a monastery, but hadn't dealt with or integrated personal anger.

Old spirituality taught us that anger is bad, that we should be *good*, that our shadow should be cut out, purified, or cleared. In the new paradigm, we explore our complex totality—our light and our shadow. The focus is integration and intention, clarity and reality. Our intent is to become a simple person, allowing the flow of our totality to express in the fluidity of life.

Live your life, freely. You have a body for a reason: to feel, to love, to experience, to hate, to explore your shadow—this must occur. The body is a vehicle for the soul: nothing more, nothing less. The body is not intended to store repressed feelings, past hurts, and disintegrated selves—dying under the strain and stress.

We are complex creatures with conflicted impulses. Sex, violence, rape, murder, rage, lust, and terror flow through us. Look at these impulses consciously, with clarity and vision. Bringing these deepest, darkest, most unacceptable parts into the light, into our conscious mind, is to live a whole, spiritually centered life.

All spirituality is a myth; that is, a story about inner insights. You are not your stories or your mythologies.

You are Not Your Myth and You Never Will Be

You are not your myth. Your myth is a creation generated by received personal and impersonal messages of morality, judgment, survival, and discernment passed down through your lineage, your soul, your parents, your DNA, and your bloodline.

Six major impersonal myth generators govern and guide our daily lives: religion, business, government, education, media, and entertainment. Without all six, society as we know it would cease to exist.

These six major institutions of the physical world are based on the same underlying principal of evolutionary survival: this thing, person, story, religion, or idea is good and that story, person, idea, thing, or religion is bad. Bucket two. This is good, and I will survive and be rewarded and therefore thrive, and that is bad, and I will be punished and die, and suffer the fires of hell.

Society and social order depend upon the individual and group's abilities to discern and honor this simple distinction of good and bad, right and wrong.

The morality of the group and/or society that we live within is created, governed, and handed down in the way of received, inherited knowledge; that is, myths are passed down from our forefathers through the six major institutional methods. Received knowledge, in the form of myths and symbols, is interpreted by the brain/mind/body/central nervous system as absolute knowledge—that is, knowledge that is fixed and unchanging—absolute truth—the way it is, the denotation. Herein lies the first internal conflict.

Received knowledge is composed of general knowledge of our time that could be false, but people believe to be true, and act on that knowledge externally. A clear example of this is the myth of the flat earth. People believed the earth was flat, that the horizon was the edge of the earth, that if you went far enough, eventually you would fall off. At one point, this was considered absolute knowledge, absolute truth, even though now we can clearly see it as received knowledge, a denotative misunderstanding—a myth.

When we embark on a path to freedom, we must see that the thing that offers us redemption, whether it is money, God, religion, education, or the pursuit of right living, is the thing that thwarts us on our path of enlightenment and spiritual evolution.

Exercise—Discovering your myths. Keep a journal, and write down what you believe is so. Here are some initial questions.

What are the flat earth myths in your life?

What do you feel strongly about—that you would be willing to die for?

Write down ten things in your life that you know about yourself that are absolutely the way it is. Where you perceive denotation.

List your myths about who you think that you are. The mind and senses may see imperfection, but entertain the possibility that you are already whole and perfect.

Why not live in freedom and perfection now? What myths are you living that prevent you from feeling incredible?

Is it bad to have money?

What is your belief about money?

Is it bad to feel good?

How do you feel about sex?

Is sex bad?

How do you feel about war?

How do you feel about your religion?

How do you feel about abortion?

How do you feel about birth control?

How do you feel about stem cell research?

How do you feel about cloning?

How do you feel about technology?

How do you feel about the Internet?

How do you feel about pornography?

How do you feel about women?

How do you feel about men?

How do you feel about love?

How do you feel about same sex marriages?

What is marriage to you?
What is the purpose of marriage?
How do you feel about God?
What is God?
How does your God expect you to feel and behave?
What does your relationship expect from you?

We make everything that doesn't fit our mythologies bad and evil. We moralize that our way is the right way. Nothing we believe is absolute truth.

Human Beings are Moralistic, Moralizing Machines

We are moralistic machines, moralizing at every turn of our lives. We make anything that doesn't fit our paradigm, our vision of the world, wrong, evil, bad, etc., and everything that does fit our paradigm, rightly, and Godly. We do this individually, within the group that we identify ourselves with religiously, as a family, as a community, and as a society. We are warring tribes, forced to live on top of one another as the world population continues to expand.

Everything you think you know is metaphorical reference to either your own, or someone else's internal experiences, and not factual reality. Everything.

If you interpret your life as metaphor, symbolism, and poetry, your life will radically transform. Nothing internal is absolute truth—it is a construction.

When we live life from our center, when we know who we are beyond all of the forms, all the conditions, and all the morals, we no longer live in fear of the end of the world, the cataclysm, the catastrophe, which is simply a metaphor for the death of the ego/mind.

Our fear is just a projection of our own lack of centeredness that exists beyond the external world of the ego. When we know ourselves as infinite, we know life as the infinite. When we identify with the infinite, there is no longer fear of external, impending doom. The body is seen as a vehicle, and eventually, all vehicles must be returned to the manufacturer.

The earth will cease to exist at some point, as will your body. The cycle of life and death simply is. You must say yes to that. Everything that comes into existence will go out of existence. You are a symbolic representation of everything and nothing.

You are a Symbol of God

Sense and feel into the possibility that you are a symbol pointing back to the infinite, a symbol of God, created in the image of God. How does this change your image of yourself?

The cycle of life and death simply is, not because you sinned, nor because of karma. The cycle of life and death is a part of physical life on planet earth. Your life is no more real than the words on this page, or the thoughts in your mind, or the clouds in the sky. You are simply because you are—not because of anything that you do. You are. Your life is meaningful in the same way that a sunset is. What is the meaning of a flower?

Your life is. You are a symbolic representation of God, a symbolic representation of nothing and everything. You exist because you exist. Your form will come and go. Life is not inherently significant, except for the symbolic representation that you choose to live by. Realize that all symbolic representations are just organizations of energy, and energy organized is a construction, a mythology, a symbol, and a story. Change the symbol that you are living your life by—if it isn't serving you, change it—change the symbolic representation and approach to your life. Let go of your story. So many times, I've heard people say life is hard or you have to work hard to earn a living. Their stories are about struggle. Change your story to life is fun and joyous or something similar that serves you, or let go of your story all together.

Without a story, you are free. All energy is freed to return to the center point of consciousness. You are the center—the creation point—the place where all things begin and end. This lives within you. You are everything and nothing. Let your energy be free.

Don't be any symbol at all—just be a field of potential that is waiting to express, as needed, right now. Here and now.

Who are you? You are.

Each time you ask that question, let go of the symbol that you are living your life by. Let go of the force of your stories. Let go of your beliefs in whom and what you should be. Free yourself of the symbol and find out who you are in your freedom.

All Life is Symbolic Metaphor— Including You

You are nothing more than a symbol to somebody, including yourself. In order to change your life-organizing symbol, you must recognize that symbolic energy is all that you are. You are a symbolic representation—not a reality. You are a metaphorical reference.

Everything that you know yourself as will come and go. It will all cease to exist. You are a symbol, and all life is symbolic. You are a representation pointing towards a greater truth. You are not ultimate reality. What is your symbol? What is it that you think that you are? What do you live by? What symbol would your closest friends use to describe you?

You must choose your symbol wisely because the symbol is the organizing principal that attracts the energy of your life. If you sit for a moment and watch others, you begin to see the symbol that a person is living under and by. Each symbol organizes the energies of your life. I was with a group of students on an outing when one of the students asked me, "What do you see when you look at people?" I answered by describing the physical appearance of a person in the room and the symbol that was dominating that person's life. A person's physical demeanor reflects their symbol.

A symbol is a way of being. Our choice of symbol represents how we organize our life energy. Nobody exists as an inherent reality, just a symbolic representation that we believe is real. Life is composed of symbols, and we merely step into them. The ones that are shared by all humans are called archetypes; which is just a big word for the organizing power of a symbol. Redneck, alcoholic, druggie, stoner, yuppie, dink, generation x, generation y, punk, rocker, hip-hopper, lawyer, doctor, student, seeker, guru, teacher, millionaire, genius—these are all symbols that organize our life energy.

What symbols are you living your life by? These are also called roles. What roles are you living your life by?

If you dropped all symbolic organization of past and future, then who are you? Who are you when you are free of your symbols and metaphors?

Symbols Evoke the Release of Energy in the Body

Take a moment to look at the clothes that you are wearing. Do they have a logo? What color are they? Why are you wearing the color? Why do you stay away from some colors? What car do you drive? Does your car say anything about you? What about your shoes? Do you own any expensive brands? Do you have a favorite number?

Take a moment to look around your room. Do you see anything not a symbol, not a metaphor, referring to something else?

Take a book. A book has a picture on its cover, a symbol trying to capture your attention, and give you a metaphorical reference to the contents. What about the author's name? That's a symbol referring back to the person. What about the picture of the author? That's a collection of dots creating a symbol that refers to the author. What about a cup? Does it have a logo, a phrase, a picture, or an abstract image? Is it an unusual shape or color? Why did you acquire it? Maybe it was symbolic of your vacation, a reminder to laugh, or breathe?

Symbols Release Energy in the Body

Do you have T-shirts with logos or cute sayings? Do you have socks with little hearts or bright colors? Do you have a brand that you love? Why? In an extreme example, how do you feel about the American flag? How about the flag of the Taliban? Did you have a reaction? That is the power of a symbol.

Symbols evoke energies within you. Symbols are energy releasing. They release sensations, chemicals, and feelings within your body. They appear to cause you to feel things.

Everything around you symbolizes something. Everything external expresses an insight, an idea that someone had in thought, and then manifested in three-dimensional reality. Symbols compete to release the energy in your body—most of it happening beneath your conscious awareness.

You have heard the phrase, "Sex sells anything." You think that if you wear the right clothes, drive the right car, or drink the right beer, you will have your deepest desires met and fulfilled. The symbol evokes the release of energy in the body, and makes you spin into action. "If only I buy X (fill in the blank), then I'll be happy."

Look around. Do you see anything that is not a symbol? Everything means something—even if it is nothing. Nothing certainly means something.

What metaphors have you concretized about your life? What insights about yourself have you made real and are you expressing through your thoughts and actions? How does the symbol that you think you are affect what you will do or not do in your life? The symbol that you believe that you are is your box, your comfort zone.

External life is composed of symbols, from the food you eat, to the car you drive, to the clothes you wear—everything is symbolic, communicating something to somebody.

Symbolism and the Brain

Symbols are everywhere in life, and all life is symbolic. As you come to understand this truth, you become conscious of how all of your life is experienced. You are a symbolic creature living a symbolic life. You are not a person, separate, but a collection of borrowed symbols that propel you on the way to your life. You identify with symbols, and are guided by symbols.

Millions of symbols pass through your brain's inner pathways everyday. Every feeling and emotion is triggered by a symbol. All problems are symbolic reactions to underlying realities seamlessly projected onto the inner screen that make the perceiving old brain think that it is under attack most of the time. The old brain communicates in emotionally-charged symbols that reflect deep, interior parts of self that are continuously trying to heal themselves by recreating the initial trauma reality over, and over, and over.

If you listen, you will hear individuals talk to you about their intimate inner symbols. They share these emotionally charged inner symbols, and think of them as if they are real. Often a client will ask me, "Is this real?" They are asking me if the symbol in their head is real. Why? They can't tell the difference. Neither can you, unless you train your brain to see mythological images as symbols.

Train yourself to recognize the language that your brain is speaking, and realize that no matter how real it feels, it isn't. You are living your life based on symbols filtered through the ego/mind.

Humans created the ego/mind as the brain developed. Prior to our modern brain, humans had no memory—no way to store and access information. In order to further our evolutionary fitness, we learned to store information symbolically. There is only so much room within the three-pound brain. Information has to be stored symbolically, and be very effective in releasing energy in the body to create a full sensory approximation of the original experience.

This is commonly experienced as fear, passion, anger, and rage. Most of the time, these emotions come from what is happening inside your head, not what is actually occurring in three-dimensional reality.

What makes us uniquely human is that we have this tremendous ability to recreate and generate energy and sensation in our bodies, from what is happening with the symbols in our heads.

Train yourself to recognize the language that your brain is speaking, and realize that no matter how real it feels, it isn't.

History of the Ego/Mind

Imagine for a moment that you have no memory, no way to store your experiences or history. What exists is an experience of here and now—no past or future—a simple sense of presence revolving around the seasons, sun, moon, awakening, hunger, tiredness, sexual desire, and fear of death.

What we call enlightenment looks a lot like the experience of what life was 10,000 years ago, before the modern mind. Without a mind, a way to store and access experiences, life is blissful because all that exists is right now. This second is mostly okay unless we are under attack—then we fight, flee, or freeze. Other than those exceptions, life simply is.

Soon after this no mind period, the modern ego/mind began to form in response to the increasingly complex systems of tribes and interdependent societies. The brain needed to further develop to rapidly store and access various life experiences, detect and store facial expressions, recognize danger, friends and mates. The brain needed to cross-reference stored patterns that tended to organize around pain, shame, guilt, and fear experiences. The simple distinction of this hurts and that doesn't; this is good and that is bad; this is right and that is wrong began to evolve. The drunken monkey was being born. Pain was the greatest teacher to the newly evolving brain. With this teaching of pain, the mind ensured that our progeny would survive the perils of the physical dimension.

Our modern memories were created out of painful experiences, which seared their way into the folds and cells of the brain/mind/body/central nervous system. Memories were created out of fear, pain, suffering, guilt, and shame. This became our normal way of being, a part of our shared human experience. The experience of shared pain made us feel human. In pain, especially intense pain, we experience inexplicable aliveness.

The modern ego is made up of the same storage *stuff.* Anything negative, hurtful, shameful, guilt ridden, harmful, etc., becomes the thing that burns its knowledge into our hearts and minds. This, in turn, is passed along, generation to generation, as the knowledge base of *experience.* Because of the nature of the brain, this shared knowledge base is taken as absolute truth—denotation. It sets a pattern within the brain/mind/body/central nervous system that says life is supposed to feel painful.

All of our modern stories tell us that life is hurtful, painful, and burdensome, that the highest order of this life is sacrifice, known as the hero's journey. Like God, sacrificing his only son in an effort to show us the way to freedom. Sacrifice, pain, and suffering are the organizing principles of survival; therefore, the organizing principles of the modern human.

From this perspective, it is kill or be killed, eat or be eaten. Human life exists in this structure of pain, suffering and sacrifice. The areas where you feel stuck in your life are the result of being fixated in this paradigm of pain, and having no references or teachings for anything beyond pain.

Pleasure is considered bad, an impulse that you are told to control and subjugate along with the rest of nature. This is the work of the modern mind. You are told to control your lower nature and lift yourself to a higher spiritual life. However, as I said earlier, nearly all of your dysfunction comes from this space, the inability to know another way. Few reference points exist for joy—and many, many more for pain, suffering, and sacrifice.

Those involved in spirituality and religion share their insights about enlightenment and sacrifice, believing their way is the right way. However, their way is not the absolute truth. Question everything.

We must make reference points within ourselves that create new paradigms of bliss, joy, peace, openness, and freedom.

Sacrifice—Your Main, Unconscious Operating System

We exist today because something else died. Our organs survive due to the death of other things. We call this eating. We must consume other living things so that we may live. We wipe away guilt and pain about this daily death through stories and mythologies that we tell ourselves about this life.

Any thought we have that justifies an action or behavior is a story. We use stories to psychologically survive in the face of the daily horrors of life. We justify why things happen by judging we are either good or bad, and had it coming. The general idea that underlies our existence is sacrifice. Sacrifice is the story that one thing gives up something for the good of another.

Sacrifice has its roots in the beginning of physical existence. Our one-cell, nonverbal ancestors lived in a frightening world of annihilation. Each moment was fraught with death and destruction. An organism is alive and in front of us in one moment, and then in another moment is not alive. Every cell in the body experiences this daily struggle. Within the body, cells die daily so that the entire organism can survive.

The physical universe is organized around the reality that, in order for one thing to survive, another thing must die. This is the reality of the world within which we live. For example, the chemical reactions that give us light from our sun are slowly killing the sun.

The endless cycle of death in the physical world creates some serious issues for the developing brain, central nervous system, and physical body. How do we handle the daily horror of physical existence? We tell stories.

For example, imagine what it was like for our ancestors on the savanna plains trying to figure out why the person in their tribe died. One minute the tribal member was alive and breathing, the next, cold and hard. The surviving tribesmen begin to add meaning to their previous actions and circumstances in an attempt to figure out what lead up to the death. The mind's way of doing forensics is to wonder how or why that death happened. Were the Gods angry? Did the person accidentally offend someone or something? It is easy to arrive at, "If only I had done X instead of Y, then this person might still be alive."

Even today, we analyze life situations in an attempt to discover the underlying cause. For example, if someone has the flu, a new ager asks, "What's that about energetically?" We, as humans, assign meaning to practically everything. The need to know, understand, and assign meaning to any and all events leads us to the development of systems of religion, which try to answer the difficult question of why bad things (e.g., death and loss) happen to good people. It becomes clear that, though we may not understand why X (fill in the blank) happened to us at this time, Santa God has been keeping a list, checking it twice, and we are likely being punished for our naughty sins that we committed either recently or long ago. In this world, if sin is the cause, then sacrifice is the answer to the problem of how to erase a sin.

Sacrifice exists in all human cultures. Sacrifice this person, place, or thing, so that person, place, or thing can be saved. Religion is filled with stories, images, and symbols of sacrifice. Sacrifice is at the core of the human condition. To live is to sacrifice. We are constantly sacrificing competing systems, impulses, or ideas, for other competing systems, impulses, or ideas. By choosing anything, we sacrifice something else. Life can be seen as a series of decisions that sacrifice other potential opportunities.

Sacrifice is an integral part of the human condition; however, here's the catch—we are not the body that we inhabit. Sacrifice may be a part of life on planet earth, but it is *not* the reality of the soul. The soul exists in energetic reality, and that reality is closer to our true self. From the soul's perspective, there can be no *reality* to sacrifice, because how can something that isn't real sacrifice something else that isn't real?

Nothing is actually lost, because physical existence isn't soul reality. Yes, there is physical reality. However, without the soul, there is no underlying life to this reality; there's just a body. That's why there is neither sin nor karma. The *reality* that we live in isn't reality at all. Physical reality is a metaphor, a story, or a symbol that points back to the infinite—which is beyond our three-dimensional reality. Human beings are symbols of God. God is a symbol that points to the great mystery of existence.

Sacrifice is a story, a ritual, a mythology of death and rebirth. Sacrifice is a system of morality. One person's sacrifice is another person's murder. There can be sacrifice only if we don't know who we are. If we know who we are as soul, then, in this physical reality, there can only be what is.

All that is actually happening is what is. Everything else is an overlay, an idea, a concept, a philosophy, and a story. Sacrifice is a symbolic representation of life on earth. One thing dies so another can live. Even God practices sacrifice, sacrificing his only Son, so that all of our human sins can be washed away. Of course, any God worth his or her weight in salt could easily recognize that man was created in the image of God, and that therefore, man is simply a symbol of God. That is to say, man is of God. How could anything of God be in sin? God knows the truth—in this life, there only is.

You are a symbolic representation of God consciousness. Sacrifice is an attempt to understand and give meaning to your life and your death. From God's perspective, you are not the body and everything on earth is an illusion held in the mind of God. From the earth perspective, everything is a sacrifice, a sin. This is why life on planet earth can be awful. No matter what you do, any action you take is bad for someone else, somewhere; hence, sin, karma, and debt to be paid.

In what areas of your life are you still living in a space of sacrifice? What is your belief system about sacrifice? What is it about sacrifice that is compelling to you?

Your life is continuous change. Everything on this planet is a symbolic representation pointing back to the infinite, and the divine.

Religion, Spirituality, Enlightenment, and Slippery Slopes

Life is a slippery slope of constant and continuous change. Everything is uncertain—except death, and most of us are in denial about this eventuality. We want to live forever and will pay just about anything for the possibility. Organized religion is all about eternal life, guaranteed. All we have to do is follow these conflicted and confusing steps, deny our human impulses, suffer, struggle, and tithe at least 10 percent of our income.

Yet, everything points to the truth that nobody lives forever. Religion answers this by teaching that *eternal life* actually comes after *death*, after we've suffered here sufficiently.

At best, life is a sticky super spider web of trials, tribulations, hurt feelings, love, confusion, and uncertainty. We are told this life is an illusion. That it is a punishment for our sin, or payment for our past karma; that the *good* life will follow in heaven if we are good, or end in hell, if we are bad. Bucket two.

I call this the Santa God universe. We want what we want when we want it, and God is (sing along now) making his list and checking it twice, gonna find out who is naughty and nice—that is to say, judging who receives what, who goes to heaven, and who goes to hell. We are told it is not spiritual to judge, yet we believe in a God that judges our every thought and action. If God judges us, then can judgment be that bad?

Few have come before us to help us sort through this quagmire of life's mythologies, to see this life clearly. Many claim that they are enlightened thinkers. Yet, when their teachings are closely considered, one must wonder. Sadly, there are few—if any—clues to substantially help us out of the dark, fear spaces of the ego/mind that predominantly make up our experience of this life.

Mostly, what we call *spirituality* is cluttered with confusion, partial truths, mythology, morality, smoke and mirrors, judgment, greed, fear and shame, power and money hungry leaders, and opportunistic parasitical relationships that promise to save or enlighten us.

Whatever enlightenment is, it is your natural state. If it is your natural state, then simply relax into the naturalness of your being. Enlightenment is about lightening up. If you feel heavy about your spiritual path, or your life work, then you are likely heading in the wrong direction, whatever the path.

Enlightenment: What is It and Will It Kill Me?

Enlightenment is the revolution that occurs when you realize that your ego/mind/identity—you who calls yourself you—is no longer at the center of your life.

Enlightenment is the awareness of being aware. Enlightenment is freedom from the animal, terror impulses that drive the physical life. Enlightenment is living in a continual state of freedom and being vulnerable about the places where you are not free.

The enlightenment process is facilitated by your own awareness and infinite nature. The mind, fear, paranoia, and terror might still exist, but they no longer run the show.

When your infinite nature is at the center of consciousness, you find that you are completely free to experience your life as a human being, rather than as a human mind of solidified fear. This defining moment in the life stream of a human being is crucial to psychological, emotional, and spiritual development. As you realize who you are, you uncover the true, infinite possibilities of your life.

Another way to say this is that when you live free of fear and allow desires to move through you, you live in a field of awakening.

Enlightenment is a field of awakening awareness, which includes the knowing that you are infinite: you are not the body—your physical form will die; you are not the mind—the mind will disappear with the body; you are aliveness, and energy, in constant creative change and motion.

In this respect, you begin to awaken to the awareness that you are God. You are the infinite. All exists within you and around you. Everything is perfect in its imperfection. You see your life in the context of a clear light, clarity. Prior to this awakening, you are adrift in a sea of endless human pain.

These simple concepts capture the tools of enlightenment:

- Everything that you think you know about who you are and what your life is about is probably incorrect—notice how strongly you feel about being right. Release your dog bone need to being right. Accept the possibility that perhaps you don't really know anything.
- You are energy—pure energy, maybe.
- Life is boundless, infinite, and constantly changing.
- All energy can be changed. The energetic universe inside your head can be changed.
- The physical universe is also malleable. When in doubt, use a sledgehammer.
- Your questioning mind is finite and can never take you to the infinite.

- Your soul and your energetic awareness will take you into the realms of the infinite.
- Pain will always lead you back to sleep. Pain feels real, but isn't. Pain is an addiction.
- Awakening is the realization that you are not your pain and suffering.
- At every moment, you have the choice to live in the universe of darkness, or the universe of light.
- Take absolutely *nothing* personally. It isn't. People have their own problems.

We unfold every moment of each day in a direction that is either on our path to freedom, or off our path—depending upon our thoughts and awareness.

If you are on your path, you move towards expansion, openness, and freedom. If you are off your path, you are where the majority of humanity lives—inside the sea of pain, suffering, fear, anger, morality, mythology, and misery. In this view, there isn't nearly enough of anything good, and plenty of bad to go around.

What becomes important is not what we do, but how we do what we do. The things that we speak of in this book are actually unspeakable. They are beyond words. They are beyond knowledge. Yet there is a part of *you that exists* beyond words, knowledge, and understanding that this book speaks to—a deeper part, soul awareness that is, even in this moment, unfolding in pure awareness and truth.

Awakening your soul and your infinite awareness is what this book is about.

Enlightenment is the process of lightening up about this crazy human existence. If you are awakening out of the darkness of fear, pain, suffering, anger, and mythology, then you are on the path of enlightening. As you awaken, your life will become simpler. You will be able to say yes to more and more—yes. If you can say yes to more and more in your life, then you are on the path of freedom. If you find that you have to say no to more and more in your life, then you should probably consider a different approach.

Say Yes to Life— Live in Your Freedom

Realize that no matter how strongly conflicted your energy feels, the conflict is not real. Whether you say yes or no to anything that you experience doesn't matter—how you say yes or no matters.

When I was in the film industry, I felt like I was always doing something less than spiritual, less than what my path should have been. This conflict completely limited my career as a director. When working with my meditation partner, he suggested to me that it's not the work that is important—it's not about the merits of the movie industry—but rather the consciousness from which I do the work. He suggested that if I do the work from the infinite, creative consciousness, the film industry was exactly where I needed to be. In retrospect, the film industry taught me about the limitations of the human brain, and how easy it is for people to be influenced by symbols created by filmmakers and image-makers. Understanding how the brain processed information led me to my discoveries about mythology.

Know the following: you are fully and completely able to let everything go—now. You can change in an instant; and paradoxically, some things you may never be able to change for the entire course of your life. You are none of the things that you are worried about. The things that you are conflicted about now, literally, don't matter. They are simply stresses flowing through your brain/mind/body/central nervous system. If you think about it, things that were stressing you out a year ago are barely memorable right now.

The bottom line is: if it feels real, it isn't. You live in a virtual reality suit called the body. Nothing here is *real* in the ultimate sense because nothing is experienced directly. Your perceptions are filtered through an ever-changing perceiver called the body/mind/spirit. What is real doesn't change; and, what doesn't change is your infinite, mysterious being.

Remember this: if it feels real to you, then it probably isn't. It is virtual reality, illusion. Consider letting it go, now, whatever it is. Let it go—just for the fun of it.

Illusion is a Trap—
It Doesn't Exist

The weirdest thing about illusion is that it appears real, feels real, and looks real, but isn't. That's what makes it strange. Even as you read this, you are convinced everything around you is real when it is not. You come to know this through awareness. If you examine your life, and what part of it is calling itself you, you realize that what you thought was you is really only a collection of ideas, beliefs, concepts, fears, memories, tastes, myths, stories, phobias, moralities, obligations, criticisms, likes, and dislikes. You are not any part of your story at all.

You are not real. Life is an illusion. If it is an illusion, how is it that one illusion can harm another illusion?

You don't exist, ultimately. If you don't exist, then how can you harm anything? What morality is it that pays attention to one illusion hurting another illusion? This concept doesn't make sense. You hurt one another because you are afraid or in pain. You are in pain and suffering because you don't remember who you are.

If you felt the constant flow of awareness, and could see through this reality all the time, you would always be in joy and bliss, connected to God. Why would you want to hurt anyone? You immediately see that if you hurt them, you are hurting yourself. You don't exist in any true form anyway; so, even if you did hurt them, they know that nothing is real. Putting it another way: if you are in a play, and you are aware that you are in a play, and your character is killed, you don't hate the actor that killed you—it is just part of the play.

With the continual awareness of our soul, we know ourselves as players in the play, and life is fully experienced and enjoyed, because we are already whole and complete. It isn't natural to feel whole and complete all the time.

You Exist Independent of Anything External—Maybe

The internal frequencies that give rise to the sense of who you are in the world, in space, in time, in the infinite, are the frequencies of consciousness to cultivate. Each time that you come back to who you are, beyond the external world, you deepen into your essence, what you truly are, behind the mask of the brain/mind/body/central nervous system.

You exist—here and now—beyond here and now. This is about the only thing that is real. You exist beyond the form of the body—cultivate the internal awareness that you exist.

Who are you who exists? What is the purpose of this existence? Why are you here? What does life mean?

You exist. That you exist is the only thing you can say that is so right now. Life means what you say it does. Life means something wherever you have assigned meaning to it.

Life is boundless, untamable. The sheer expression of life is infinite. When you think you know it all, something will happen to snap you out of that knowing, turning your world upside down.

Your religion, spirituality, beliefs, and truths will all fail you at some point, because this is the nature of life. Life is boundless, infinite, timeless, and simultaneously expanding in all directions. There is no religion, spirituality, belief, or truth that can possibly encompass boundless life.

You exist: beyond your form, beyond what you do, beyond how much money you have or make. You exist.

As you associate with the field of awareness, you experience your infinite nature, and release yourself from the grip of your inherited, moralistic, symbolic mind.

Your mind's nature is to grip, grasp, and hold. The drunken monkey loves to concretize, moralize, super-size, hyperbolize, fear, judge, reject, and conjecture. Don't worry about it—that's what the drunken monkey mind does. You cannot turn an elephant into a giraffe. They are different. Your mind's nature is fear and grasping. Stop wasting energy on controlling the mind—stop trying to calm it. You can't change it. You can't force the mind to be something other than what it is. Let it be. Learn to pay less and less attention to what the drunken monkey is saying and soon you will be free of it. Basically, most of what the mind says is worthless anyway. Scratch that—all of what the mind says is worthless, so don't bother paying attention to it. Let the drunken monkey sit in the corner, eat bananas, and play with crayons while you live your life.

The mind has power because we feed it. When we stop feeding the drunken monkey and let the mind do what it does, without being sucked in one way or another, we are truly free of the mind. That the drunken monkey is there is unimportant. That it jibber jabbers at you all day is unimportant. What's important is that you give yourself permission to ignore it. Forget about it. Let it talk. Who cares what it says as long as you aren't paying attention to it?

Give the drunken monkey a rest. Freedom is your nature. Your nature is infinite. Everything else is a super imposition upon your infinite nature. Know yourself as infinite essence. That is the only truth, and even that may be limiting.

Core of Self—
Living in Your Essence

The inner core of your being is like the sun: filled with energy, passion, and everything that you need to live your life. Essence is already there—complete, whole, together. The inner core is filled with silence and stillness, yet vibrant and alive. Essence is the unique vibration that is you, vibrating with the hum of the universe.

The deep seed of essence is planted within the being that you are. The seed will grow infinitely as an expression of self. Essence is the texture and flavor of who you are.

Essence of self is the ultimate self-esteem. That is your home. When you know yourself as full self-esteem, there are no holes left to fill. You are essence of self. You deserve to live in your essence.

If you feel anything other than your essence, you are in an illusion. You are in a story.

Essence is beyond the form. When the body is gone, what you are left with is essence, untouched by anything, and unshakable—the essential frequency of who you are as a human, the core of self.

Essence is independent of anything else, independent of life.

The core of who you are is unshakable. Self-esteem is the ultimate fulfillment—the unfolding essence of who you are—ever flowing, ever embracing, ever open to life. You are the ever unfolding of essence, of self. Total awareness. Total is-ness.

Inquire into Your Essence

Who you are is essence, presence, and awareness; that which is untouched, unchanged, and permanent.

Think about the moment of birth—a new presence emerges, comes into being. Everybody has their own essence, presence; that which is there beyond space/time and brain/mind/body/central nervous system. Each baby has its own *feel*. You know them, even though they are not adults. Presence is beyond adulthood. Presence is beyond schooling and identity.

If you learn the language of reality, of truth, there comes a great peace over your life, because you begin to identify with the unchanging, the essence, the presence that is beyond all change.

Learning the language of essence is easy—practice tuning into the language. Once you know it, once you understand it, you are completely free to explore the entire universe. Everything is open to you when you know who you are.

As you inquire into what is real, you begin to feel peace for absolutely no reason at all. As you inquire, you are putting a stop to the endless drives of the unreal.

Am I my body? If the body were *real*, it would never change. If you look up the word real in the dictionary, real is defined as something that never changes. The body is in a constant state of change; I can't be the body.

Am I my mind? The mind changes constantly. The mind goes into good thoughts, bad thoughts, struggles, and frustrations. The mind is in a constant state of flux; I can't be the mind.

Am I the world? The world is in a constant state of upheaval; I can't be that.

One simple way to know who you are, and to identify what is real, is to simply change everything that is not real on a regular basis. *Change your mind, no matter what it is telling you.* Randomly change your mind. Take control of the mind, or the mind controls you giving you exactly what it thinks it needs. Whatever you feel right now—change that. Change everything—now.

None of the things that you are basing your life on are real. Change everything that isn't real, and everything that is real will begin to emerge in the spaces between what isn't real.

Your essence is eternal and unchanging. Meditate on that, Grasshopper.

Loss of Your Essence

You live in perfection in the womb: total oneness, peace, and security. Every need is met. You are one with the infinite. You know yourself as essence. You experience a deep connection with the one who nurtures you and this sense of essence. In this respect, essence is outside of you, and you spend the rest of your life trying to connect back to essence—through the external world.

You can't connect to the external world. You can't be what you are not. All of the money, sex, power, and food can't fill you; you continue feeling empty and alone. These wounds are of the spirit, the lost self. The voice of learned helplessness tells you that you can't connect to essence. Not only have you lost your essence; you are helpless to do anything about it.

One of my students kept looking externally to fill the emptiness and loneliness, not understanding it was the desire to connect to *her own essence*. I explained that physical reality could never fill an energetic need. She understood but felt helpless when trying to fill the need energetically. I explained mythologies and how they are the unconscious operating system, similar to wallpaper that we no longer notice. As she recognized and let go of her inner operating system, her mythologies, the student practiced energetically feeding her wants, needs, and desires. Soon enough, she connected with her inner essence. With the connection comes a sense of wholeness and well-being. We can open to greater and greater amounts of pleasure, sensation, and joy. The internal hunger is filled energetically.

Call forth the reconnection to essence. Connect to the wounds, the sense of loss, and allow the flow of essence and the soul to heal the parts that are lost. Be still in the face of the wounds. Stay present with who and what you truly are. Completely surrender everything that keeps you from knowing who you are.

All roads in your life, no matter how bizarre, are trying to lead you back to your essence. You are not the identities who are messed up, confused, and filled with problems because, in reality, you are not any of these things. You are not who you think you are.

Remember who you are as essence—let go of learned helplessness. Nothing out there can rescue you. Stop acting as if mommy will come and feed you. She can't, and she won't. You have to help you.

Feeling Vulnerable and Helpless is Part of Being Human

The drunken monkey hates feeling helpless. Yet, we are all, at our core, helpless. We feel helpless in most areas of our lives. Things happen to us, either in external reality or in our heads, and we react helplessly to these experiences, symbols, and images.

We feel helpless around our outer projected symbols such as money, relationships, status, jobs, cars, etc. All of those external symbols will eventually disappear. If we are completely honest with ourselves, we don't feel as though we have much control in this life. This is the issue. The physical world is, for the most part, unbending. Money can give us an opportunity to exert some modicum of control, and can allow for tremendous creativity, but still most events are out of our hands.

However, anything that is not physical may be easily changed, altered. In fact, to overcome our learned helplessness, we *have to practice* changing our energetic reality. Everything physical can be changed, too—just not as easily. To change the physical, we tend to

Feeling Vulnerable and Helpless

need a tool of some kind.

The problem is this: we are not the body. Perhaps we don't have full dominion over the physical dimension, but we do have full dominion over the energetic dimension that exists inside our head. We don't know this simple truth because we are consciously asleep. The images inside our heads that inform us about our universe are not real. They exist in energetic reality and can be changed. The images, symbols are rudimentary constructions of the most primitive aspects of our brain and they are the things that are shaping and running our conscious experience—seamlessly.

The helplessness of humans has been passed down through the ages, and quite frankly, is one of the silent tenets of the planet and human history. Every culture has its way of dealing with the feeling of helplessness, but none work forever because the helplessness always wins. From an evolutionary standpoint, to feel helpless is to feel human.

The human lives in a chronic state of helplessness due to being mostly other than conscious. Being human is feeling helpless. Many psychological theories exist about helplessness, and I have my own. Suffice it to say, basically, we feel helpless to change anything in our life—so we constantly seek answers.

Curiously, this is why we go to therapy—to receive help healing the parts of us that we are helpless to change on our own. We believe that we need someone outside of us to rescue us. We are waiting for some external thing to come and take us out of an experience, or situation, that we feel helpless to change, and it is a subtle thing. If the mind isn't trained, then, it just does its thing. *The mind's strategy is simple: keep flashing bad things in front of our inner mind so that we can attempt to heal those bad things.* The drunken monkey believes it is helping us by creating all of this inner misery. The drunken monkey mind is trying to heal us in the only way that it knows how, keeping what is painful upfront, close, and personal.

We must re-train the mind out of learned helplessness and *into* action. We must learn to move through energetic reality, and often, action is the best choice. Energetic reality is not physical reality, though it feels that way. Consider that what we feel is just a sensation. If we are conscious that the feeling is caused a flow of chemicals running through the body, then it is possible to change the flow of chemicals simply by taking counter action—interrupting the pattern, doing something else. When in doubt, or feeling helpless and frozen, do something completely arbitrary. Take action. Move your body. Dance. Play. Laugh. Swing. Stand on your head. Do something physical to move the energy.

Learned helplessness is an energetic feeling, not necessarily a reality. Take some kind of action to overcome the feeling of helplessness.

Drunken Monkey, You Shall Not Pass!

At some point, you must take out the sword and say of the negative stuff of the drunken monkey, "You shall not pass!" Why? Human beings are creators. If you want to have smelly, awful life experiences, you are free to have that. The mirror brain always says *yes!* Yes, to whatever you desire. Pay attention and focus on what it is that you want to create, instead of the noise of the drunken monkey.

The person you were before you read this last paragraph—you are not that any more. Who are you now? You are constantly changing. Each moment gives you the opportunity to create an entirely new reality. The key is to create a safe space within yourself, where you remind yourself to focus on what you desire.

"You shall not pass!" Refuse to live in the mythologies, and the noise of the drunken monkey mind. Whether it takes ten minutes, ten hours, ten days, or ten years, eventually you will come into the silence of your mind, the sweetness of silence. It's not that the drunken monkey isn't there; it is just that you no longer listen to its endless barrage of ridiculousness, rendering it ineffective and quiet. If a drunken monkey falls off the branch in the jungle, and nobody is there to listen, is there a sound? The answer is no.

You do whatever you need to do to protect your home. Silence is your home. Protect your inner space as you protect your external home—not through defensiveness, but through command. Take command of your inner space. Take command of your silence. Claim your power, and say to the mind chatter (the insane drunken monkey), "You shall not pass!"

You are not the chatter of your mind. You are not what the drunken monkey preaches. Chatter in the mind is a form of evolutionary stress, a program that continues to run in order to help you survive. When you take command, you can say to the drunken monkey, "I don't care what you throw my way, or wherever you drag me, because I'm not going there." At some point, you must simply be, no matter where you are on the path. Be who you are, in your power, peace, silence and freedom, and you are free!

Drunken monkey mind chatter is a form of evolutionary stress, and stress injures the brain and body. Take command of your inner space, now. Make a commitment to yourself to keep it clean and clear—so that your energy is free—to give yourself exactly what you want in your life. Give yourself permission to have what you want.

The Brain, Like a Flower, Blooms when Nourished

Until recently, scientists thought we were born with a finite number of brain cells and they did not re-grow—now scientists know that surroundings influence brain cell growth. Enriched, prosperous, safe environments lead to increased growth of new brain cells and the connectedness of these cells to each other, creating a complex, intercommunicating brain. Brain cells respond to changes in the environment.

Boring environments, and excessively stressful environments, suppress the growth of new brain cells. When we are under stress, glucocorticoids (a type of steroid) put the body on a heightened state of alert. Glucocorticoids are toxic for the brain. If the stress is chronic, the brain retreats within; brain cells die; connections within the brain disappear; and the hippocampus—the part of the brain involved in making memories and learning—begins withering away. In essence, the brain begins committing suicide.

The brain has no feeling per se, so when there is trauma inside of the brain, we have no way of knowing that any injury has occurred. If we stay in the stressful, traumatizing situation, we inadvertently continue injuring the brain. We become addicted to the body sensation of lack of repair.

It is very seductive. The brain doesn't have the mechanism to stop the stress cycle—to turn off the switches of terror, blame, shame, guilt, fear, trauma, morality, mythology, pain, suffering, self-abuse, doubt, humiliation, confusion, etc. The moment trauma occurs, the brain stays in the loop.

The more trauma we experience, the more likely we are to be close to that animal part of us that is a bundle of raw nerves and primal impulses—every hair on the body is hyper alert. The sensitivity level is high because everything in the brain/mind/body/central nervous system is about protecting itself from a dangerous, hostile environment. That early primitive being is still alive within our psyche and trauma reveals that.

Trauma of early childhood lingers on as a decrease in the generation of new brain cells in the hippocampus and the inability to turn off the switches of danger. (Womb stress diminishes the volume of brain cells as well.) An early hostile environment results in feeling that nothing is ever enough, that nothing can stop the pain; that God is punishing us for something that we did wrong—even though we are unsure what that was. Further adding to that is the religious mythology that we are born in sin—the general idea is that we are punished for being alive. Vivid religious paintings of the terrors of hell, the devil, evil, and mortal sins create trauma and scarring within the psyche and brain. These symbolic images are intended to release the energy of fear, shame, and guilt in the body. Being young, we might forget the pain but the brain remembers. Furthermore, this early trauma and chronic stress is passed on and taught, generation-to-generation.

We learn to live with contraction, depression, smallness, and helplessness, not noticing when the brain starts to shut down and stops making new cells and new connections. Chronic stress and depression deprive neurons of sustenance. A newborn neuron is alone when created by the brain. All the neurons around it are connected to other neurons in massive neural networks, but the new cell is alone, desperately trying to connect, to plug itself into the network. Neurons reflect their circumstances, just as the universe mirrors back to us.

The brain can't heal itself if it is given neither tools nor permission—but if given the proper tools such as rest, food and water, exercise, and allowing the brain/mind/body/central nervous system to spontaneously act with the intent of releasing trauma, the brain can self repair. Turning off the switches, demythologizing, learning how to interpret and work with the symbols and images moving inside the brain resets the brain, and removes the traumatic image loop that continuously generates stress.

If we have a bruise, we give it time to heal. It is the same with the brain. The brain, like skin, can heal itself. The brain, like a muscle, swells with exercise and can heal itself on a cellular level by learning new things. It takes two months of consistent change before the brain begins to fully recover.

Our environment influences the structure of our brain. The brain is in a state of ongoing cellular upheaval and always giving birth. The self continually reinvents.

Exercise to heal the brain: Put on some gentle music. Lie down on the floor and draw your attention inside. Tell your brain that for the next thirty minutes, you will do whatever it needs you to do to release trauma. Do nothing. Just wait for the first random impulses to flow. Follow whatever spontaneous movement you feel. Follow the inner impulses and movements with the intent of releasing the stored trauma from within the brain. Give yourself a full 30 minutes but you will know when it is over.

This process has worked over and over again for releasing stored trauma in the body. Your body knows exactly what to do to heal itself. Tune in and give it full permission to do whatever it wants and needs in order to heal itself of trauma and stored pain.

Turning off the stress switches, demythologizing, re-interpreting, and working with the symbols and images moving inside the brain resets the brain, and removes the traumatic image loop that continuously generates stress.

Shifting the Pain Paradigm— From Bananas and Peanut Butter to Star Fruit Jelly

What is causing you pain in your life is not what is actually happening in your life, but what you fear could happen in your life. In fact, your life is fairly simple. You live in an age where life is mostly safe. What is ailing you is what could happen, in the head of the drunken monkey, not what is actually happening.

The biggest problem in your life is that you are living as if something bad is happening right now! Your emotions are ruled by the intricate release of brain/body chemicals. Deep inside your limbic brain, there is a twisted, gnarled jungle of images that are stalking you now, devouring you.

These simplistic, symbolic, but frightening images, sounds, and feelings are terrifying you, and more specifically, the inner drunken monkey. Right now, even as you are reading this, the drunken monkey is being annihilated, over and over and over again through a constant terrorizing of self-triggers, endless stresses, symbols, images, and fears from deep inside the limbic system of the brain.

The drunken monkey reacts as if it is actually happening right now. The brain can't distinguish external reality from energetic reality, so it reacts to what it sees—even if it is completely imagined.

Everything that is making you feel anything in your life is coming from how your brain interprets the symbols inside your head. The drunken monkey believes what it sees—even if it created what it is seeing itself. It's drunk, so it forgets.

Everything causing you stress and pain comes from these symbols and movies that you don't even know are there, flickering below the surface. Those images that you are aware of, you are living with in a natural human state of learned helplessness that says, "I feel/see X (fill in the blank), but I can do nothing to change it." Worse, yet, you don't recognize it as emanating from your head. You are trained to be helpless. However, you can train yourself to let go of the helplessness by practicing changing the energetic symbols, and images in your head.

You and your inner drunken monkey believe that the images in your head behave similarly to physical reality, but they don't. The drunken monkey is mistaken about this. If you are listening to the drunken monkey, then you are mistaken, too. The symbols of energetic reality are changeable in an instant. Faster than you can squish bananas and peanut butter in your fingers, you can change a symbol in your head.

The old pain paradigm can at times be a gift for the soul to transform. The soul will show you that the other side of pain is life, aliveness, infinite openness, and the universe of light. You are

Shifting the Pain Paradigm

either living a life of hell—the endless existence of living in human pain, lifetime after lifetime—or living in the universe of light. Give yourself permission to remain present with the pure sensation of pain, not the story. When you are with the pure sensation, allowing it to move, you are free of it. You can see it for what it is, which is just energy, and that energy will flow back to your center.

When you let the thing inside your head that is scaring you run its course, it no longer scares you. You begin to see that what you call pain is really just a blockage in the natural flow of energy.

Ask the soul to bring forth the healing qualities of love and light that are needed by the parts of you that have been affected by, and have been holding onto the field of human pain. The entire field of human pain is an illusion. Inwardly say, "I'm not all my stories. I'm not all my pain. I am awareness, consciousness. That is truth. The field of pain only exists if I perceive myself as somebody. I am nobody. I simply am." If there is nobody, where can pain grasp?

Out of this, there is a tiny gap that you are looking for, a tiny space between you and your pain. Feel the gap. The settling down within you lets you know there is a gap. Suddenly, there is a space, the background of your being. Feel the drop. The mind no longer calls itself you. Your body sense and feeling sense are open, flowing into the light universe. You must allow the universe of light, the only thing that really is, to surround you, to hold the space of light around you and your immense pain.

Ask the universe of light to surround you—to change the pain paradigm to the love paradigm, to the fun paradigm, to the freedom paradigm. The bottom line: if it isn't fun, don't do it.

Love Is…

Love is all there is in the universe—it holds everything together. Love is the highest frequency and the ultimate universal bonding agent. All there is … is love. What we are doing is changing the paradigm.

The old paradigm was fear, pain, sacrifice and suffering. That paradigm of the mind believed it was serving us by fearing (e.g., fear of dying, fear of disappearing, etc.). That was an old belief. Fear is contracting and limiting.

The subconscious is an entity that has its own life. Its basis is that fear holds us together; if fear died, we died—but that is false. If it were true, then it would mean that we are fear; but we can't be fear, because if we were fear and fear suddenly disappeared, then we would disappear when we were no longer afraid. We let go of that last vestige of fear by saying to the subconscious, conscious, and body, "I am total, unconditional love. I am love and be loved."

"I am the liberation of all fear, replaced by love."

"Nothing external can ever harm me."

"I replace instinctual survival fear with instinctual survival love."

Integrate love through every cell, atom, DNA, particle, light packet, and quanta of energy that holds your hologram. Love fills the space. Love is the liberation. Love has dominion.

Love is who we are. Love is a great thing. Love automatically reveals itself to all. Love replaces everything. Love is all there is. Love fills every last cell. Love is expansive. Love is free to grow. Love is a wellspring.

The paradigm is love: every thought, every belief, every desire, every word must be love—unconditional pure love.

Love feeds love. Love is self-love. Love is self-deservement. Love is freedom to live your juiciest life.

Self-Love, Self-Deservement, Self-Creation

If we are created in the image of the creator, then the highest compliment to the creator is self-love, self-deservement, self-appreciation, and conscious creation.

Self-love is our natural state: to love the body, to laugh in joy, to have fun. This is our nature. Through massive reconditioning, we lose track of this and end up in a state of self-hatred, lack, and loneliness.

Self-love is your birthright. If you love God, and you are created in God's image, then you must love yourself.

Self-hatred is a form of suicide. The biology of the cells is such that if you hate yourself, you essentially create a condition that is an internal state of war. The war is within, and the cellular structures, genes, and organs begin to break down in the confusion. Diseases happen in the breaking down of the complex interactions.

The brain, and where your awareness rests, is responsible for controlling and coordinating the physiology and behavior of the brain/mind/body/central nervous system. Most of the process is unconscious. If you are caught in a field of self-hatred, the brain is sending out mixed messages to the body/mind creating confusion.

Self-love is your birthright. Sexual energy flowing freely through the body is your birthright and a tool for healing and manifesting. Sexual energy is similar to a magnetic force that aligns all the cells of your being into self-love. You are beautiful just the way that you are with warts, impulses, desires, shadow, and all. For a moment, take a deep breath, and let it all be just the way it is.

You are created in the image of the creator. The highest function or expression of this reality is through creativity and manifestation.

Money and the Secret of the Sacred Wind Manifestation Tornado

EVERY moment there is a thought, and consistently thinking that thought affects and alters your physical reality. Things that manifest in physical reality use the technique of the sacred wind of the tornado.

That sacred wind manifestation tornado simply states, "It takes the energy of others to support you, to work on your behalf, to pay you money."

Tornado manifestation is how all businesses are manifesting. Every dollar a company makes is given to that company by someone who converted their time, thought, or creativity into work energy, and then stored that work energy in a piece of green paper that we call money. An individual then says to herself that she values what a person, company or service has to offer enough to give her green paper to them. I call it the tornado effect. Individuals give you all the money that you earn.

The manifestation dance is an inherent part of the physical

dimension. I call dollars energy converters because they are similar to batteries. We work, store our energy in the form of green paper, and use that green paper to convert our stored energy into other things that we want, such as food, homes, cars, spirituality, etc.

The tornado manifestation works best with things such as dollars. Observe what it is in your life for which individuals give you their energy converters.

For example, lawyers run businesses that fight for others rights. The product they are selling is the counter effect of helplessness. A lawyer is selling the ability to defend, to right a wrong. The little person, feeling small, comes to a lawyer for protection and safety. For this, they give the lawyer their energy converters, their money.

If you stop performing a service, or stop offering a product, you will quickly see how energy converters, money, no longer flows to you. To stay in the flow of money, you must continue to put yourself in the game of money. The natural state of cash is flow.

Money doesn't come from God, trees, the universe, or the tooth fairy. Money comes from individuals who give us their money in exchange for goods and services. Money is sex energy manifest. Money is creative energy, life force energy, and catalyst energy stored. Money is the blood flow, the circulatory system of planet earth.

Money as Creation, Money as Love

Money is the circulatory system of life on earth—a creative force seeking motion. Money is dynamic, and the core desire of the consciousness of cash is to be used, held, shared, spent, and exchanged.

When money feels loved, it is happy and says, "I will go out and I will find more ways to bring money to you now that I know you love me." Money is like an excited child living inside you, that you denied and locked in a dark room. You have been rejecting money and all it wants is love.

Your current relationship with money is no more than a reflection of the aspects that you have imbued into the universe about money. All the universe can ever do is mirror back to you; however, the consciousness of money wants to give back to you—to co-create with you. You are the one blocking this relationship from blossoming. You do this by unconsciously creating from your past prejudices, inherited opinions, perceptions, denials and blocks.

From this moment forward, declare to the universe that you want the creative flow of money, *cash*, to come to you and integrate into your consciousness, and you in turn, embrace the integration of money. Money is eager to embrace you and fulfill its purpose in creation. You are the one putting up the barriers to keep it out of your life, because you are afraid of its magnificent, creative power, which is basically a reflection of your fear of your own magnificent, creative force.

Invite the essence of the soul and consciousness of money to merge and integrate with your soul manifestation consciousness, so that there is no aspect of money that is in any way external. Give the soul essence of money permission to fully weave and blend into who and what you truly are—letting it become part of the fibers of your being.

Say within yourself, "I ask the core and soul essence of money to embrace and fully integrate into my creative manifestation consciousness *now*." Feel the rush of the waterfall of cash, money, and riches. Step into that golden waterfall with your soul, and let it fill you and flow through you. Feel the sense of cooperation with the universe in co-creating your abundant, external reality and desires. Inwardly say, "I claim my financial enlightenment *now*."

Give the soul permission to fully integrate into the cash aspect of creation energy right now. Give your soul permission to create with cash. Let the power of cash merge with your sexual centers, into a unified flow of creation. When God created the earth, she said it was good. Well, if that creation story is true, then money is also good. Wherever it came from, however it came into existence, whoever dreamed it up, it is an aspect of creation, and it is good. Therefore, it should be acknowledged as an integrated part of you.

Cash, creativity, and money are already a part of you anyway, but you have been in a state of stuck-ness, resistance, and denial of it because of your fear of your power. You are afraid of its power, which is an external manifestation of your own fear of embracing your own powerful self. But you can't hide who you truly are forever, and you wouldn't be reading this book if you didn't want to free yourself from your box of pain, lack, and limitation.

Embrace your full-powered, full-throttled self now. Embrace your vastness. Embrace your creativity. Embrace your animal manifestation force. Embrace your true soul self. Let all parts of yourself step out of the shadows and into the light of cash, money, abundance, creativity, and creation. Let all parts of you drink this manifestation power deeply. Fill yourself completely.

We must learn to give ourselves energetically exactly what we need right now, in the here and now. This in turn relaxes our bodies, minds, and spirits into the natural flow of energy that is the infinite, prosperous, creative universe.

Cash Flow—The New Paradigm for Receiving Money in Your Life

Much of my recent work is about stripping away mythologies and stories so people can see for themselves what is actually happening—instead of what mommy and daddy told them is going on. I want to help you learn to perceive cash flow clearly, then to act based on that clear perception, not on the tired old stories you inherited about money. It is the equivalent of driving down the road with your hands on the steering wheel following the road versus looking at a map and trying to drive with your hands on the rearview mirror. Concerning money, most of us have our hands on the steering wheel with one foot accelerating and the other foot braking while staring at the map wondering why we're not getting what we want. Meanwhile, some of us don't even have our hands on the steering wheel. We've turned the steering over to the drunken monkey while we steer with the rearview mirror, worrying about our decisions of the past.

In the old paradigm, people thought the world started with a

Cash Flow

big bang and was slowly working its way back into contraction. The universe seemed finite, and ultimately would collapse in on itself. What we know now is that the universe is expanding infinitely at ever increasing speeds. If you want to put yourself in harmony with the flow, and in harmony with the action of the universe, realize that the natural movement of the universe is expansion, and who you were yesterday is insignificant. What your problems were yesterday are insignificant. What your problems were a week ago, a year ago, ten years ago, 20 years ago are irrelevant. Drop the map and take your hands off the rearview mirror. Let go of the past. Focus on what is happening right now.

Trillions of dollars are being exchanged. I want you to feel into that exchange, the flow of that cash. I want you to take a funnel, or whatever it is for you, and tap into that cash flow as if you were diverting a flow of water from Niagara Falls. You wouldn't need to divert that much to get massive amounts of water flowing your way. The same is true here—just a little tap, a little diverter into that infinite flow, infinite expansion of cash, and you can fill up your tank. If the container gets full, then expand the container. Put yourself in harmony with an ever expanding universe and keep expanding. Expand your ability to take in more and more cash, more energy, more joy, more fun, more pleasure, more health, and more contentment.

Take something that has been messing you up about money—a thought, a fear, a problem, a limitation, a mythology, or some old idea—throw that into the cash flow and watch it disintegrate. Step into the cash flow. Take your whole being into the flow for a moment. Let the cash pound you, move through you, change you, shift you, and shake off anything that doesn't serve the flow and movement of cash into your reality. You are the cash flow.

You literally can have anything and do absolutely anything you want in your life. Just breathe that into your body. Give yourself two minutes right now to be the cash flow—a million dollars, no problem, what else? Infinite expansion, literally to do anything you want. Want to go up in the space shuttle? Buy your ticket and see earth from outer space. Feel that possibility. The cash flow instantly fills it. Have a big fat mortgage on your house? Handle it—pay it off.

Money is flying around the world at the speed of light. That's 186,000 miles per second, and that's the speed of cash. Feel the infinite supply of cash in your body and make more space. When everything is filled up, you begin to feel peace and joy, inside and out.

Notice that the more money you have, the more creative you can be—infinite creativity, resource, and flow. We have a duty to contribute to this life as fully and completely as possible. In the world that we currently live in, we *need* cash to live in our freedom and create. Give yourself permission to be free. Cash is a metaphor for infinite creative flow.

Where you get confused is that you don't need cash to have happiness, you can have happiness right now—without cash. You can have peace right now, too. In the physical dimension, you don't use cash to buy energetic things, because energetic things are infinite and you can have them right now in energetic reality. What you need cash for is to create in three-dimensional reality—infinitely. If you want to participate in the expansion of the physical universe, you need cash. If you want to participate in the flow of expansive creativity that the physical universe is expanding in, you need cash. Cash is a beautiful thing that can bring joy and happiness, but it is not an energetic resource—that is where you get confused. You think external reality will impact, or have an affect on the internal, energetic reality—that is the mistake.

The drunken monkey knows that money will solve all problems—including internal pain, suffering, and emptiness—not true. Money is great for physical things that make you feel good, and expand three-dimensional creativity, but cash will not affect energetic reality. You can have anything you want energetically right now regardless of your cash supply. Right this very minute you are free, with or without cash. But as my Grandpa Mike used to say, rich or poor, it's good to have money. Cash is fun, too. Begin focusing on that reality, and continue to ruthlessly expand your cash container in physical three-dimensional reality.

Our Experience of Money is Energetic Reality

Our worth, our sense of self, the value we place on the quality of life are all tied to how much money we earn, the possessions we own, and our myths about money. For example, being rich is better than poor. We judge others and ourselves by the size of our financial portfolios and our possessions. We equate money with living the good life forever. Our fears and myths keep us locked in place, feeling helpless to change our financial situation, and unable to experience happiness.

The thoughts that cause you difficulties are the ones dealing with survival and your possible annihilation. You probably have never felt that you measured up in your life: whether it is because of money, real estate, relationships, marriage, divorce, children, no children, not loving your work, not loving your life, too much education, or not enough education—you get the idea.

I have news for you—you feeling inadequate, or a failure, isn't helping the world. Moreover, it definitely isn't helping you.

Our Experience of Money is Energetic Reality

Consider the possibility that the whole experience of being human is an internal experience, an illusion. Nothing in the universe is static. Nothing. To combat the unending change and shifts, we constantly look for stability and search for meaning in our lives—a way of seeing the world as more than just an assemblage of matter and energy from which consciousness inevitably arises. This is too much to bear. The natural human need is to seek security, organization, meaning, and purpose. This need clutters our ability to see ourselves clearly.

No thoughts are necessary for your survival—none. You can do perfectly well without a thought, without a mind. You want to be *happy*, but you don't know what it is that you are looking for—even if you got it, you wouldn't know you got it; similar to driving a car without an objective or a place to go—you won't arrive anywhere—except wherever you are. In addition, the mind constantly shifts. What makes you happy today won't be the thing that makes you happy in ten minutes, or tomorrow.

Energetic reality is unaffected by physical experiences; however, physical experiences change when you give yourself permission to receive everything you want and need in energetic reality. Give your energetic desires, dreams, and wishes permission to express themselves and have everything that they want—regardless of your external circumstances or reality. Give yourself what you want, right now, in your imagination—in energetic reality. Give it to yourself fully. Completely. This will change your energetic experience, and eventually your physical experience.

The natural human need is to seek security, organization, meaning, and purpose. This need clutters your ability to see yourself clearly. Give yourself exactly what you need in energetic reality, and you will come to know yourself beyond your ever-changing field of needs and desires.

Energetic Reality and Manifestation

All life is energy. Energy can be changed. Energy can be exchanged. Energy is alive. You are energy. You are alive.

The truth of what and who we are is energy. We can call this truth Energetic Reality. We are energy, a field of potentiality that comes in and out of existence based on where we focus our attention. Where the attention goes, reality flows. Reality exists because we are aware of it. Without perception, without awareness, there is nothing.

Whatever your attention is focused upon will continue to expand and grow. If you focus on money problems, situations of lack and unworkable things in your life, then your soul energy and your awareness will flow to where your attention is. You are energizing with creative life force the very things that you don't want. You are watering your inner seeds of thoughts with your life energy. If your life energy is spent watering seeds of destructive thoughts, then that's what you will grow. That is what you will manifest in your life.

You can shift your entire energetic field in an instant, and the entire universe must adjust to this new reality. The whole universe shifts every time you shift. Everything changes although you think that you are in the same place. All manifestation is done from the realization that you are composed of energy, and therefore you are the composer of your energy.

Begin by stating your goal clearly. Check for any fear and resistance. Keep adjusting the goal. Repeat it and bring it into each of the chakras and the entire being—until all say yes, until the energetic field around the body says yes. Everything resonates yes. Your cells and organs say yes. Give it to yourself abundantly. Be clear about it. Bring it into the present. The goal is the seed. Wrap the seed in trust and creation with all the events, individuals, and situations needed to magnetize the creation to you—all that it needs to come into manifestation.

Grant this to yourself now—no matter what. Wrap this seed with the energy of creation. Bring it from nonphysical to physical; this is the birth process. Surrender the goal into divine consciousness, into the center of the universe and let it go.

Give yourself everything in your life. Completely surrender to the flow of energy that the mind thinks that it wants. Let the experience flow until there is nothing left causing attraction or reaction. Abandon and surrender to your own creative, magnificent energy field; experience the vastness of your life, unfolding in the moment, expanding into the infinite, saying *yes*. The universe is in constant, creative expansion. Align yourself with that freedom.

Formless substance desires expansion and more life. Look around you. Expansion in nature is everywhere: more and more and more and more and more. You are that expansion. You deserve that expansion. You create that expansion. You are expansion. You are. Expand now.

Give yourself permission to have everything that you want in your life right now—give that to yourself energetically—now.

How to Manifest—
Create in an *Infinite* Field of Creation

In its original state, the formless creative substance contains a thinking stuff from which all things are made—that permeates, penetrates, and fills the inter-spaces of the universe.

You produce images in thought, and impress thought upon the creative substance, causing the thought to create and form out of the thinking stuff.

In order to do this, images must pass from competitive mind to creative mind. In your creative mind, form clear mental images of exactly what you want; hold the vision with intent, commitment, and purpose. Use your will to keep your mind working in the creative manifestation way. Contemplate your pictures, deeply and intimately.

Action must accompany thought in order to create. To receive what you want when it comes, you must act now upon the individuals and things in your present environment.

Do whatever you can do from where you are now. Be bigger

How to Manifest

than who think you are. Do more than just fill your place in this life. Expand freely, infinitely, in all directions.

The universe is a reflective universe. What you are thinking, feeling, desiring, and imaging is exactly what you are receiving, moment-to-moment. Nothing is out there—no God. All is inside you. You are God.

As this impression, image, feeling spreads, all things are set moving towards its realization. Every living thing, inanimate object, and things yet uncreated are stirred towards creating what you desire. All forces begin exerting in the direction of your creation; all things begin to move towards you. The minds of individuals, everywhere, are influenced towards doing the things necessary to fulfill your desires, and they work for you, possibly not even understanding why they are doing what they are doing.

In the energetic reality realms, enter into the full enjoyment of the things that you want. Without the body, you are thought. You are energy. Energetically, completely love and experience whatever it is that you want and desire.

Know that what you want is already fulfilled. The tornado manifestation is key. See and feel individuals giving you their checks, money, cash, and credit cards. Money is coming to you in a powerful, energetic tornado. All of the creativity of your highest life will flow from having lots of money with which to create.

Offer tons of gratitude towards the creation.

Interest yourself in the world of richness. See the cash that is coming to you, through the physical world, by impressing the creative substance.

The underlying truth is that all things are moving towards greater fulfillment, fuller expression, and complete happiness... this is the great one life moving behind all life. Everything is expanding in this universe or it is dying. Make sure that your cash is expanding, too.

Create with intent, commitment, sexual energy, and desire—consciously—and the whole universe manifests consciously with you.

Given a Choice, Choose Conscious Manifestation

You are conscious and unconscious in your manifestations. When you were pre-thinking this future, you were pre-thinking this life without all of the details necessarily worked out. There was a momentum of thought, actions that mobilized you in a specific direction. This is a form of conscious manifestation.

Active, conscious, creative manifestation is extremely helpful to master on this planet—as is mastering the filtering of thoughts that create the energetic patterns of fear, pain, and suffering. Even the way we ask life questions is fear based. Deep inside, we are angry and unconsciously shooting bullets into the creative substance that creates more fears.

If you manifest unconsciously for your whole life, you will have a tendency to create from a space of pain and suffering. So, you ask, "Why must I be here on earth suffering?" There is no purpose, per se, in suffering. Suffering is just one small part of the three-dimensional experience of life on planet earth.

In many ways, our capacities are limited in the physical dimension. Ultimately, all thoughts come from *infinite* consciousness as an impulse. That pure energy is given to us to do with what we will. In this respect, we blame the universe for being neutral but, in truth, we are given full authority to live this life any way that we want. Once we master rapidly manifesting in matter, life on planet earth no longer is an issue.

Experience God flowing through the physical body, experience pleasure and ecstasy. Many wonderful sensations can be experienced in the body if you stop the thoughts of fear and terror that take up much of the day-to-day, unconscious manifestation energy and experience.

Most of your life force energy is filtered through the barrier of the unconscious brain/mind/body/central nervous system and this is the problem.

Manifestation is done in thought and you need to recognize the depths of your unconscious consciously, right now. Wrap the soul around your unconscious and conscious mind. Create from your power, clarity, and desire.

Soul Manifestation and Creation Meditation

If we sit with the soul and change all thoughts, conscious and unconscious, we can change unconscious manifestation energy to soul manifestation energy. With the tools of intent, commitment, and total self-deservement, we can work with the natural energetic flow of the universe to manifest anything in physical form.

As you breathe into your body and wrap the soul around your conscious and unconscious mind, acknowledge you who observes. Once you begin to recognize the soul embracing the conscious and unconscious, there is recognition that you are the observer, and not the conscious, unconscious mind. When the brain dies, your unconscious and conscious mind cease to exist in their current form. The remainder energies will take over the causal body.

The universe is neutral substance and is created by you—however, you create it. Judgment only exists in the human condition and the human supportive hierarchy structure of the angels, spirit guides, and other beings that support the moral hierarchy of good and bad, right and wrong. That structural hierarchy is itself an illusory-based idea.

Anger and frustration in the physical dimension have to do with frustration that manifestation abilities are apparently being limited; because, in the physical dimension, we try to manifest, to do things through the physical form, even though our true essence is non-physical.

Our essence is no different from God itself: divine energy in motion. A divine thought holds us in place, contains us. To this degree, we exist in a form of separation. However, seeing ourselves at the level of true soul essence is like looking through a pane of glass. We see separation, but we also see the clear light of who and what we truly are. The life most of us live in the physical is much more dense and condensed.

To truly manifest, you need to clear these dense areas and recognize the truth of who and what you are, and let that awareness flow through the body so deeply that it becomes natural.

Intent of soul essence manifests and creates, evoking your willingness and commitment. Your commitment focuses spiritual energy into able energy. Form, like a Rubik's cube, reconfigures to support the changes in consciousness, and what you truly, deeply desire manifests because space and time reconfigure to support the new possibility. Manifestation is commitment, from a level of soul essence, in motion. The flow of manifestation is related to the flow of the soul, and the alignment of your soul with the flow of *cash*.

To commit to something fully, with all of your being, is to ensure manifestation in physical form. Let go of the human conditions of judgment and morality that inhibit manifestation—let go of your need to be right. The flow of manifestation is related to the flow of the soul, and the alignment of your soul with the flow of cash, which is already flowing around the planet.

The Human Need to be Right

Part of the human limitation is not recognizing that we have to step out of the box of thinking that our way of thinking is the only way of thinking.

The universe is infinite, infinite possibilities in all directions. Your mistake has been thinking your way is the only way. The overwhelming need to be right is the human condition. Being right has nothing to do with anything. Things you fought to be right about last week, last month, or last year are completely lost in the sea of nonexistence.

What was important, what you may have been willing to die for, is now past—gone. Being right means nothing. Surrender the need to be right—it is simply a disease of the mind. Be aware of the need and do your best to release, in your being, the need to be right. Take a moment and sense how meaningless being right really is. Being right is another way of becoming stuck in the mud of what you don't want. Focus on what you want. Let go of the need to be right—practice dropping it in an instant. When you find yourself stuck in being right, drop it. On my grandfather's deathbed, he shared a secret with me that he told me he had regretted for 80 years. I told him that I would listen, and that it would be okay if he shared the secret with me. Reluctantly he did, and when he did, I was shocked—not by the secret, but by the fact that he had been secretly beating himself up for over 80 years. His inner judge, his inner critic, was there all the way to the end.

The need to be right is based in survival fear. Fear thoughts fire into the causal body, the plane of energetic creation, energizing fear and manifesting it back in thoughts that affect the physical body. Simply put, you are afraid because you are afraid. I repeat this. You are afraid because you are afraid. The fear itself is the causation. The causation is the creation. I cannot iterate this enough. The thoughts themselves feed back instantly to create a sense of reality in thought, which creates reality, sensation, in the body, which goes to the causal plane and bounces back in a continual feedback loop.

The thought itself is the causation. Part of your work, part of your healing is coming to terms with the fact that thinking is creating your reality instantaneously. Not in some esoteric way, but rather in this way: your thoughts affect your behavior, and your behavior affects your experience, and the way people react to you. It is internal—energetic, but it ends up affecting your external reality—and ultimately every part of your experience. This is not an easy concept to grasp or understand. Take a moment to consider how your thoughts create your internal reality. Stay aware. Pay close attention.

Exercise: think of several examples that you needed to be right about, perhaps even fought fiercely about, that are insignificant now. Think of things that were once upsetting, that are insignificant when considered in the field of existence—in the field of *now*.

Thought is the causation and causation is the creation. Just as humans erroneously seek cause and effect, they also attempt to create order out of chaos. Being right and two dollars will get you a cup of latte. The days when being right meant life or death for the tribe no longer exist. Let go. Drop it. Put it down.

Humans are Addicted to Chaos

Human beings tend to make order out of chaos—they explain anything. Chaos emerges in your life because you are unwilling or unable to face your deepest, darkest demons. What are your money or sex demons? What symbols, myths, stories, or past history cause chaos in your life?

Your personal, past history is a field of consciousness resting in a quantum field of potentiality—infinite potential until you look. Quantum theory suggests that observing is what creates and solidifies reality.

The field of chaos, which we call the past, comes into consciousness and is often debilitating. We project our past into the future, and that becomes our future reality—a field of is-ness.

If you are waiting for something to happen, don't waste your time, because it would have already happened if it were going to—move on—do something different *now*.

The tragedy of human life is that we are fragile, that no matter what we do, at some point it will all be meaningless. The only way out of this life is death. On our way to death, we need to find creative ways of earning cash—no matter how high our awareness. Part of this life is working with *cash flow*.

At this second, one part of your mind is devising some way for you to feel messed up about some other part of your life, or some disintegrated aspect of your life. This inner conflict is caused by conflicting mythologies—misunderstandings about the way life truly is. Even right now, as you are reading, a part of you is devising a plan to make you feel horrible about something. Therefore, you won't have to pay attention to the subtle flow of your inner life. You can stay on the surface of your life, being right, focusing your energy in fight or flight situations, living a life totally trapped by the *Maya* illusion.

Basically, on a human, mental level, we are screwed if the confused, mythological mind remains in control of our lives. An easy mind is fine. A mind at ease with life is great. It can be a great asset. However, a mind occupied with conflicted operating systems feels horrible.

Pay attention to what you are thinking beneath the surface, to your need/addiction to chaos. That plays more of a role in who you think you are, and your life situations, than you know. You repeat chaos because it is familiar and safe. Listen deeply to what is going on beneath the surface, and you will see that you are actually defining yourself by these conflicted conversations of the mind.

Externally projecting the answers to our internal energetic

reality needs causes pain and conflict. We can't heal energetic needs with physical stuff. This is why, when people finally solve their money problems, they find it isn't enough. Money does not heal the internal, energetic need that drove the desire in the first place. Money is just a tool that allows us to do more of what we want, when we want, on the physical plane; however, we can do anything and everything we want in energetic reality *right this minute*. Yes. Right *now*. For example, what do you think that you need money for? What do you think having that physical thing will bring you? Whatever that is, give it to yourself now—energetically—in your imagination.

Everyone and everything is an energy field, a particle field, and you influence that particle field. You have to ask or you will never receive. Ask specifically, directly. Give yourself energetically what you desire; it is absolutely overwhelming how great you can feel doing this simple exercise. Energetic reality is infinite, and its source is infinite. The key to total ecstasy in this moment lies here.

Pay attention to your addiction to chaos and to the thoughts feeding your energetic reality. Being human includes making mistakes—stop feeding your inner critic and beating yourself up.

Ask specifically, and directly for what you want. Give yourself energetically what you desire right now. Energetic reality is infinite, and its source is infinite. The key to total ecstasy in this moment lies in integrating this awareness.

Stop Beating Yourself Up

A hypercritical, mean spirited, prison guard part of yourself is relentlessly beating you up over all of your guilt, shames, and regrets. Not only are you imprisoned by these feelings, your relentless prison guard is the part of you that brutally beats you up because your life is not the way you think it should be—you're not rich enough, not doing the work that you love, not physically perfect, not admired by others, not in the perfect relationship, not manifesting what you want in this life, and on, and on.

That is hell. Every thought that you think that beats you up, leads you deeper into pain and suffering. Track your thoughts, and you will find that the pain and suffering is morally based—based on conflicted, internal judgments and stories about your life.

You are trapped in the beliefs of how life is and what you have done in your life. Often these parts pose as God or your higher self. They trap you in thoughts of no forgiveness, damnation, and hellfire. The part of you that cannot and will not let go of the past sits in continual moral judgment of all of your actions; relentlessly judging your life, day in and day out: the super critic, on top of the mountain, sitting in the capacity of *official judge*, the arbiter of truth. This is what many of you experience as life.

We don't do much of anything because we feel imprisoned, listening to the prison guard, our inner critic. The inner critic listens to the limbic system, which is basically listening to fear and terror, and trying to take control of the sympathetic nervous system.

You are a human being, and human beings make mistakes—that's reality. Acknowledge that you made mistakes, perhaps a lifetime of mistakes—and so what! Your point is what? That was yesterday, or an hour ago, and now you are here. That was the past, and in this moment, you can move on. Turn and face your past, your mistakes. Grieve your past, your mistakes, and move on. Yes, mistakes were made—experience the grief of that, and free up the energy. Let the energy move again, let it flow.

You deserve your self-compassion and self-forgiveness. Do you believe that? That is what is important; that on the deepest levels of yourself, you know you are willing to meet yourself with compassion.

You were innocent and naive in the beginning. Be innocent and naive now concerning your healing, your life, your soul, and your consciousness. Go to your heart to find forgiveness. When you find yourself lost in a sea of self-abuse, anger, criticism, morality, judgment, and lack of compassion, always come back to your heart. By focusing on the heart and embracing the oppressive feelings with your awareness, you will find an expansive feeling opening you to the infinite universe. Stuck energy is freed and returns to the center. Turn and face what you feel is unforgivable, offering yourself the love and compassion of your own soul—your infinite awareness.

Offer your inner critic compassion, and free yourself of moralities and judgments that keep you coming back to earth.

Morality and Judgment— the Double Bind

Morality is the thing that keeps you in line and coming back to earth. Nearly every thought that you have is a moral thought—one that forces you into a double bind. For example, morality is a way of keeping you on the straight and narrow in your external behaviors; however, if you are completely honest about your impulses, then you are in constant conflict. You have thoughts, desires, and impulses that you are unable to act upon. These create tensions in your body. As my acting coach, Judith Weston says, "Depression follows your inability to follow your impulses."

Morality is the constant and continuous judgment of our actions and impulses. Judgment is an endless thing: another's judgments about us, our judgments about others, and our judgments about ourselves. Even God is a judge, constantly and continually judging our actions and desires. Our stories capture the essence of the idea by saying, "God will be the ultimate judge of X (fill in the blank)." However, this assumes that there is ultimate truth in the universe, which is false. The anthropomorphized God only says *yes* to whatever it is that we want or desire. Just look at creation and we see that life is infinite in its creativity.

Morality will draw you back into the cycle of life if you do not realize that there is no ultimate morality. There must be clarity with respect to laws, because you see clearly that there is a strong cultural morality that must be respected. You must be able to pick out the moral issues so you can function on the planet without being arrested, but also realize that there is no real morality. Stop at stop signs, of course. Pay your taxes, absolutely. Free your consciousness, *yes*.

We inherited a cultural morality about sexuality, money, and life itself—this is good and that is bad. Society discourages us from exploring our sexuality, from being selfish, from feeling angry, from experiencing too much joy, and from discovering what turns us on. That's your job. Find out what turns you on, and give that to yourself—energetically—right now!!!

Sexual Essence

What is it that turns us on? That is sexual essence. Sexual essence lights up our energy circuits. We inherited a cultural sexuality that is running us, whether we know it or not. The cultural sexuality has a split: this is good, and that is bad. (Bucket two.) Cultural sexuality is based on a masculine, male, penis-centric, missionary position, vanilla sex that is *the way*, "God intended it to be." Functional. Sex has only to do with procreation and ensuring paternal certainty (i.e., no cuckolding)—using God as the enforcer, a malevolent, unseen agent that is waiting for us to mess up sexually—to catch us cheating; an invisible man, who is making his list, checking it twice, finding out who goes to heaven or hell, Santa God is coming to town. Human control of sexual energy is accomplished by making up stories about an invisible God who watches and judges everything that we do sexually.

We need to awaken from this delusion. God doesn't care if we self-pleasure. Sex energy is just that—energy. Controlling sex energy is ludicrous, pointless. Sex energy is the essence of the human experience. Everything on planet earth is driven by sex energy. All problems arise out of us not knowing who and what we are as energy. Sex energy is catalyst, creative, powerful, uplifting, profound, earth shattering, and heart pounding. Sex energy is the most transformational energy on planet earth. In addition, the flow of sexual energy is directly related to the flow of cash and money in our life.

Every building, every road, every tunnel, every town, every bridge, every city; for that matter, every tree, every mountain, and all food is a reflection of sexual energy. Sex energy is part of the abundant cycles of life and death, and rebirth. Sex energy, creatively harnessed and expressed, is the fuel responsible for every manifestation in the physical dimension. Sex creates: figuratively, literally, and abundantly. Who gave us this abundant energy, and the ability to experience infinite pleasure? God—infinite, source, creation. We were created in the image of God, and that includes our genitals, and our sexual energy. Moreover, God said, "This is my creation, and it is *good*."

Your sexual essence is the starter sequence that ignites your catalyst energy—creating flow, stimulating you, and awakening your sexual fire. Sexual essence is the fuel that fires up your life and can be a tremendous source of pleasure, creation, and *cash*. Life is delicious, yummy, and scrumptious when you allow your sexual essence to express in its naturalness.

God wants us to be happy, creative, healthy, and joyous—to

infinitely create in as many directions as we desire. Life is creative. Sex is creative. God wants us to infinitely create happiness, joy, energy, and abundance for ourselves, in the here and now—in energetic reality as well as in three-dimensional reality.

Sexual Essence and Thought Exercise: The best way to discover your sexual essence is in thought. Thought and imagination is a powerful way to fully and completely—fearlessly—explore what starts your sexual motor. You may be in a relationship and think that you just don't like sex. I assert to you, you haven't yet explored your sexual essence. Your sexual essence is big, bold, and beautiful. Listen to it. Discover it. Find it. Follow it. Explore your sexual essence in total freedom—in your wildest imagination. Let your energetic sexual essence run free. In that freedom, give yourself permission to create.

To further explore your sexual essence—examine your sexual myths about the feminine and the masculine.

Sexual Myths and the Unconscious Mind

The roles and identities of the masculine and feminine have changed many times through the ages, as well as the myths associated with them. As we progress on the path to freedom, the messages we've received about sex (and the masculine and feminine) mostly remain unconscious. To spiritually mature and evolve, we need to examine our sexual myths.

An insignificant amount of brainpower is devoted to your genitals, making the experience of sexuality mostly an unconscious experience. Moreover, because it is unconscious, sexuality exists in the realm of mythology and symbolism.

Attraction is based on the appearance of external and internal symbols, often in the form of people that awaken physical sensations in our bodies. This symbolic realm often determines our physical actions. Who we are attracted to is largely symbolic, and has little or nothing to do with the person in front of us.

Because most of what we experience of our sexuality is unconscious, and only a tiny fraction of our brain power is available for the genitals, our sexual experiences tend to remain unconscious over the course of our lifetime, mired in judgment, condemnation, blame, guilt, shame, self-hatred, and self-criticism.

Sex energy is similar to the great white shark—so big and powerful that it doesn't need a big brain. When you have that much raw power, the brain is small. The sexual brain is small, so that we continue to reproduce without much thought. We see this all the time with *unexpected* pregnancies and confused, conflicted, emotional feelings regarding sex.

Our lack of conscious brainpower is what creates the hell, confusion, and conflict in sexuality and sexual situations. Sexual desire is the drug of unconscious sex. Unconscious connections create overwhelming feelings of love, lust, and desire that we project on the person outside of us. We take those projections as reality and act accordingly. Then one day we wake up, and have no idea whom the person is that we have been sleeping next to for the past few years.

We are like radio receivers walking through life, being pulled one way or another by the energies of sexual impulses. The impulses driving the survival of the species are the most dark and unconscious. How this unconsciousness manifests is different for each person.

You have the false impression that some external woman or man will take you back to God through love and sex. This is the realm of the unconscious. Nobody outside of you can take you to

God. You must first do this inside you, and the external world will follow because you have done the work of clearing your myths and uncovering your impulses and desires, along with developing your feelings of self-deservement. When I first introduced clearing myths to one of my students, she recognized the myths she was willing to release, but couldn't yet see the myths that were unconsciously running the show. She worked with me on a regular basis and remained open to looking deeply at those unconscious myths. She continued to clear her myths and in doing so increased her self-deservement. She now understands how sexual myths impact our lives, and in releasing them increases sexual freedom, creative freedom, and life freedom.

We must accept that we are a total mess when it comes to our sexuality. It helps to acknowledge the problem so that we can consciously heal it.

Rushes in sexual energy always follow spiritual insights and awakenings. Whenever I lead a workshop, participants often report on the increased flow of sexual energy and desire, and how intense it is for them. The flow continues for about a week to a month and is completely natural. Give yourself permission to feel sexual energy within you. Sexual energy is spiritual energy in motion. When the flow of sexual energy expands, you can be sure that there will be an expansion of consciousness as well. In addition, when spiritual energy expands, you can be sure that there will be an increase in sexual energy.

Sex energy is life energy. To deny sex drive is to deny the impulse to live, thrive, and create. Denying sex drive also limits your ability to clearly see the myths you hold about love.

Relationship Mythology—
An Endless Barrage of *True Love* Symbols

When it comes to sex and relationships, the drunken monkey is running the show. Some of the strongest, most tenacious myths people have are about love and relationships. From the beginning, we are bombarded with stories, symbols, and images of *true love*, soul mates, and finally finding our missing piece. From movies to fairy tales, from prince charming to mermaids—myths of true love rule our psyche. People are on endless quests to find their other half in this life. Marriage and partnership have been held up as the noblest, most challenging path of transformation. Relationship is considered a fulfillment of life purpose and meaning—the highest act of submission to the divine.

However, for most people, the reality of this path is quite the opposite. They find that the person who once completed them now causes pain, constriction, and suffering. Often times people stay in relationships they have outgrown because they feel obligated, or are bound by religious mythology to stick it out—till death do us part. As one friend of mine said, "Well, I bought the farm on this one."

Essentially, relationship has to do with long-term healthcare, the sharing of resources, and ensuring the survival of progeny. To understand the societal purpose of marriage, all you have to do is look at divorce court. The end of marriage always deals with the splitting of resources—who gets what, and who gets the kids. Therein lies the purpose of myths. If you agree to marry someone, you agree to take care of them, and your children for the rest of your life—thereby eliminating the societal burden to care for you or your loved ones. *Until death do you part* means you agree to feed, clothe, and support this person until one or both of you dies.

Relationship has nothing to do with love. Love is akin to cocaine. It has the same high and drives you crazy. Love is about the free flow of chemicals in the brain that impair your judgment so that eventually, you take enough risks to end up with a new soul being born. Love is a chemical high—period. Love feels great, and I highly recommend it. However, any stories that you tell yourself about love are myths. Chemicals are chemicals—nothing more, nothing less. You can tell yourself all kinds of stories, but they are not *the* truth.

Relationships are no higher or lower a path than *anything* else. Relationships are what they are, and if you want to share resources and have children, marriage is an excellent ritual and system. Unfortunately, such a practical view is not how the drunken monkey sees it. The drunken monkey prefers myths about seeking true love, completion—deep fulfillment and oneness—to any kind of clarity. The key here is to understand what is going on inside of you—this deep desire to merge actually exists in energetic reality not three-dimensional reality. You want to feel infinite love from someone, and you are fine with this myth; that is, until the *from someone* part.

An external person will never give you what you long for and desire in energetic reality, in thought. It is simply not possible. Sure, an external person will take care of some superficial need for a while, but they will never access the deepest, energetic longing parts within you, because they can't. The drunken monkey mind constantly confuses two *different* systems of reality—energetic and three-dimensional—causing you confusion and pain.

One reality is three-dimensional external, physical reality, and the other reality is inside your head, your feeling world, energetic reality. If you want deep un-ending love, then give that to yourself right now, energetically, symbolically, in any way that you desire to experience it. Merging with the Divine, and feeling oneness and love is about you giving yourself what you want *now*—in energetic reality. Go directly to the symbol that's in your head—the one that you are looking at when we discuss your *true love*. Look at it closely. That person in your head is in your head; however, you are projecting that person onto the outside world.

The drunken monkey is simply confused. The person in your head doesn't exist in the real world. You are letting the drunken monkey steer your car. So, if you want to do something radical, and snap out of your deep sleep state, then go directly to the symbol right now, and receive the true love that you so want, desire, and deserve. Get into the habit of giving yourself, energetically, exactly what you want the moment that the thought or feeling appears.

Learn to flow and connect to the symbols in your head. Like all good symbols, they store energy that is just waiting to be released and make you feel awesome. Release that energy right now, and let it flow through and heal your body, mind, and spirit so that you can feel deeply relaxed and connected to the infinite—energetically.

There is no one or nothing out there that can save you, heal you, or make you finally whole. There is the flow of chemicals, and a temporary delusion. Eventually, one or the other will wear off, and you will be left seeing the person, the human being before you. The brutal truth is that love is about losing your rational mind so that you bond, share resources, and have kids. Of course, not all love includes kids—but love does bind humans together. From a social biological perspective, love serves to create strong ties between individuals, families, and groups. Those with strong ties are more likely to thrive and survive together—to build community and social order—and ensure the survival of their progeny.

I hate to break the bad news, but when it comes to relationships, the drunken monkey runs the show. The monkey is loose. Contrary to what the drunken monkey believes, love is chemicals—drugs—temporarily flowing through your body, making you crazy. If you want eternal love, God's love, human love, give that to yourself now *by releasing the energy of the symbols in your head, and letting that energy flow through your life and body—energetically– because that is all it is anyway. You may as well give it to yourself freely, and have fun doing it.*

Sex Drive: Source of Creation

The body was built as a vehicle for the soul and to perpetuate the species. Sex drive is the drive to procreate. The drive can be overwhelming when fully engaged, and it can put us through many changes. When active, sex drive can be a tremendous source of creativity, expression, and creation.

What I can tell you is this: stop worrying about desire. Desire is the way that it is. Sex drive is the way that it is. Sexual desire is in your cellular programming. Without it, life ceases to exist. If you realize that sex drive is something biomechanical, programmed into your DNA, and not *bad*, you have already gone a long way towards healing your shame and unconsciousness around sex.

Sex is a dark universe. Over time, it has been mired in fear, guilt, shame, humiliation, blame, etc. This was done to create formal society in which individuals of many different backgrounds could live together. Religion, government, and socialization/education became the main way in which sex drive was controlled.

These took the basic human impulses, and imposed the ultimate tax: eternal damnation—eviction from the physical and spiritual tribe—if the impulses were followed.

For many, there is nothing worse than the fear of being ostracized from society because of their sexual impulses or preferences. We needed to control our impulses in order for society to exist. Society's attempt to control sex results in men and women feeling guilt and shame about their sexuality. The naturalness of sex is sublimated and wounding occurs. On the spiritual path, however, this becomes a hindrance. We have to bring sex energy out of the depths of fear and unconsciousness in order for us to heal spiritually, and to break free of the bindings of guilt, fear, frustration, shame, and blame. Sex is just energy, an impulse that is as tall as the highest mountain, and as strong as the pull of the moon on the ocean. All physical creation is a testament to either the sublimation or the open cultivation of the sexual impulse.

Men and women live most of their lives feeling wounded around their sexuality, amounting to a refusal of life. We still use the 7,000 year-old idea that sex is bad, is part of nature, and must be controlled. Women feel wounded by men's sexual energy—and men feel that they can't express what it is that they truly want.

As you begin to focus on sex energy, you will see that in energetic reality there is a big, scary, dark, and conflicted world. The one thing that has potential to bring you pleasure really brings you pain, because of the intense fear and emotions, and the depth of vulnerability associated with it. This is the joke. The one thing that brings pleasure is mired in darkness, shame, and guilt; therefore, no pleasure can come from it.

The physical body is simply a vehicle for the soul to reside in. That's it. Everything else that we do with the body, including sex, has to do with the biology of the body. The physical body should be tension free, open to the moment—a housing unit for the soul, an ingenious way for the soul to experience physical reality, separation from the whole, and a complete immersion in an illusion that feels deceptively real.

Sex drive is natural. Women and men are wounded due to the guilt and shame attached to this naturalness. The world population has more than doubled since the 1950's. Therefore, you can extrapolate that people are having more sex than ever—all around the world—sex is happening.

Articulating the Masculine Wound

Men are wounded because of their nature. Men are wild animals with insatiable impulses. They experience instant conflict with laws, rules, drive, and desire. The sex drive is so strong and profound that men learn deep ways to mask, hide, and suppress their natural impulses. By expressing their true desires, men feel that they will be rejected, shamed, and unloved. Moreover, because these impulses are continuous and in the wiring, men often feel angry about their lack of control, or their inability to be able to have what they want. So much of masculine sex ends up being pushed into dark rooms of anger and suppression, coming out and expressing in strange ways, often in the form of hatred towards women.

The natural impulse of men is to have sex and orgasm quickly. The impulse begins in the genes. All men who are alive today come from lineages of survivors. These survivors were men who were able to fertilize many, many females, quickly, and often, and ensure the survival of their progeny. If *you* are alive today, it is likely that you owe your life to one of your male ancestor's ability to sire many children with different women—quickly, randomly, and often.

The masculine wound is this: the appetite for sex is strong and constant. Desire and longing impulses can overwhelm. They are crafty, and something to be reckoned with; or, they become dark and hidden, expressing in less than uplifting ways. Men feel shutdown, ashamed, and unable to ask for what they really want. Men feel guilty and confused by this naturalness.

Religion, doing its part, teaches that these impulses are sinful, dirty, evil, and lead to hell if not overcome. Yet, we know from the sheer volume of priests involved in child molestation scandals that religious denial and shame isn't working.

Sexual energy drives the planet. Everything on earth is created, one way or another, from sex energy. These sexual impulses cannot be *controlled* and overcome. The impulses are vibrating with the creative energy of the universe: the creative energy that creates all life.

The sexual impulse in man has the potential to feed him deeply and assist him in physical creation. The act of creation is sexual in nature. This beautiful sexual energy, if cultivated, is beyond description as to the intimacy, self-love, appreciation, and joy that can be felt in the body.

The first step is to heal your wounds and self-judgment about these impulses, and how they express in your life. What you can't accept within yourself is what you can't heal. Where you feel shame within yourself is where your relationship will shame you. Your own impulses are your salvation. What are your true desires? Accept and express them to yourself as facts, and you will find that you are completely free in your flow of sexual impulse and desire. Make more and more space in your body to feel exactly what it is that you feel. Explore your impulses freely in energetic reality.

Give yourself whatever you want energetically, and you will free up your sexual energy, and paradoxically, your ability to attract more cash into your life. Accept the sex drive and impulse within yourself. Be comfortable with all desires. They are natural.

Desire:
Secret Language of God

Desire is something that human beings experience many times, every day. All human desire is the impulse to merge with the infinite unfolding of creation. Love, song, music, yoga, dance, prayer, sexuality, partnership, and creativity are all part of the desire to merge with God in the divine flow of infinite creation.

Religion and spirituality traditionally teach us that desire should be controlled, pushed down, and overcome; that the only path to awakening is the overcoming of desire. This begs the question, who or what part of us must overcome desire? Why is desire bad? The misperception of our teachers was that the source of desire was the ego, not God, which is simply wrong. Desire does not cause pain, but the denial of desire—blocking the movement of this energy—causes pain. Desire is just the movement of energy.

Desire lives outside of the brain/mind/body/central nervous system. It flows from something infinite, and therefore is not to be *controlled*. Desire is the threshold to the doorway of the impulse to merge with God. The ego wants to love and be loved in a way that no external being can ever do. Only our relationship with the infinite can truly nurture us in the way that our insecure ego needs—infinitely.

Nurturing is attained by opening to the impulse of desire and allowing the infinite, from which the impulse emerges, to take over the ego and embrace your endless needs in love, compassion, and understanding. Completely surrender to the impulse. The secret to quieting the mind is to not effort and suppress, but rather to understand that the nature of the mind is to be in *continuous action*, and this action is *not* who you are. It never will be. The secret to quieting the mind is to realize that the mind exists within you, within your field of infinite awareness. A relaxed mind is actually a pleasure to be around.

Desire is a path, a spiritual path, where you follow its divine impulse and allow that impulse to wash over you like a sacred Hawaiian waterfall. Desire is rich, life affirming, liberating, if it is allowed to flow back to the essence of God, from which it emerges.

Make peace with your desire body and discover peace in your mind. You are not your mind, and you are not your body. You are simply awareness; and desire, if followed diligently, will lead you back to infinite awareness from where you emerge.

Sexual Energy Creates and Destroys

Sexual desire impulses flowing from the rudimentary, primitive parts of your brain often drive you crazy. They are in constant conflict. The primitive part wants raw, unbridled sexual power, while the newer, more *evolved* judgmental, fearful, and shameful parts of the brain fight those impulses. An inner war erupts. Your brain wants to keep your cake and eat it too, and wants to acquire everyone else's cake, and eat that as well—another example of the human dilemma.

Sex, and expressions of sex energy externally, is a healthy need impulse of the brain and body—as you need food and water, or exercise on a daily basis—in an ideal world, there would also be the flow of sex energy. When sexual energy openly flows, your body stays younger, your brain suppler, and you are more honest with yourself about the flow of impulses moving through you. These sexual impulses are natural and necessary. They are powerful, and depending on the organ that is taking over at the time, they create what they want.

Sexual energy can confront and destabilize if you are not prepared. It can potentially rip through your life, similar to a wild fire during a drought. Sexual energy can rock your foundation, and create volatile transformations in your life. Sexual energy is powerful, and much as the sun can help you grow crops or burn your skin beyond recognition, sex energy can create or destroy.

When faced with overwhelming feelings of sexuality and desire, you have several options:

- Follow the desire impulse completely, to its energetic conclusion. Simply take action as consciously as possible.
- Deny the desire impulse completely. This creates internal pressure and does nothing to integrate sexual energy. Denial is the preferred method of every major religion on the planet, though not particularly helpful.
- Allow the two conflicting impulses to communicate. See if you can reach a third way—a solution that takes into account all parts and impulses, arriving at a third solution.
- Relax into the sensation and make space in your body for the powerful energies to flow and move through you.

The general idea with sexual energy is to allow and open to your flow unrestricted. Allow your body to take in greater amounts of sexual energy. Try saying yes to the energy, allowing it to flow through you, as you would allow a river to flow, impersonally, appreciating it exactly as it is.

Actualizing sexual desire externally is a completely different thing than what is triggering energetically inside your head, two percent of which is flowing into the conscious mind, telling you that you need sex. Your brain is searching for something that doesn't exist externally—an attempt to find a solution to the pain and suffering that it feels continuously because it can't have what it wants all the time. The Buddha's solution was to simply have no desires; but the cosmic joke is that physical existence is dependent on desire. Desire drives creation. Desire is causation. Desire drives movement and change.

Perhaps the easiest thing to do is say yes, energetically, but don't necessarily try to physically actualize the impulse. Feel it come and go, ebb and flow. One way or another, our external needs are trying to heal internal issues, which doesn't happen, because physical reality has little or no affect on energetic reality and vice versa. We externally seek the perfect relationship to heal our internal issues. The unconsciousness of this creates pain. The external will never permanently heal or feed the internal wound. That's why we are continuously seeking.

Allow for greater and greater amounts of pleasure to fill your body, mind, and spirit. Sexual energy can literally feed your soul.

Relationships and the Pain Paradigm

Human relationships are composed of pain. That's how we bond—our unconscious pain meets the unconscious pain of someone that we love or are attracted to, and bam—relationship. We are each attempting to heal our unconscious pain through another person.

Repeatedly, we hear stories of couples living together for years, and one day waking up to find that they don't know whom they are married to. This happens because we see what we want, or expect to see, not what is. We see what our brains tell us is there—highly processed data and symbolic imagery, especially around sex and relationships.

Pain and suffering is the paradigm. Some incredible *love songs* reflect this paradigm of pain, heartbreak, and suffering.

Humans live for pain. Our movies are about pain, television is about pain, and the news is about pain. The more vivid the image, the more likely it will make the top TV story or front page news, and the more alive we feel as a result. Relationships are birthed out of the same energy. See that the paradigm is pain, and be willing to give that back to source.

Give away your need for pain and suffering in relationships. Why not experience love, joy, peace, intimacy, and other delicious things in relationships? It is time to update your myths about sex, death, money, and relationships.

Pain and Suffering Do Not—
and Will Not Ever—Lead to Bliss

As far as pain and suffering goes, well, what is the point? Think of it this way. We are created out of energy, and many agree that this life is an illusion. Which, in a way, is true. Life feels real while we are experiencing it, but once the experience is gone, it is gone. For example, the time we spent a few weeks ago is only alive inside the synapses of our brain. Events are stored symbolically in the brain; they no longer exist in physical form, and often we have to trigger the memories with pictures, videos, music, tastes or smells.

We are in physical reality only in the instant of perception. Everything else falls into the unreality of the brain/mind/body/central nervous system's energetic, memory storage capacity, and our ability to access those memories. We convert standout experiences into symbolic images that when referenced cause a massive release of energy throughout the body.

Spiritually, we refer to the instant of perception as living in the now, being present. However, it is all an illusion; even the perception of now isn't real. Now is just a moment of perception that is instantly over, followed by another instant of perception. Each perception of now consists of jumbled information, incoming data, and random sensory stimulus that the brain/mind/body/central nervous system filters and assembles together sometime after now. The perception filters through all of our painful, hurtful, and fearful experiences; recycling those past memories, mixing them with the incoming stimulus of the moment, calling it a *new* experience, a new reality. There is no direct experience of anything. The brain is the perceiver and the assembler of reality.

There is no tangible reality other than this instant, which as I said before, is only itself a perception of the brain/mind/body/central nervous system's past experience seamlessly blended into this current moment. None of it is *real*. No reality exists, per se, but rather there is a constantly changing field of moment-to-moment unconscious experiences that the brain cobbles together, filtered through our worst, most painful memories called life, truth, and reality. This is truly the way that we create our reality.

What you call reality of self is continually being cobbled together by the brain, and is in a constant state of flux. Who are you now?

Seat of the Problem of Humanity—
It is in Your Brain

The underlying problem of humanity exists deep in the brain. The core issue is that the brain uses the *identical pathways* for seeing objects as for imagining them; only it uses those pathways in reverse. That is to say, what you actually see, and what you imagine that you see, uses the same screen, the same internal brain hardware. The screen is a buffer zone. The screen is the place where the brain processes and makes use of visual information, carrying out preliminary analysis of incoming visual image stimulus. The fact of the matter is, your eyes don't see; *your brain does.*

In a movie theater, where the movie is projected from in front of the screen and in back of the screen, simultaneously, it would be impossible to determine which is which. From the screen's standpoint, it is all the same. From the viewer's perspective, it is all the same as well.

The problem for humanity is that internal reality is indistinguishable from external reality. Memory, thought, self-image, ego, dreams, imagination, language, visual perception, and mental imagery are all using complex processing and storage powers deeply rooted within the substructures of the brain. Furthermore, they are using the same perceptual brain structures that your five physical senses use. Thoughts, dreams, imaginations, fears, etc., are not ethereal at all. From the brain's standpoint, they are real. Inside/outside is all the same, whether it is photons of light tangibly projecting through the eyes from the outside in, or internal light that is being generated from electrical impulses and static noise deep inside the substructures of the brain. They use the same physical screen of perception.

Putting it another way, every area of the brain that sends information upstream and inward for processing through the neural nets, also receives information back from those areas. Similar to a Los Angeles freeway, information is flowing in two directions simultaneously at all times, freely. However, the two sides of the freeway are not clearly marked in the brain. It's a bit of a free for all when it comes to the flow of information—inside or out, it doesn't really matter—it's all *seen and processed* by the brain.

The brain contains limited space, so everything that is experienced must be stored symbolically to create a memory. In addition, the brain has a limited lexicon of symbols from which it constructs complex visual images that help us make sense of our experiences. These symbols are the alphabet through which our memories, thoughts, dreams, fears, hopes, and experiences are written back to the brain and stored. A picture is worth a thousand words. Pictures and symbols are economical ways to store information within the small space of the brain.

The eye's ability to perceive light relies on a specific class of protein that captures the basic qualities of light, and translates them into electrical signals that brains can understand. Whatever we *see* is a translation of reality that a brain can make sense of. The same is true in reverse. The stored memories, traumas, fears, hopes, dreams, references, inner seeing, etc., must be translated into electrical signals that brains can understand. That's what makes it confusing from the brain's perspective, and therefore from our perspective. We are not seeing what is real, but rather a highly processed amalgam of *reality*.

In this respect, life truly is the way we perceive it, and everything we perceive about ourselves is a lie, a myth, and a story.

Be Conscious with any Discomfort— This is Stuck Energy

Everything that you think you are is a lie. Even you who think you know who you are—is limiting. Imagine that everything you've ever thought about yourself is a lie, because it is. Everything you tell yourself, everything that you don't tell yourself, is all a lie.

Who you think that you are has *nothing* to do with what you really are. Your mind tells you who and what you are. The drunken monkey tells you where you are going and what you will be. The mind is endlessly shifting and changing.

You are living in a world, where you must stand your ground and be who you really are. You are to face and embrace your whole self, your range of emotions, your disparate feelings, your demons, your childish and neurotic selves, etc. Some call it discipline. Mostly it is turning and facing the thing that is driving you to act out, run, hide, or indulge. You either are being, facing, or running.

Being present means being fully here and now: no distractions, no running away, just a pure second to second opening to the discomfort. Be comfortable with feeling uncomfortable; this must happen for you to fully actualize. You must be able to stay conscious and current to the discomfort in your life, mind, body, and spirit—so that energy can be made conscious. The body's natural state is peace, and that's the way it should be. A body, as a vehicle for the soul, is at total peace.

Eventually, your soul will emerge fully. The soul is a divided reality. The soul exists here, in your simple life of illusion, and in the grand universal essential life. You are not one or the other. Allow the soul to work through your life—transforming you as the sun transforms the night to day. Your soul will unfold and guide you into the light of your true self. The soul has infinite space and compassion for your life. Infinite.

If you understand this one concept, you are well on your journey: your soul has infinite compassion for your life. As you develop a relationship with your soul, you begin to understand that compassion is your key to healing. From the soul's perspective, everything can be embraced—even that which you believe can't be embraced.

Healing Sexual Abuse and Trauma

To overcome sexual abuse and trauma, you have to understand the physical reality of the body's survival mechanism. The body runs programs that tell you to *not* recognize abuse. That simple program affects every area of your life, and draws you into situations where you can't defend yourself against abuse, because you are blind to it—you go into a frozen, survival trance. This is also identified biologically as the *freeze response*, a survival mechanism that all creatures do as a last resort of life. The freeze response gives an appearance of helplessness and mimics death; then wears off at a later time, so you can escape once the predator thinks you are dead.

When confronted with abuse, the body squirts chemicals that cause you to not see abuse clearly, masking the awful sensations in your body that are caused by abuse and trauma. That is why individuals suffer from sexual abuse. When the body freezes, you can easily be guided into dangerous situations by sexual predators that feed off sexual abuse energy. Your body protects you by creating chemicals that cause you to feel numb. "I will not recognize abuse," is the end result.

The syntax of the release that is needed around the brain, the heart, the tummy, the sexual organs, and the root chakra, is the freeze response program, "I will not see abuse." As you begin to see abuse clearly, you can identify it, shake yourself out of it, and then work towards healing accordingly. To heal abuse, you must actually reprogram the body. I have been working with one of my students for more than a year to recognize the freeze response when it occurs, shake out of it, and then re-live the occurrence in energetic reality choosing behaviors that break the freeze response. The student shared with me how painful it is in the beginning to work on this in energetic reality, how experiencing freeze translates into feeling a failure because the freeze response is tough to interrupt, how confusing it is not knowing what is a healthy response, and how boundaries are blurred or nonexistent due to the abuse. Repetition of choosing different behaviors to the freeze response in energetic reality enabled the student to respond differently in physical reality. I also worked with the student to build self-confidence by practicing to physically fight off an attacker and loudly say, "No."

Abuse serves *no* purpose. Sexual abuse serves no purpose. We must choose to clear out the programs feeding off the energy of you feeling frozen. We must blast out the freeze response.

Understand that abuse and trauma are frozen energy, and that energy must be dissipated, and replaced by action, movement, sound, and freedom. To move is to live. To speak up is to experience victory. When you feel frozen, as soon as you recognize the feeling, look around you rapidly, similar to a cornered animal seeking an escape route. Move your body: breathe, yell, and shake. Move your spine.

It helps to have a professional work with you when you are releasing trauma and abuse. Seek out the help of others who can help you to connect with your inner resources and learn to dissipate the stored trauma in your body.

Be compassionate and gentle with yourself when releasing trauma and abuse. Nothing is more important than having compassion for what is happening in your life and body as you open to the flow of your sexual energy. One way to become familiar with the ebb and flow of sexual energy is through yoga practice. Yoga incorporates breath, movement, sound, and strength to help move frozen, stuck energy in the body.

Sexual Energy and Yoga

Moving the body in yoga class is akin to making love. You give yourself fully to commitment, sensuality, passion, sweat, exertion, exhaustion, and finally, dead pose. Post-coital bliss. Awareness of the relationship among sexuality, sexual energy, yoga, and spirituality is crucial to awakening your consciousness and lifting you to the highest levels of freedom.

How do we, as conscious beings, come to understand the impact of this formidable force of sexual energy in our lives? One way to become familiar with the ebb and flow of sex energy is through yoga practice. Yogis have long understood the power of harnessing sex energy for the evolution of higher consciousness and refinement of the body. What do you think down-dog and up-dog are all about, anyway?

However, in our high speed, digital age, we have lost sight of the transformation potential of this energy. Through opening the channels to sex energy, we can experience the divine. Bliss,

Sexual Energy and Yoga

emptiness, openness, and vulnerability—these are all aspects of the infinite. We can know God through discovering, uncovering, and exposing our raw, unexpressed sexual energy.

As we move our bodies together in yoga, in a symphony of sensations, emotions, sounds, and self-love, we discover the truth of who and what we are as energy in motion. A constant flow of truth and being that expresses moment-to-moment.

Refining the body through the movement of sexual energy is key to psychological, spiritual, and mental health. Yoga encourages and helps us to create sexual polarity, one of the keys to healthy, abundant, sexual attraction. Polarity occurs when, through our yoga, we move towards our feminine (lunar) or towards our masculine (solar) orientation. Ideally, throughout our practice, we are moving in and out of the masculine/feminine polarity. In some moments, we are pushing, thrusting, and piercing, in other moments we are yielding, softening, and receiving, all the while intimately listening to the body's ever changing voice.

In your yoga practice, begin to notice the shifts of polarity when they occur. Follow your body's impulses. Be gentle. Be piercing. Be forceful. Be soft. Listen closely. Intend to allow your unconscious sexuality to emerge and flow consciously into your practice. The sensuousness of yoga is key. Bring it into your conscious mind. Feel the emotion of your sexual power and life force moving through you. Taste your sweat. Breathe deeply from your belly. Open your hips. Deeply relax your sex center. You are moving into a ritual of breath, humidity, and life—a tussle with your mind on your yoga mat.

At the end of practice, bring the energy you have cultivated up into your heart and into your brain. When sitting in meditation, or lying in corpse pose, focus on opening the pleasure centers in your brain. Feed the brain and soul your sexual energy, pleasure, exhaustion, and joy. Circulate it freely. Open and relax your heart completely. Allow the unbridled flow of sexual energy to deepen your connection to the divine. Steep in the bliss of yoga. Feel the interconnectedness of all life through sex energy.

Circulate your sexual energy—feed the pleasure centers in your brain—feed your soul.

Opening the Sacred Geometry of the Pleasure Centers

There exists a matrix for pleasure in the brain/mind/body/central nervous system. The matrix is composed of sacred geometry as to how pleasure is experienced, a combination of switching on hormones, centers, neural pathways and various components within the brain. You have to invoke this sacred geometry of pleasure and feeling good. Ask your soul to establish the sacred geometry matrix for feeling good in your life. Awaken the parts of the brain and central nervous system that are responsible for feeling good, pleasurable, and ecstatic.

Your juiciest center in the brain is what you want to connect with. If you imagine a line that goes through the center of the head, like a skewer that runs from the crown to the front of the throat, and then across the top of the ears, the intersection is the pleasure center. At this central point, when you activate awareness of this space, you will feel a tingle in the head, and a shiver through the spine. You will feel a vibration in your awareness that will spread throughout the whole body. When you feel this part of the brain, you can stroke it with an inner finger, rubbing its little belly.

Experiment with the sensation. Let your awareness, your own inner wisdom, guide you in the direction that you need to go. Just be aware of the brain. The brain loves feeling itself. The brain loves the awareness. You don't have to create anything. You are simply giving yourself permission to receive your pleasure.

Awareness itself awakens the pleasure centers. As you clear contraction, and your mind quiets, pay attention, because as things open, you become a creator in your life, receiving exactly what you focus your attention on.

Focus on what you want. Focus on what you desire. Focus on exactly what you want, the way that you want it—this is important. Rest your focus on the openness, in the juiciness, the pleasurableness, the ecstasy, and the fluidity of now—awareness, being, and freedom. Continue to stay in an open state, resting your awareness predominantly on the things that you love and enjoy, things that make you feel good! Granting yourself permission to feel and have exactly what you want and desire in your life (even though you are in the habit of doing the exact opposite) is a spiritual discipline.

The natural flow of feminine energy is about opening to more and more pleasure.

Divine Feminine

Feminine sexuality is not the Madonna or whore polarity. Feminine sexuality is about receptivity—receiving pleasure and opening to feeling good—opening to more and more pleasure. All major spiritual shifts emerge from our feminine, receptive, self-opening, whether we are men or women.

Receiving is the most powerful dynamic—opening us to receive our whole life. Without receiving, there is no life, only doing. How we receive depends on our willingness to let go—to completely let go and open. Opening can feel extremely vulnerable. However, opening to these subtleties creates an abundant flow of divinity in our lives. This abundance is rich and full, ripe with life. Give and receive, love and be loved. Everything in life is giving or receiving, creating and un-creating. The deepest levels of receiving bring tears of gratitude—how deeply grateful one can be for receiving the gifts of spiritual awakening and enlightenment.

The divine feminine is responsible for transmitting spiritual energy into the physical body. Every major spiritual transmission is an opening of the universe, an opening of the feminine nature that allows our consciousness to enter her hidden, higher frequencies. The universe is feminine. She opens herself to give us her insights and gifts ... allowing her divine infinite essence to flow, within and without.

Divine feminine teaches us how to truly love ourselves so deeply that we no longer allow any type of disservice to our being. We have strong boundaries, and we stand up strongly for them.

Self-love, self-appreciation, and self-knowledge are the work of the divine feminine. Learning about self-pleasure and self-deservement is also the work of the divine feminine. When we truly love ourselves, we love all that there is about ourselves, infinitely, including our impulses, desires, and wounds.

Defining the Feminine Wound

The unconscious feminine wound is triggered by, and at a polar opposite to, the unconscious masculine wound.

When a man feels badly about his sexual essence, his sexual drive, he inadvertently wounds the feminine by losing interest in her the moment he has her and orgasms, seeing her as either a Madonna or a whore, discarding her due to projecting his own sexual shame, losing interest as the chemicals leave his body. He shunts her aside and often loathes her power. She feels this and, of course, takes it personally. She feels that there must be something wrong with her. Perhaps her face, breasts, thighs, or butt aren't desirable.

Then the endless mythologies around sex are added into the mix for total chaos and confusion: that holy sex, or correct sex, is *the immaculate conception,* and that somehow we are doing something inherently wrong and sinful, that our bodies are naturally unclean, that desire is sinful, that Prince Charming will come to the rescue, that we will find the perfect soul mate. Mythologies obscure our ability to see what is actually happening and the real person who is physically before our eyes.

Through union, a woman is looking to heal herself and bond in the deepest, most intimate ways so she can *find herself*, learning more and more about who she is in the act of loving, opening, and sharing her being. She wants to experience a symphony of sensations, and a man, more often than not, wants release. This is confusing to the feminine. She wants to be seen in her fullness, in all of her gifts, in all of her vastness. He wants to come, but feels badly about that.

The feminine unknowingly takes the wounded masculine, the unconscious desire and drive to release, into her body in an attempt to *heal* him, so that he will love the real her, and find value and worth in her beyond her ever-changing form. In his inexperienced, unconscious vulnerability, he projects his sexual shadow onto her, for which he hates her. On one hand, he is trying to heal through the feminine womb, through sex, through the vagina; on the other hand, he hates her for needing this healing, and for being so helpless in his desire for her form. Man often loathes his lack of *self-control*, and blames that on the *evil, misguided woman*.

As a result, woman feels that she isn't enough, and she hates the masculine for not receiving her gifts. Hurt, shame, guilt, closure, and blame are heaped generously in both directions.

Woman, often ashamed of her body and genitals, can't let a

Defining the Feminine Wound

man see her nakedness, vulnerability, and insecurities. Moreover, to feel a man's unconscious sexual desires, without any sexual training and awareness, can be very disconcerting for woman. The vulnerability can be overwhelming, and often too much to see directly.

Through the feminine, a man can potentially heal himself, but he must surrender to his own nakedness and vulnerability, and to woman's nakedness and vulnerability. He has to soften into his body, and feel the tension of his impulses and desires, and his conflicted beliefs, and then *share that vulnerability with her.*

She wants to share her deepest gifts, wrap around his vulnerability, and see and be seen. When this doesn't happen, woman feels unseen, unheard, un-listened to, and unappreciated. She falls back to the question, "What is wrong with me?"

Woman knows about man because she is the one who gives birth, and therefore knows the source from which he came. Men are worried about finding truth; women are living.

Through menstruation, woman is thrown into adulthood and into the world, whether she likes it or not. It's done to her. Her body changes and suddenly she is faced with the power and attraction of her body, and the call of her eggs. If her mythology about this is loving and supportive, then she transitions smoothly. If it is not, her sexual development will come to a halt, she will compress herself, make herself small, and hide her true expansive capabilities. She chooses smallness and being liked over social and intimate conflict. When the masculine shames her for her attractiveness and for his overwhelming, unexpressed desires, she shuts down, cutting herself off from her *lower chakras*, her sex center, her pleasure, and her womb. She feels ashamed of the sexual energy beacon that she has no control over. Therefore, she hides, moving far from her deepest truth.

The deepest pull of the feminine is to suck in, to devour, and to create through the vagina and the womb. It is so natural, and yet this is the thing that both the masculine and the feminine are most afraid of in each other. Man is afraid to die, to be devoured by the vagina. Woman is afraid to reveal or even know this desire to devour, and out of that energy, to create and to destroy.

Both the masculine and feminine wounds are born out of the human field of shame, where pleasure and natural impulses are abominations. The paradigm of pain is passed down generation to generation, through received knowledge. Once the mythology of original sin was created, once there was a split between man and God, God and nature, nature and man, the whole world was at war. Masculine and feminine were at war, organs and desires within the body were at war, and the blame game was created: man against nature, nature against man, man against woman, woman against man, God against man, man against God, God against nature, nature against God, good against evil, evil against good, etc. Everybody is victimized by what they don't have and can't get, by what they desire but shouldn't want. Moreover, it goes on and on to this day.

Becoming human happens as we recognize these inherited

wounds and paradigms, taking them out of the realm of mythology and into the realm of conscious awareness, where they can be healed.

By continuously exploring ourselves and eventually revealing ourselves to our partners, and most importantly to ourselves, we can accept our deepest, darkest, most unlovable parts, and bring them into the space of wholeness and integration.

The divine feminine and infinite masculine are aspects of your soul. The infinite masculine holds the accepting space for the small self that endlessly desires. Make a commitment to see your sexuality with clarity, to listen clearly, and to unabashedly ask for more and more of what you want.

Infinite Masculine

The infinite masculine is not what we generally think about when it comes to masculinity; that is, testosterone run amok, someone who doesn't cry, doesn't feel, is bulky, able to fight, powerful, hard, strong, overwhelming, and forceful. These concepts of the masculine are part of the reason that we lost our way in our culture. We lost touch with the essence behind life, the energies that existed before there was matter.

You are not the shell you walk around with. You are born naked and you die naked. Your body is a temporary, disposable vehicle. If you think that you are this body, you are lost in the fog of the finite, masculine zone. All strength and power comes and eventually goes. The strongest cultures in the world crumbled through the ages. Strength, in the old sense of the word, is not what it appears to be.

I first discovered the infinite masculine while working with a student of mine. He was salivating over a Lamborghini that he wanted to buy. Since we had been meditating all day, I suggested that we feel into the energy that created the Lamborghini. What created this vehicle? In feeling into the object, we could feel that the car was made of masculinity, strength, and power. However, most individuals are attracted to the object, thinking that it is the object that will give them the energy, quality, or power that they desire. They believe that the car, the woman, the man, the relationship, the house (fill in the blank here) will be the thing that makes them whole. Nothing could be further from the truth.

The new definition of masculine is the masculine that is infinitely aware of its self and holds the infinite, accepting space for the small, insecure, worldly, neurotic self that endlessly desires.

The infinite masculine is an aspect of your soul—the masculine aspect—and it is infinite because you are not at all limited by anything on an energetic level. Who you are is so far beyond what you can imagine that you may never know it with your conscious mind; however, the infinite masculine knows first hand, and it is this energy, this ocean of life force, that we are speaking about. Who you are, is who is living right now. Some of the experience you can see, feel and perceive; however, who you are, is well beyond your conscious perception.

The infinite masculine energy is so in touch with your infinite life stream, that when you encounter it for the first time, the sheer volume of energy that you experience will be a shock—though normal and natural. Encountering your essence for the first time can be disconcerting.

Realizing that you are much greater than you ever imagined can be a bit overwhelming. The divine masculine is energy of infinite power, ability, potential, and action; greater than any problem that you will ever have or encounter. Meeting the infinite masculine is like meeting your best friend. The power of the infinite masculine is unimaginable.

Sex Drives Everything— Stop Trying to Control It

Behind all creation is a drive for sex. Sex powers the planet. Sex drives life. All the creation on the planet comes from sex energy. This powerful force ensures the perpetuation of the species. As long as there is life—there will be sex. Stop trying to control the impulse. Put yourself in accord with the impulse. The impulse to sex is the impulse to life. Boundless life. Boundless creativity.

On the path to freedom, sex can be confusing. Most of what we learn about sex is received knowledge, mythology, and stories passed down through the ages. All religions try desperately to control sex—and it isn't working. Individuals are having sex more than ever, and sexual dysfunction is at an all time high.

Sexual energy drives most human transactions one way or another. Whenever you have a problem in your life, think dirty first. That's where the physical problem is based. Putting it another way, you are a physical being with sexual drive, sexual desires, and sexual issues. The best way for you to address these issues is to know that you are facing the drive that has kept the species alive.

Sex drive is strong. Sex is a hormone blended cocktail flowing through the brain/mind/body/central nervous system creating and satisfying needs, emotions, and desires. Sex energy is a fact, and to understand it and how it works you must see it clearly. Sex is a drive, similar to a machine. You don't go out to your car and complain because it has pistons, you just drive your car. Sex drive is similar. Properly functioning, your body needs sex as much as it needs food or water. Sex is simply a need—it is not personal.

The body is all about self-preservation and perpetuation of the species. The body is really dealing with simple programs that govern its experience. The largest of these are avoidance of pain, pleasure seeking, and sex drive. All of these are specifically based on this temporary physical vehicle, and have no recognition of the energetic reality that underlies life.

We are filled with desire, but we are seeking to tangibly manifest that desire, which is impossible. For example, we desire the perfect partner but we will never feel completely loved by anyone or anything external. The love we're looking for has to come from ourselves, in energetic reality. We must energetically give that love to ourselves in the depth and infiniteness that is needed and desired.

Feed yourself the love you desire—and life with that perfect partner—in energetic reality. Give yourself what you need, energetically, right now, and you can have it all.

Live the Fairy Tale—Drink the Energy

We are all looking for the perfect partner to make us feel whole and complete. The energetic reality in your brain holds the image and feeling of this perfect other. The perfect other exists in a Frankenstein way inside you, an amalgam of what it is that you think that you are looking for. This image, if attained, if found in the physical, will supposedly bring you peace, fulfillment, and happiness. However, the physical world is a ton of work to move through with logistics, timing, attraction, density, fear, history, location, desire, interest, phone numbers, diseases, boyfriends or girlfriends, communication, opinions, religions, economics, drives, money, and on and on the list goes.

An out to this dilemma is to explore the energetic reality of your mind and give yourself full permission to have that life with that perfect person right now, over and over, triggering within you feelings of happiness, joy, freedom, peace, etc., making you feel really great. You can do this as often as you want, whenever and wherever you want.

We must generously offer the symbolic brain the inner food that it needs to feel whole and complete. Give it the fairy tale life that it desires. Deliver it that life by allowing the whole *fantasy* to run its complete course from beginning to end. Then, do it again, and again. For example, I met someone I was attracted to but I knew that pursuing a physical relationship would not fulfill either of our needs. I knew that I was projecting my energetic needs and wants onto this perceived perfect other. Soon after in a meditation session, I pursued this relationship in energetic reality. I gave myself everything that I wanted in this relationship—falling in love, having a family, living a wonderful life, and agreeing that our love was so great that we would find each other in our next life time. I lived life time after life time with this perfect other in energetic reality until we both agreed that we wanted to try something different in our next incarnation. I felt completely loved and fulfilled when I finished the meditation session.

You can finally have the thing that you want—inner freedom and contentment. You can live an entire lifetime in a matter of minutes or even seconds, giving yourself the life that you would, under any other circumstances, spend the rest of your life trying to work out.

Allowing the energetic reality to play out within your mind is a beautiful thing. As you cultivate it, you begin to live a life that is pain free, because you learn to give yourself exactly what you want, the exact way that you want it, right in the moment that the desire arises, freeing up your energy and allowing your creativity to flow.

The above is especially true of sexual impulses. Allowing your energy to flow freely, perfectly, and completely in the moment, opens the floodgates and allows you to come back to your freedom.

Making love is an inside job. Do it often, let the energy flow. Love yourself enough to give yourself exactly what you need right now.

Loving from the Inside Out

The human being is in a beautiful state of flowing sexuality in the protected womb. Your sexual energy is flowing deeply and openly, unimpeded; an inherent sense of I am loved, an inherent sense of genital self-identity.

Every human being needs to feel that, no matter what they do, they are loved, completely. We all must internalize the person in our lives who lets us totally, feel love and be loved: grandparents, teachers, someone who looks out for you and allows you to feed off their strength. I am loved, no matter what. Most humans are operating at ten percent capacity of the experience of love. Inherently feeling loved reconfigures our energy system. We have to transform the entire experience of love and be loved. This is key. Total and complete love and be loved.

The whole system of human love, love and be loved, is broken. The system of conditional love is part of what makes life on earth such hell. Pull all the energy out of your story until love becomes a fact. The dark vestiges of the brain need to inherently feel love. Light up every part of the brain with your soul's light, brighter and brighter.

    Making love is an inside job. Give yourself permission to make love from the inside out. When your body is in pain, let the pain be touched by your love. Whenever the body speaks, love your body, and allow the energy to flow. Love yourself. Love everything that you are. Let go in love.

Love everyone, and everything about yourself—from the inside out. Love becomes your background experience. At any given moment, you are buoyant with love, floating on the sea of love.

Our Natural State is Buoyant, Abundant and Must Be Cultivated

Creating new neural pathways is the beginning of reconfiguring our energy system to love and beloved. Through meditation and awareness, we begin closing down the pathways to the parts of the brain that are addicted to pain and suffering. The neural rewiring is an important aspect of transformation.

In the opening of that new stretch of neural freeway, your life experiences change. As you develop new neural pathways, you develop new choices and new experiences. Freedom in the deepest pathways of your brain is freedom in the widest expanses of your consciousness.

Rewiring the brain/mind/body/central nervous system is akin to the natural buoyancy of a sailboat on open ocean water. No matter how high the waves, the sailboat stays afloat by riding up and over the waves, responding moment-to-moment with natural buoyancy.

The turmoil in life is the result of the subconscious, sub-mental, and sub-emotional movements of energy within the brain/

mind/body/central nervous system. These are the energetic freeways to the old patterns, beliefs and thoughts that we come into this life with and that develop and deepen over time. The new wiring, the new neural pathways are the buoyancy above those ancient, disempowering thoughts.

Even as you read this, your sub-thoughts are being rewired along with all the other sub-consciousness patterns. The spiritual brain, the conscious mind, and the developing prefrontal cortex are all beginning to re-route around the neural pathways of the old ways of being.

The new freeway is buoyancy. Give permission to the highest enlightened awareness of your soul to assist you, right now, in the rewiring of your brain to create a new paradigm, a new way of being. As you have the beginnings of a natural tendency toward buoyancy, life will change.

The gift of buoyancy is that it is not something you have to think about. It becomes the tendency of the entire brain/mind/body/central nervous system. Your system will learn to remain buoyant no matter what tumultuous circumstances appear. The true nature of your being is buoyancy. As long as there is buoyancy, there is freedom. As long as there is freedom, there is buoyancy. Each supports the other.

In life, there is buoyancy. If cultivated, buoyancy can become your natural state. There is no question whether or not life will present circumstances that challenge your focus and commitment. The only question is when, and have you been practicing on the small stuff, so that when the big stuff comes you are already in your natural buoyancy?

Awakening from the Dream— Some Reminders

Always ask the simple question, "What do I want now? What is my intention?"

You are part of a universe that is in infinite and continual expansion. This is the universe that you live in.

Life is expanding infinitely. It is boundless.

Creativity is expanding infinitely. It is boundless.

Cash is expanding infinitely. It is boundless.

Know that to facilitate infinite creative expansion, there is an ever present, infinite flow and expansion of cash supply. Creativity thrives on cash. Since creativity is in infinite supply, there *must* be enough cash to facilitate that infinite, creative expansion. They go hand-in-hand. You can't have one without the other.

Cash is the circulatory system of planet earth. Cash wants to be loved, shared, held, spent, and created with. Track your money myths and clear them. You deserve to live in your freedom with plenty of cash.

To tap the cash flow, you must learn to tune into it, to recognize it, to feel its presence. Unlike many things that you are told to take on faith, cash is concrete. The movement of cash is concrete and in a continual state of flow, creating its own energy. Your task is to tap into that movement, tap into that supply, and find ways to allow that infinite supply to impact your daily life.

Everything that impacts your daily life in three-dimensional reality is part of the movement of cash and creativity.

Live as if the only thing that is real is what is in front of you to do right now, in actual, three-dimensional reality. Everything else is, well, BS (belief systems). Beliefs and thoughts affect your reality!

Continually ask yourself, "What myths and stories am I living my life by? What symbols in my head are driving me crazy?"

When you find yourself feeling obligated, ask yourself what beliefs you are operating under that make you feel that way. What myths create your sense of obligation?

Pain is caused by the collision of myths and beliefs inside of you. Where two myths collide, there is suffering and conflict.

Live as if pain and suffering are over in your life. Live as if pain and suffering are arbitrary. Therefore, choose something else—like joy, peace, cash, ecstasy, pleasure, fun, etc.

At this point in human evolution, you have the potential to give up your myths entirely and see what the next evolutionary step will be. Can you really be free? Can you feel good? What happens when you are no longer driven by your primal, drunken monkey fears?

Live as if everything in your drunken monkey mind is incorrect

100 percent of the time, which for the most part is true, even when the drunken monkey comes at you with continuous urgency. Stop paying attention to the content. Even a broken clock is right twice a day. That doesn't mean that it's working, and it doesn't mean that the drunken monkey is right.

The drunken monkey has been running the show, but now it is time to retire the drunken monkey. From now on, when the drunken monkey speaks, tell it to be quiet, sit in the corner, and play with crayons. When you can't do that, then let it run crazy until it tires itself out.

Remember, "You shall not pass!" as an inner attitude. Your space is your space, inside and out. Keep it clear.

Morning time is brain vomit time. Beware. Clear your energy of the residue from the nighttime sleep state. The quality of your day begins with the quality of your night. If your night is bad, your day will be, too, unless you take control of your brain and emotions the minute you wake up.

Live as if nobody and nothing external causes your experience. Your emotions are your own. Take responsibility for them. Feelings may exist beneath your conscious awareness, but they are still your own. Pay attention. Stalk sensations to their source, realize that they are not who you truly are, and surrender them. Stalk feelings, emotions, and sensations consciously, fiercely, and then let them go. For now, let them go to the infinite, Creator self.

Ask yourself, "What am I afraid of now, and do I have any real evidence at all of the validity of this fear, or is it emergency symbols flashing in my head? What is happening right *now* in physical reality?"

Learn to deeply feel/see/listen to the other parts of your brain trying to communicate with you; practice developing the sensitivity to the other parts of your brain and consciousness that are beneath your conscious awareness. Learn the symbols that the various parts of your brain use to communicate with you.

Live as if you understand that your brain and consciousness are evolving. There is no *there* to get to. *There* is actually right here, now. That is to say, there is here. You are infinitely expanding awareness, living in an infinitely expanding universe.

Happiness has to come from within. Your brain is still evolving, and it is your duty to push the boundaries of evolution. The brain and body can respond and adapt to practically anything. You have to teach your brain to perceive what is actually happening in your life and break free of the voices, images, symbols and delusions that dominate the experience of the drunken monkey. Evolve your brain into happiness. Demand it. Accept nothing less than total freedom, joy, power, cash, and peace. Happiness will never come from stuff outside, and if it does, it will only be temporary. Happiness comes from giving yourself everything that you want, inside, in energetic reality, right now. Let yourself be happy and filled with pleasure now.

Give yourself everything that you want right now. Be kind to yourself. Have fun. If things are complicated or too serious, then you are probably heading in the wrong direction.

Eat the world; realize that it is all a part of you. You are the very thing that you do and don't want to experience—all of it—the worst of the worst, and the best of the best. Eat the energy!

Live as if you do not cause other people's emotions. Their emotions are their own. Their reactions are arbitrary. See what happens if you live free of what other people do or think. Take nothing personally. Nothing.

If you are telling yourself anything, please tell yourself this: I am a good boy, or I am a good girl. Give yourself, sweetly, the love and acknowledgement that you have always wanted from your parents. Give it to yourself *now*.

Have more fun in your life. No problem or situation is so big that you can't run away from it for a spell. Take a breather. Take a nap. Put it down for a while. It's okay.

Understand that nobody really knows much of anything—and neither do you. Become comfortable feeling uncomfortable with the fact that you just don't know, and neither does anybody else. In this respect, you are free!

Live as if today is your last day on earth. Energetically, in your inner space, give yourself permission to have everything that you want and deserve, right now.

Make death your ally. A way into spiritual adulthood is to know that death is always on your shoulder. You are six minutes away from death at any moment.

Pull out all of the stops. Let yourself completely fall into your experience of life.

Know that your senses grasp. It is simply what they do. The grasping makes the senses feel alive. There is no morality to their grasping. Sometimes it is called attachment, but really, it is just the nature of the senses.

Use your sexual energy and drive to create what you want. Sex drives most human transactions one way or another. Be conscious about sex and use the energy to create.

Most sexual interactions come from a place of wounding. Sexual desire is steeped in shame, guilt, and blame. Be conscious with your sexuality. Hold a space for the wounded feminine and masculine.

The feminine and masculine aspects ebb and flow through you. You can be soft and receptive, piercing and direct, or anything in between. Allow the sexual energies and desires to flow freely through your body. Make noise. Let the energy move. Let yourself be free to explore.

What is your sexual essence? What turns you on? Explore your sexual essence in energetic reality and when you're feeling really good, feed that energy to your brain and soul.

The need for sex is the same as your need for food, water, and exercise. It just is.

Live as if the perfect people surround you. The people around you are your path to freedom. However, if you don't like who is around you, feel free to make a change.

Be gentle, caring, and forgiving when it comes to your heart. Take it easy on yourself.

Take a love bath from time to time. Energetically bathe yourself in all the love that you desire and deserve.

Live as if you are already awake. Awakening is experiencing awareness, which exists before, during, and after images, symbols, thoughts, and feelings appear and disappear.

Evolve your brain. The brain hides its insignificance through mythology. See what happens when you drop all the cute little fairy stories of your life. You are nothing more than a pea, floating on the ocean of a planet in a solar system in a galaxy, that is only one in an infinite number of galaxies expanding infinitely, each powerfully exploding towards infinity. The paradox is that by recognizing your insignificance (which the drunken monkey desperately denies) you can find your significance. On one hand, life is meaningless, and on the other hand, life is rich with meaning. Instead of unconsciously creating meaninglessness, contemplate your insignificance and recognize the significance of every moment that you consciously work towards creating meaning for your life, exactly as you want your life to be, and then extracting the juice from creating your deepest desires. In this way, desire catapults you to your freedom. Life simply is. What are you going to make of it? Exactly how free do you want your life to be? Life is. Ask for what you want. This is your life. This is it.

Everything in this book may be wrong someday. As soon as you think you have the answer, know the truth, or understand the meaning of life, take in your insignificance. Whatever you believe or understand today will be erroneous in a few minutes, a few days, or few years. Life is infinitely creative. Expand infinitely into the freedom of your meaninglessness, the freefall of nobody into nothing.

ABOUT THE AUTHOR

Lawrence Lanoff's first spiritual awakening came at age nine while backpacking through Egypt with his artist mom. This experience led him on a 30-year path of self-discovery and study with several attained masters. During this time, Lawrence also studied physics, yoga, spirituality, neuroscience, photography, meditation, magic, semiotics, advertising design, computer science, philosophy, tantra, Taoism, anatomy, meta-physics, psychology, hypnosis, NLP, art therapy, massage therapy, film, television, fine arts, marketing, and business. He applied the practical essence of his spiritual and artistic skills over a 20-year span directing music videos, commercials, and movies, and was vice president of an international cosmetic manufacturing and marketing company. Lawrence's visionary producing and directing style, and strong aesthetic style put him on the cutting edge of the film industry, and led him into an even deeper understanding of spirituality, symbolic communication, and the inner workings of the human brain.

Lawrence is currently refining his work on a revolutionary new theory of consciousness that includes mythology, evolution, human awareness, business, money, symbolism, metaphor, neurobiology, and their relationship to healing, brain function, spiritual evolution, and neuro-economics—the neural pathways that influence our deepest feelings about self worth and money.

Lawrence is truly and fully enlightened, retaining functionality, creativity, and humor in three-dimensional reality. His life's mottos are fun, joy, laughter, freedom, empowerment, and most importantly—ease and simplicity. He teaches people how to live in this life fully empowered. He loves playing the role of the coyote, turning tired old stories and mythologies about spirituality upside down. As a master energy tracker, Lawrence carefully observes unintentional verbal and non-verbal energetic signals from students and participants in workshops. Lawrence deeply taps into and utilizes the group energy that he cultivates for transformation of awareness and experience. He naturally knows how to profoundly shift group consciousness.

Lawrence is a leading scholar of dismantling mythologies, which are the misunderstood stories, ideas, rules, laws, and cultural values that determine our decisions and choices of action both consciously and unconsciously. Lawrence asserts that we are energetically trapped within our interwoven stories of *thou shalt*, which are ideas about reality that we've inherited—but are not *the truth*. His intention is to help groups and individuals realize their true potential by ridding themselves of their inherited mythologies and beliefs—the unbridled voices and emotions of the drunken monkey. Lawrence's remarkable gifts accelerate energetic clearing, psychological transformation, and spiritual development. He has the ability to clear the depths of core issues, as well as facilitate the expansion of consciousness to enlightening levels. Lawrence currently thrives in joy, fun, freedom, and simplicity in Sedona, AZ.

Meditation CD's by Lawrence Lanoff

Entering the Heart of God: The doorway of your heart connects you to the infinite universe. This meditation is designed to synchronize your heart with the heart of Mother Earth, The Infinite Universe, and God for transformation and healing. (44:20)

Energetic Reality and the Quantum Field begins with a talk that explores the nature of Energetic Reality, Being, and Transformation. The talk is followed by a mediation that is an in-depth exploration of silence and the quantum field. It extensively explores the power and vibration of silence and then uses the force of that potential energy to heal the physical body. This is an advanced meditation. (56:28)

Clearing and Neutralizing Karmic Patterning: This CD is an intensive, active, working meditation designed to help you break the binds and illusions of Karma. This is a very practical CD that is to be used over and over again to help free your body, mind, and spirit from the ravages of the illusion of Karma. This CD also gives a clear definition of the underlying energy of Karma. (38:58)

Body Awareness and Being: This live meditation takes you into an exploration of the field of awareness that lies behind the experience of the body. Powerful energies of transformation are evoked and recorded to help you further release your attachments to the ego, body, and mind. (29:24)

Death and Rebirth: In order to truly live, you must learn to face your fear of death. This CD will lead you through an intensive look at death and rebirth. Each time you do this work, you will continue to cut the ties that bind you to your fears of death, allowing you to truly live in your freedom. (67:30)

Dynamic Prosperity, Dynamic Abundance explores the relationship of abundance to all areas of life. You must expand your view in order to experience total and complete freedom. This meditation will help you to integrate this dynamic, universal force of creation. (61:33)

Seeds of Creativity and Manifestation explores the nature of desire and its relationship to manifestation. You align with the life force energies of the *universal* creation vibration, using the ancient technique of planting seeds of desire into the fertile ground of the causal plane. This CD includes connecting to the Heart of God Blueprint that causes creation. (23:19)

Cash Flow Code: In order to tap into the flow of money, to tap the cash flow, you must learn to tune into it, to recognize it, to feel its presence.

Release and Expansion into the Cash Flow: This meditation deeply releases the blocks that keep you form receiving in your life. The release frequencies move into expanding you towards what you want. This meditation is a deep and powerful exploration of the Infinite Cash Flow Principal. (43:57)

Freedom, Power, and Prophet Expansion: This highly advanced material deals with expanding your circle of influence into 3-D reality. This CD includes an exploration of consumerism. This meditation will put you squarely in charge of getting what you want in your life. (57:18)

Prophets II–On Floating in a Pool of Mythological Feces: This CD is the unedited content of a live dialogue with the beings known as

The Prophets. Their message is direct, clear, and often challenging to listen to. In this session, The Prophets speak directly about the planet that we live on, our consciousness level, and the trap of life and karma. Please note: these are advanced teachings, and not for the spiritually feint of heart. (57:38)

Prophets III–On Ice Cream Containers and Prison: This is highly advanced material and must be listened to at your own risk. For entertainment purposes only. (73:46)

Prophets IV–Peas and Meaningless: This is highly advanced material and must be listened to at your own risk. For entertainment purposes only.

Visit www.acourseinfreedom.com to order Lawrence's CD's and book, and to view workshop dates and locations.

Multiple copies of *A Course in Freedom* are available at a discount:
10-25 copies at 5% discount
26-50 copies at 10% discount
51-200 copies at 15% discount
201 or more copies at 20% discount

Order Form

Qty	Description	Cost
BK	*A Course in Freedom*	$30
CD	Entering the Heart of God	$25
CD	Energetic Reality and the Quantum Field	$25
CD	Clearing and Neutralizing Karmic Patterning	$25
CD	Body Awareness and Being	$25
CD	Death and Rebirth	$25
CD	Dynamic Prosperity, Dynamic Abundance	$25
CD	Seeds of Creativity and Manifestation	$25
CD	Cash Flow Code	$25
CD	Release and Expansion into the Cash Flow	$25
CD	Freedom, Power, and Prophet Expansion	$25
CD	Prophets II–On Floating in a Pool of Myth. Feces	$50
CD	Prophets III–On Ice Cream Containers & Prison	$50
CD	Prophets IV–Peas and Meaningless	$50
Pkg	*Starter Package: A Course in Freedom* plus 4 CD's (Entering the Heart of God, Energetic Reality and the Quantum Field, Clearing and Neutralizing the Patterns for Karma, Body Awareness and Being)	$115 ($10 ship)
Pkg	*Money Package: A Course in Freedom* plus 5 CD's (Dynamic Prosperity-Abundance, Seeds of Creativity-Manifestation, Cash Flow Code, Release-Expansion into Cash Flow, Freedom Power Prophet Expansion)	$140 ($11 ship)
Pkg	*Master Package:* Two copies of *A Course in Freedom* plus 13 CD's plus two 50-minute phone sessions with a fully trained associate student plus two Lawrence tele-meditations plus one 50-minute intensive demythologizing session with Lawrence…directly going after mythologies that limit your life…not for the feint of heart	$1500 ($20 ship)
Ship	U.S. Shipping $6.00 first item + $1 each additional item	
	TOTAL	

Name on credit card: ─────────────────────────
Your cc billing Address: ─────────────────────────
City: ───────────── State: ──────── Zip: ────────
Visa or Master Card No: ───────────────── Exp: ───────
Security Code: ─────── Order: www.acourseinfreedom.com or fax 800-880-6247

Signature: ─────────────────────────

Order Form

Qty	Description	Cost
BK	*A Course in Freedom*	$30
CD	Entering the Heart of God	$25
CD	Energetic Reality and the Quantum Field	$25
CD	Clearing and Neutralizing Karmic Patterning	$25
CD	Body Awareness and Being	$25
CD	Death and Rebirth	$25
CD	Dynamic Prosperity, Dynamic Abundance	$25
CD	Seeds of Creativity and Manifestation	$25
CD	Cash Flow Code	$25
CD	Release and Expansion into the Cash Flow	$25
CD	Freedom, Power, and Prophet Expansion	$25
CD	Prophets II–On Floating in a Pool of Myth. Feces	$50
CD	Prophets III–On Ice Cream Containers & Prison	$50
CD	Prophets IV–Peas and Meaningless	$50
Pkg	*Starter Package: A Course in Freedom* plus 4 CD's (Entering the Heart of God, Energetic Reality and the Quantum Field, Clearing and Neutralizing the Patterns for Karma, Body Awareness and Being)	$115 ($10 ship)
Pkg	*Money Package: A Course in Freedom* plus 5 CD's (Dynamic Prosperity-Abundance, Seeds of Creativity-Manifestation, Cash Flow Code, Release-Expansion into Cash Flow, Freedom Power Prophet Expansion)	$140 ($11 ship)
Pkg	*Master Package:* Two copies of *A Course in Freedom* plus 13 CD's plus two 50-minute phone sessions with a fully trained associate student plus two Lawrence tele-meditations plus one 50-minute intensive demythologizing session with Lawrence...directly going after mythologies that limit your life...not for the feint of heart	$1500 ($20 ship)
Ship	U.S. Shipping $6.00 first item + $1 each additional item	
	TOTAL	

Name on credit card: ─────────────────────────
Your cc billing Address: ─────────────────────
City: ──────────────── State: ────── Zip: ──────
Visa or Master Card No: ──────────────── Exp: ──────
Security Code: ────── Order: www.acourseinfreedom.com or fax 800-880-6247

Signature: ───────────────────────────────

A Note to the Reader by Masaru Kato

Summary of Lawrence Lanoff's claims: One of the top claims Lawrence makes is that you confuse what is real or factual (denotation) with what is symbolic (connotation). This confusion is the source of the crisis, individually and globally. I want to reframe and reemphasize this claim because it is perhaps the very core point you find hard to grasp. This is not to say that you cannot cognitively understand it. However, it is difficult to assimilate this claim and to move out of the confusion into clarity. Mixing up *connotation* and *denotation* in your head is an inevitable thinking habit for you and, honestly, for me, as well.

Why do you so easily mistake what you imagine in your head as *real?* As Lawrence explains, the answer resides in your head. The brain does not differentiate internal reality from external reality. When you see your girlfriend in a dream, from the brain's standpoint, the image of her internally created in your dream is no different than an actual image of her projected through your eyes from the outside, when you physically look at her. In other words, as Lawrence points out, when an image is projected on the screen, the brain does not distinguish whether it is projected from inside or from outside.

Another example is your mom saying to you, "You should marry and have a child by the age of 25." You now perceive a sensation of obligation in your head. This sensation actually emerges from within; however, your brain perceives this sensation as external reality, denotation from your mom. This confusion creates a tangible quality, a sense of burden, as if your mom actually placed a physical weight on you. Your mom becomes your enemy. Your experience of the burden is an illusion, due to the error in your head. In this book, Lawrence presents many examples of illusions such as sin, guilt, shame, feeling responsible, karma, sex is dirty, low self-esteem, financial anxieties and worries, etc.

To liberalize you from this horrible mess, Lawrence repeatedly presents his most important spiritual insight: everything is internal, created by the mind; therefore, everything is not real. Whatever you feel, perceive, or recognize is a byproduct of the translation that the brain makes. When you see an object or a thing, your brain processes the stimulus from your receptors, interprets the stimulus, and cobbles together a symbolic image that it conveys to your mind. The symbolic image is perceived as *real*. As Lawrence states, "your eyes don't see; *your brain does.*" (p.288) Everything is experienced within you. You should be aware that everything exists in your awareness. Therefore, nothing is *real*.

To grasp this insight more deeply, I would like to challenge the basic assumptions of your cognitive orientation. You assume that there is external reality *out there* prior to your own experience of that reality. You also assume that your mind is *passively interpreting* that reality. You believe that your cognition is similar to a camera. As the figure on the photograph reflects the external features out there, you firmly believe the image in your head reflects the external world. However, it is actually the other way around. The external reality reflects the picture in your head. Your experience or imagination precedes what you perceive as external reality. Your mind is *actively creating* the reality out there. This is another claim Lawrence makes, "The external world is a reflection of your inner consciousness." (p.29) Can you believe this?

Here is another example. When you think of *river*, *ocean*, and *rain*, you probably believe that these three are completely different things. Please think about this carefully. Are these three separate in external reality? They are all water, the fundamental element of this planet. They are one, aren't they? Look at the water circulation on this planet: water evaporates from the ocean forming clouds in the atmosphere that create rain, which forms rivers on the land that flow into the ocean. They are one, not three things. You perceive that *river*, *rain*, and *ocean* are different because you believe these three are divided in objective reality. This is wrong. Can your eyes capture the actual border between *river* and *ocean*? Your categorization or conceptualization is arbitrary. You believe that they are different in external reality, simply because you believe so. This is how you create your world.

Please turn your cognitive orientation from *outside in* to *inside out*, and try to capture the world from the viewpoint within. You will soon realize that nothing is external. Everything is internal. Thus, whatever you feel is real is an illusion. This includes everything that you think or know about yourself and your life: name, job, identity, nationality, race, relationships, body, mind, etc. Then, there is nothing to worry about. This is one of the most important messages to you from Lawrence. *"You think something is real because it appears real to your senses. However, senses can be erroneous—often, and so can you. In fact, if you pay close attention, you will see that you are mistaken most times about everything ... so relax."* (P.43)

You are confused about what is internal or external, real or unreal, aren't you? Do not worry! You are not alone. Everybody is confused. Practice releasing what you feel is real, which is not *real*, one by one, step by step. All human conceptions are illusions, not real. Release any identities or ideas: where you live, nationality, race, what you have, what car you drive, how much money you should make, who your mother and father are, what your friends say to you, even your own name. Then, what is left? The sensation or feeling that you exist right now, right here. What is absolutely certain is *I AM*, aliveness of being. When you get this, you are awakened. Lawrence is helping you to awaken by assisting you in recognizing and releasing mythologies, which are not real.

Arguments to possible criticisms: I would like to offer some comments for those of you who are probably dismayed at Lawrence's arguments. If you think you are a moral person, who is concerned with social order or security, Lawrence may appear as an anarchist who loves chaos. He states, "...there is no ultimate morality." (p.260) Your question to Lawrence may be whether your freedom could coincide with a societal order. In a collective sense, you wonder if the society becomes a better place when many people awaken, free from their mythologies. You may be afraid that if the many are liberalized from the rules and laws, your town will be filled with villains or scamps, robbing, stealing, killing, raping, and so forth. Please remember that Lawrence is not saying, "You are free, thus you can rob a bank." What he is saying is that you should not hallucinate, by *energetically* attaching yourself to laws and rules. There is a clear line between if you act in compliance with laws and if you view the laws as *absolute* facts. If you cannot grasp this point, you misunderstand the arguments in this book.

Rules and laws are necessary to live in a systematic society. It becomes a problem when you energetically imprison yourself in the rules. Recall the story of the woman whose marriage was at risk because of the direction to face the toilet paper on the roll. (p.130) She sets one direction as an absolute law, as if her God commands it. The opposite direction is *real* for her husband, as if his God requires it. The mythology of toilet paper forms the war between her God and his God. Can you see how insane it is?

If you are an orthodox Christian, please do not become upset with Lawrence when you read the part where he disenchants the *myth of God.* When Lawrence mentions, "God is a mask..." (P.85), which means the personified quality of God is created by humans so that humans can understand God; Lawrence is talking about God as a symbol. He is a true believer of God beyond the symbol, which is beyond the mask, beyond human conception about God, beyond what the term God means. He believes in Infinite Consciousness, which is a source of Creation, filled with Love. As do I. How about you?

If you are a theorist or thinker of anti-modernism, who encourages re-enchanting the world, you probably misunderstand this book entirely. Please reread it carefully. Your logic is this: the crisis of modern days is originated from the denial of spirituality. In your eyes, the world becomes a meaningless skeleton of vulgar materialism. The value or meaning of life is lost because God is killed by scientific empiricism. People lose the direction of life and become dead, and then a society becomes fragmented and unsafe. This crisis is nicely summarized by Max Weber's term, "the disenchantment of the world."

Then, your prescription for modern crisis is simple: the cause is *disenchantment*; therefore, the solution should be *re-enchantment*, binding or molding people under the name of God, Goddess, Gaia, feminism, the quantum self, the quantum society, non-dual state of consciousness, and so on. Thus, in your eyes, Lawrence, who advocates *disenchanting mythologies*, appears to exacerbate the crisis. In short, you believe that people need more *mythologies* to put a society in order and make it safer. If you are a serious follower of Joseph Campbell, the authority of mythology, you probably favor this idea: re-enchanting the world.

This approach gained popularity through recent decades, as confirmed by the rise of fundamental religious movements all over the world. Ironically, it is this approach that exacerbates the crisis, because what religion does is tie people up with the rope of *mythologies* of God. In other words, you are imposing your own ego, the desire to control other people, onto the world at large. When you bring in a *mask* of God under the noble slogan, "My God offers you unity and harmony," other people, of course, bring in their masks of God, and say, "My God is better than your God." As a result, the countless conflicts of Gods versus Gods, mythologies versus mythologies, stories versus stories arise and the world becomes much more complicated, fragmented, and violent.

I believe that the key for the solution lies in what Lawrence offers. Spirituality is lost in this modern technological era. The real crisis is the confusion between real and unreal. Without clearing this mess, you cannot gain a healthy spiritual awareness.

For instance, when orthodox Christians read, "Jesus ascended to heaven," they believe it physically happened as stated, interpreting the Scriptures literally. They mistake connotation for denotation. Then, modern science reveals that there is no place like heaven in the universe where Jesus could ascend. Here is the gulf between science and religion. If you believe science is *real*, you deny God. If you believe the scriptures are *real*, you deny science. When both stances view their position as absolute fact, there is no room for God within this conflict.

You need to detach from what the symbols of religions and science are literally saying, which is not real. *Jesus ascended* is a metaphor that signifies internal transformation, the depth of inner consciousness that is the source of everything, the heaven within. *Jesus ascended* is simply encouraging you to tap deeply into your inward reality where you can directly connect with God beyond symbol. To capture the reality behind your eyes, you need to be pure and free. You need to disenchant each story told by the scriptures, science, media, other people, etc. This is key to dealing with the modern crisis, where countless mythologies fight against other mythologies, without the presence of the Divine.

Asking courage to awaken: The biggest challenge to you is whether you have the courage to follow the *path of no path*. When you are liberalized from the prison of mythologies, it means that you do not accept, "Thou shall…" from anyone. You are not bound to the instructions that you should do A, B, C; who to marry, where to live, what kind of job you take, how to behave in a certain situation, and so on. You are not given a yardstick to measure what is good or bad, what is desirable or undesirable, etc. It is similar to standing in the deep forest without a map, where you cannot see any path. This is scary isn't it? As Lawrence mentions, the mythologies hold you in a comfort zone, like an unborn baby safely held in a placenta.

As Lawrence describes, it is not easy for you to disenchant mythologies, to escape *mommy's belly*. However, it is worth the effort, because when you awaken, your decisions and actions will spring from the Divine wisdom that is filled with love, peace, harmony, calmness, and other positive qualities. At this level of awareness, you will experience deeper happiness, intense pleasure, and more laughter. You now allow your joyfulness to emerge in its purest form. Pain and suffering disappear because you released their causes. You might be afraid that transcending human conceptions, which are mythologies that give you values and moralities, may make you inhumane. As you can see, the opposite thing will happen. You become a human with great happiness. Lawrence is proving that in his life.

Please reread this book, taking off screens, filters, philosophical frameworks, your religious background, and thought forms. Simply read his texts and taste what he is offering. Please do not try to grasp it contextually or deductively. Otherwise, you cannot get Lawrence's spiritual insight. Lawrence is offering you liberation from political standpoints, philosophical points, and all other viewpoints. Do not take time to categorize his claims or name his position. Do not think about whether he is utopian, a Democrat, or if his view relies on the phenomenology of Husserl or deconstruction of Derrida, etc. This is simply wasting your time. All of these intellectual frameworks are illusions. You cannot see the truth when wearing eyeglasses of illusions. Let go of every thought you have. Lawrence is offering you freedom through disenchant-ment of mythologies because he believes it will make you happy. Taste his claims. Okay, are you ready to reread this book? Go for it.

Masaru Kato
Christmas 2006
Hoffman Estates, Illinois